THE WIND RAGES

ELEMENTAL ACADEMY BOOK 4

D.K. HOLMBERG

Copyright © 2019 by D.K. Holmberg

All rights reserved.

No part of this book may be reproduced in any form or by any electronic or mechanical means, including information storage and retrieval systems, without written permission from the author, except for the use of brief quotations in a book review.

If you want to be notified when D.K. Holmberg's next novel is released and get a few free books and occasional other promotions, please sign up for his mailing list by going here. Your email address will never be shared and you can unsubscribe at any time.

www.dkholmberg.com

1

Tolan stared out at the vast expanse of the waste, his gaze lingering on the rocky ground stretching before him. There was nothing in the waste. No sense of the elements. Nothing of the elementals. No shaping. For the first time in his life, that scared him.

There was another emotion that needed to be dealt with first. Anger.

Running his hands across his jacket, he smoothed it out, wishing he had his furios or other bondars, and yet here he was, empty-handed, about to be asked to head into the most dangerous place in the world.

"Why did you bring me here?" Tolan asked.

"This is the next step in your training," his father said.

Tolan looked over at him. In the hours since his rescue from Amitan, his father had been on edge. Partly, that came from the fact he was running from the potential shapers of Terndahl, and partly it came from the fact that it seemed to Tolan as if his father didn't want to answer him.

All he needed was the answer to a simple question. Did they serve the Draasin Lord?

Despite wanting—needing—that answer, his father had been silent, racing away from Amitan and everything Tolan knew, and toward something else. He didn't have any idea what would be asked of him.

All he knew was he'd been banished from the Academy. The Inquisitors had done it. Aela had done it.

And he couldn't return.

How many left behind had been hurt by the Inquisitors? He hoped none but considering what they had done to him and the way they had been willing to attack, he wasn't convinced that was the case.

"You haven't told me anything yet."

"I've told you what it's safe to tell you," his father said.

Tolan tore his gaze away from the waste. It was emptiness. Desolation. Nothing but rock and desert. Even the power of the element bonds had abandoned people out in the waste. There was no reason for him to venture out there, nothing other than the test the Academy used on young shapers.

"Do you know what they said about you in Ephra?" Tolan asked. They weren't so far from Ephra now. They were on an edge of the waste unfamiliar to Tolan, closer to the northern border than he'd ever been, with Ephra a few days from here. The shaping used to carry them had been impressive, but now Tolan had experienced it, he thought he could recreate it.

"I'm sure they said a great many things," his father said.

"They did. They accused you of serving him."

There it was. He'd managed to say it, and even though he had, he watched his father, waiting for him to give him some sort of sign he didn't serve the Draasin Lord.

"They said it out of fear, I imagine," his father said.

Tolan looked up at him. In the chase from Amitan, he hadn't had the opportunity to really look at his father and try to understand what had happened with him. Now he was here before him, Tolan saw the same man he'd known growing up. The same dark hair, now peppered with much more gray. The same sharp chin. His hair was shorter. The wrinkles at the corners of his eyes ran deeper. The clothes he wore were a different style and cut, but otherwise, he was still the same man.

At the same time, he wasn't. The man Tolan had known had been a craftsman, an artisan, and had served Ephra.

"How could they say it out of anything other than fear?" Tolan asked.

"They said it out of ignorance, as well."

"You haven't denied anything."

His father sighed, stepping toward the waste. He seemed unmindful of the fact one foot was on the border of Terndahl and one foot practically across the border, very nearly in the waste.

"You shouldn't have needed rescue yet."

"You expected this?"

"We weren't able to bring you with us. You were too young, and the road too dangerous. We wanted to."

"You're saying it's all true."

His father turned to him. "I'm saying there is much you don't understand. I don't know you *can* understand."

"I understand my father and mother abandoned me. You left me for the Draasin Lord."

Now he'd said it. Tolan ventured a glance behind him, looking over to where the disciples remained. There were three with his father, three disciples of the Draasin Lord, men and women who served, who wanted nothing more than to summon the power of the elementals in order to serve the Draasin Lord. Ones who wanted to release and control the elementals.

That might be why Tolan felt the most conflicted. In his time here, he'd come to understand the elementals were nothing to fear, and he didn't want them controlled. He'd felt their pain when they had been forced back into the bond. He had known the agony the elementals had known, and had felt the desire to do anything he could in order to ensure they no longer suffered.

His father—and the disciples of the Draasin Lord—didn't just want to free the elementals from the bond. They wanted control over them.

"It was dangerous for you to come. You weren't ready."

"And I'm ready now?"

"Not as ready as your mother would have liked, but the time had come."

"Why now?"

"Because now you can touch the elements."

Tolan licked his lips. "I'm not supposed to be a shaper,"

he whispered, looking out at the waste. "I'm not supposed to be anything here."

"Not supposed to? And who decides what you are and are not supposed to do?"

"All of this," he said, motioning toward Terndahl, waving back toward Amitan and the Academy, "was an accident. I went to a Selection to support a friend."

"You did what?"

Tolan felt a flush work through him. "I couldn't shape. I had some sensing ability, but not enough that I would even be interesting to the local shaping academies. I went to the Selection in order to support Tanner."

"He wouldn't even have known."

"I didn't know that at the time."

His father chuckled. Tolan tried to decide if there was any darkness within it but couldn't tell. Maybe there wasn't. Maybe his father really did just laugh at the idea that Tolan had gone to a Selection to support a friend. The Great Mother knew he had laughed about it often enough.

"It's unfortunate we weren't able to be there with you, to guide you, to help you understand the world as we know it."

"As you know it? Had you stayed, you would have forced me to serve the Draasin Lord. You still want to force me to serve the Draasin Lord."

"And what do you think that means?"

Tolan looked around him. Strangely, he felt almost as if he was just as much a prisoner now as he had when in the Inquisition. When he'd been there, there had been a desire to break something out of his mind, though at the time, Tolan hadn't known he needed anything in his mind broken free. He understood that much better now.

"I know it means you want to release the elementals from their bonds."

His father nodded. "That is true."

Tolan thought of the various elementals he had experience with. Since going to the Academy, he had known many of the elementals, and even felt as if he had communicated with some of them. He wasn't sure if it was true or not, but there was the feeling he had, and the feeling the elementals had wanted him to know what they were thinking, wanted him to know how he could help them.

It was how he had known they didn't want to return to the bond. There was pain within the bond, and fear.

"And the Draasin Lord seeks to use their power."

His father's eyes twitched a moment. "In a way."

Tolan licked his lips. Saying these things out loud left him scared and troubled, but it was better than keeping them to himself. It was better to admit what he feared, to share what he believed, than to hold it inside and continue to worry about it. That worry did nothing other than leave more worry.

"And you want the Draasin Lord to control the elementals."

His father's gaze drifted to the disciples. They were standing guard, peering away from the waste as they looked toward Amitan. There was no reason for them to focus on the waste. There was nothing out there. There wasn't even any sense of the element bonds, so there really was no reason for them to keep their attention fixed anywhere but toward the settled places of Terndahl.

"This is the part I'm not sure you're ready for."

"To talk about the Draasin Lord? I suppose you're more like the Academy than I realized."

"The Academy doesn't want to talk about him?"

Tolan shook his head. "I know he studied in Amitan."

"That is true in a way."

"You know him?"

A slight smile curved his lips, one reminding Tolan of how he'd smiled at his mother when she asked him to stop tinkering in his shop. "Very well."

"And you want the same things he wants?"

"I do, but not for the reasons you think."

Were it any person other than his father, Tolan thought he might run, to escape and get anywhere but here. But this was his father. It had been years since he had seen him. He'd known they weren't dead—at least, he'd hoped they weren't dead—but knowing a thing and seeing it play out were very different experiences.

For so long, Tolan had wanted nothing more than to return home. He had wanted to feel the comfortable embrace of his mother, to hear his father offer the kind of advice he often would offer while sitting in his shop and working. When they'd disappeared, so much had changed for him. So much had been harder.

And here his father now stood before him, trying to tell Tolan he didn't understand the things he'd seen and heard.

Worse, the man in front of him, the man responsible

for the things he now knew his father to be responsible for, wasn't the kind of person he remembered as a child.

That made him question how well he'd ever known his parents. Could they have hidden that side of themselves so well, even from him?

He never would have believed it before, but now… now he wasn't sure he could believe anything else.

"Why don't you help me understand."

His father took a deep breath, and then he nodded. He stepped forward, making his way out into the waste. "Join me out here."

Tolan hesitated. The last time he'd been out on the waste, he hadn't been nearly as attached to his connection to shaping as he was now. He could shape, which meant being separated from that ability would be a far more startling experience than it had been when he'd come through here before.

At the same time, Tolan hadn't cared. He had been willing to venture deeper into the waste than anyone else in his class, anyone other than the Grand Master.

He took a step forward.

When he did, everything shifted. There was a sense of loss; suddenly, the power he knew within himself, the power connecting him to the elements and the element bonds along with the elementals, was gone.

It was a hollowness. An emptiness. And through it, Tolan felt the pain of the absence acutely.

"What do you notice out here on the waste?"

"I notice there's no way for me to shape."

His father nodded. He motioned all around him. "This place, this waste, is a barrier."

"A barrier?" In his time growing up in Ephra, they'd been taught the reason for the waste was because of the Draasin Lord and his destruction, though Tolan didn't even think that was necessarily accurate. If it were because of the Draasin Lord, then the waste would have been there only since his attacks, and those who lived near it understood the waste had been here far longer than that.

"It is. It's a barrier isolating Terndahl."

"Let me guess: you would break that isolation?"

His father chuckled. "I would, but probably not for the reasons you think. What do you feel when you're out here?"

"I don't feel anything. That's the whole point of the waste. We're separated from the bond."

"I understand we're separated from the element bonds. What I'm asking is what do you feel?"

His father continued walking, leading Tolan deeper and deeper into the waste. A part of him hesitated, wondering if he should follow, but this was his father.

"I feel emptiness," Tolan said as he walked. It had always been that way, always the overwhelming sense when he had been out on the waste. There was nothing.

"Where do you feel the emptiness?"

"What are you getting at, Father?"

"It's a simple question, Tolan. Where do you feel the emptiness?"

"I feel it everywhere."

"Everywhere?"

"It's an absence of the elementals."

His father regarded him for a moment. "Most would say it's an absence of their connection to the bond."

Tolan cursed to himself silently. He wasn't sure how much to reveal about his connection to the elementals just yet.

"You are aware of the elementals, aren't you?" his father asked.

"You already know the answer to that," Tolan said.

"I know the answer, but I'd like for you to admit to the answer, to the truth, as well."

"There is no truth."

"None? I think you missed the point. What do you notice about this place?"

"I already told you," Tolan said.

"What does that mean to you?"

"I don't know."

"See? That's why you aren't ready."

"I don't understand why I'm not ready."

"The Academy and people of Terndahl would have you believe the elementals are dangerous."

Tolan met his father's gaze.

"I can see from your face that you already know they are not."

Tolan shook his head. "I don't think they are."

"Why?"

Tolan shrugged. "I just don't."

His father smiled at him. "You need to answer a little bit better than that."

"Why do I need to? I don't think they're dangerous. Not the way the master shapers at the Academy do."

"What has been your experience with them?"

"What's the point of all of this?"

"The point is to help you to understand the nature of the elementals, Tolan."

He looked around the waste. What was there to understand? He recognized the elementals were dangerous. How could he recognize anything else? He had been around them enough that he knew they wanted to help. They wanted their freedom. They didn't want to be trapped within the bond.

And that might be the most compelling reason.

"I can believe the elementals don't want to be trapped within the bond and also believe the Draasin Lord would like to harm them."

"That's where the Academy influence reveals itself. The Academy fears the elementals, but for reasons different than you know. If the elementals are pulled from the bonds, they are weakened."

"The elementals are weakened?"

"The bonds. The shapers. Everyone is weakened. Everyone other than the elementals."

"Why do you believe that?"

"Look there," his father said, motioning toward Terndahl. At the edge of the waste, everything began to change, shifting from deep green grasses and trees to the barren and unlivable rock. It was an abrupt line, a clear demarcation between the boundary of Terndahl and that of the waste. He had always thought it strange. It was more than just a separation. It was a distinction, a point where power shifted, and it was where there was nothing beyond it. "You can see the effect of the element bonds. You can see the power that having access to shaping grants the people of Terndahl." He turned and motioned to the waste. "And you can see what happens when the elementals are pulled free from the land."

"The elementals are pulled free in Terndahl, too."

"No. They want you to believe they are, but there are places where the elementals are trapped. They aren't held within the bond so much as held within the land, confined so they can't escape. It keeps Terndahl from looking like the waste."

A Keystone. That was what his father was getting at.

And he had felt the elementals within the Keystone, and knew exactly how they were there, the power they were holding.

"I've seen one of those places."

His father looked at him, reaching out toward him. "You know where they are? Then you should show us."

"I only know where one Keystone is."

"Keystone? Is that what they have taken to calling them?"

"Do you have another term for it?"

"Probably not that's any better. We've been looking for these places. Searching, knowing the power of the elementals is trapped within them, and if we could free them—"

"Then Terndahl would look like the waste?"

"No. Then the waste might begin to return to the way

it should be." His father stretched his hands out in front of him, motioning to the vast expanse of the waste. "Everything here is artificial. It might look as if it isn't, but the fact of the matter is shaping has changed this place as much as it's changed any place. By pulling the elementals free of this land, by forcing them into the bond, the waste has been changed, diminished. The power within it has been altered, and the people who once lived here have suffered."

"There were people in the waste?"

"A great many people."

Tolan stared out at the waste. There was no sign of life, no sign of anything, and he found it difficult to believe anyone had ever been here, and yet, the things his father said resonated with him.

"Why are you telling me this?"

"We wouldn't have told you before now. Had you not experienced what you had at the Academy, we probably wouldn't have told you even now."

"How are you aware of what I experienced at the Academy?"

"The protections placed around you are missing."

Tolan looked at his father. "What protections?"

"Your mother and I wanted to ensure your safety. Living in these lands as we were forced to do, we didn't want you to have to experience the danger existing here. Not before you should."

"So, you protected me."

"I know it doesn't feel that way."

"You don't know anything about how it feels."

"Know that had they understood what you could do, they would have taken you, and would have forced you into a different kind of service."

"And what kind of service is that?"

"That of an Inquisitor."

Tolan turned away. Spirit shaping. His father had known.

Stranger still, he had attempted to protect him from it.

"Why would you keep that from me?"

"We intended to teach you ourselves. We never expected to be called back quite so abruptly, but…"

"But what?"

"But there was a need."

"What need was that?"

"If you come with me, I can ensure you know. You might not be ready yet, but perhaps it doesn't matter."

"What if I don't want to go with you?" Even as he said it, he knew what he needed to do. In order to return to the Academy, he would need to do this, to know what might come next.

A flash of pain worked across his father's face. "I won't force you to come. You might not understand this, but the Draasin Lord doesn't force anyone to serve. He doesn't force the elementals to serve him, either."

"What does he do if he doesn't intend to have the elemental serve him?"

"What he does is try to free them. He wants to restore the world as it was."

"Why?"

"Because we recognize a greater danger will occur."

Tolan remained within the waste, standing there. Part of what his father said felt true, and he thought he could believe, but part of it didn't fit. He'd seen followers of the Draasin Lord and the way they'd attacked Amitan. That wasn't the kind of man his father was describing.

"How do you cross the waste?"

"What?"

Tolan motioned to the waste. "How do you cross it?"

"I don't know what that has to do with anything."

"It has to do with everything. How do you cross it?"

"Tolan, there are things you can't understand."

"So you keep telling me, but I wonder if that's true or if you only want it to be true."

"Why would I want it to be true?"

"You're trying to use me."

"I'm your father. I wouldn't try to use you."

"The same father who abandoned me to follow the Draasin Lord. The same father who left me in Ephra, letting them believe you were abducted by the Draasin Lord. The same father I had to defend to others in Ephra, and yet, shouldn't have."

Tolan took a step back toward Terndahl. He wouldn't be able to do anything until he reached it, and now they had this opportunity to talk, he wasn't sure he wanted to —or could—remain.

His father continued to watch him, and a frown deepened on his face. "I'd like you to come to take the next step in your training, but I won't keep you here."

"You brought me to the waste, where I don't have any connection to power. You are trying to hold me here."

"You're not seeing things correctly," his father said.

"Maybe not, but I recognize what you're doing."

He took another few steps, and as he did, his father took a step toward him.

Tolan ran.

When he was nearly to the edge of the waste, he felt his father behind him.

Tolan lunged.

The moment he crossed the border of the waste, he felt the return of his shaping ability. He wrapped earth and wind around him, a barrier he held, turning to face his father.

What was he thinking? His father was a disciple of the Draasin Lord, and because of that, he was likely a very powerful shaper. What did Tolan think he could do against someone like that?

Nothing. That was what.

"You're making a mistake," his father said.

"I'd be making a mistake if I went with you."

"We can't protect you if you return to Amitan and the Academy."

Tolan stared out at the vast expanse of the waste. "And you can protect me if I stay with you?"

"Better than we could otherwise." His father stood, his hands clasped behind his back. "Let me show you. Once I do, you can decide what you want to do."

Tolan glanced over at the disciples. They had made no move toward him, and despite the violence he had seen from them before, this was still his father.

That was the hardest part to wrap his head around.

Why would his father be like this? Why would his father attack like this?

It didn't make any sense.

If he turned away now, he would never know why his parents abandoned him. He would never understand what reason they had for leaving him in Ephra alone. Potentially tormented. He would never know why they had left him.

If he went with them, he would be everything the Academy feared. He would be going and potentially serving the Draasin Lord.

That was something he would never do.

Yet he couldn't shake the sense he needed to go with his father. He needed to know.

"I'll go with you, but I'll return if you've been lying to me."

He said it with far more confidence than he felt. It was possible he wouldn't even be able to return, but his father nodded nonetheless.

2

Although he followed his father, Tolan had no idea where they were going. He had suspected they might cross the waste. The rumors of the Draasin Lord and those who followed him suggested he would be found there, though when his father had taken him to the edge of the waste, the other disciples had remained within Terndahl, almost as if they had no interest in crossing the waste.

There had been hesitation. Not just hesitation—almost a sense of fear.

That wasn't the sign of anyone willing to cross the waste in order to find the rest of their people.

And if they weren't on the other side of the waste, where would the disciples hide?

In his time within Amitan and while working at the Academy, Tolan had experienced attacks from the disciples several times. Wherever they hid had to be someplace reasonably accessible.

As he watched his father while they headed north, skirting along the edge of the waste, Tolan couldn't help but feel as if this was a mistake.

He had left Amitan. There had been only a little choice on his part, and as much as he had wanted to remain, he no longer even knew if he could.

This was safest.

That was what he told himself, despite the fact he no longer felt that way.

His head spun, trying to wrap his mind around everything that had taken place, trying to grasp the strangeness of his father being with him once again. Even harder was the idea his father truly had served the Draasin Lord. All the years he'd defended his parents had been for nothing.

It made him feel like a fool.

In the back of his mind, the taunts he'd heard over the years, those from people like Velthan and others within Ephra, came crawling back.

How could they not? For every attempt he'd made to deny his family's connection to the Draasin Lord, they actually had been his servants.

And now Tolan was heading in that direction.

His father turned back to him, watching him. It was almost as if he recognized the hesitation within him, and Tolan couldn't deny there was significant hesitation on his part.

"We need to keep moving," his father said.

"I'm coming with you, aren't I?"

"Tolan—"

Tolan took a deep breath and picked up his pace. They no longer were shaping their way along the edge of the waste, preferring to go by foot. Somehow, he suspected that mattered. They had traveled as far as they could, farther than Tolan had ever gone, and in a different direction than he had traveled before. By following the Shapers Path this way, they had skirted north of Ephra, heading to a desolate part of Terndahl. There were no cities here. No towns or villages. Nothing.

And yet, the Shapers Path had carried them all the way out here.

That surprised him. There had to be a reason for it. Everything he knew about the Shapers Path suggested there was a purpose to them. The people of the Academy had formed them over the years, often to make it easier to travel from place to place. Why would they have needed to travel out here?

Glancing back toward the distant sign of the Shapers Path, he tried to understand. They had moved far enough away from the Paths that he could no longer feel the energy used upon them. As he focused on that absence, he wondered if there was anything else he could detect from it.

"We need to keep moving," one of the other disciples said.

He was a dark-haired man, older than even Tolan's father, and wore a dark cloak and, surprisingly, heavy leathers more suited for colder climates.

"I'm coming," Tolan said, nodding to his father.

A part of him didn't know if he was making a mistake

or not. Leaving the Academy, regardless of what had happened and how he was doing so, pushed him away from everything he knew. It pushed him away from everyone he knew, and from the opportunity to continue to learn how to master his shaping.

And now he would have to learn something else.

Then again, Master Minden had suggested he go. She claimed he would continue to learn, but what could he learn?

The elementals. That was the only other aspect of his training he wouldn't be able to acquire within the Academy and in Amitan.

One of the disciples in front of him started to shape, and there was a strange sense to it. It was different than the kind of shaping he often encountered within Amitan, and yet there was something distinctly familiar about it.

Why was one of the disciples shaping?

That was the part of all this that Tolan needed to better understand. The more he focused on the way the disciples shaped, the more certain he was that there was something off, but why?

"Regan?" one of the disciples said.

Tolan looked at his father. What was taking place?

His father drew upon power. It was incredible, a mix of shapings, far more strength than Tolan ever would've expected.

Bondars. That was what he was using. Then again, Tolan had known his father had the ability to make bondars. He'd used one himself.

It made sense his father would have bondars with him,

and it made sense he and the other disciples would be able to use them.

It was a wonder anyone from the Academy had ever been able to overpower the disciples of the Draasin Lord. If they all had access to bondars, then it seemed even more surprising the masters from the Academy would have been able to stop them.

Tolan pulled upon a shaping, drawing upon earth. If there was something to be worried about, he'd want to use earth in order to sense it.

He pushed that sense out from him, letting power flow through him, connecting him to the ground, to the grasses, to the trees, and everything nearby.

He didn't often use his connection to shaping in such a way, but in this case, he thought it necessary.

The more power he pulled, the more he felt something off.

Not just something off. There was some*one*.

And they were shaping.

Tolan recognized the nature of the shaping, if not who was doing it.

He looked at the other disciples, at his father, and couldn't help but feel as if they had no idea there was something out there.

"Father?"

His father glanced over his shoulder but continued to head along the border between Terndahl and the waste. The waste was only a dozen or so steps off to their right, far enough that he didn't have to worry about the separation from his bonds but near enough that he was acutely aware of just how it would happen if he stepped over the border.

"What is it?"

"Do you detect anything?"

His father frowned, closing his eyes, and a shaping built from him. It swept outward. As it did, it radiated through the ground. An earth shaping, but unlike most earth shapings he had experienced.

"You detected this already?"

Tolan nodded. "I can feel it."

And as he did, he realized not only weren't they alone, but there was someone shaping nearby.

His father made a motion to one of the disciples, and they started off. Tolan veered toward them, but his father grabbed his arm. "You shouldn't go with them."

"I'm the one who detected it."

"Just because you detected it doesn't mean you should accompany them."

Shaping built from the disciples who started off, and Tolan watched as they disappeared. It troubled him, and he didn't care for the fact he was being left behind.

"I'm going," he said.

He raced forward and chased the sense he detected. There was only one shaper, he was certain of it, but couldn't tell who they were and what they were doing.

This far outside of Amitan, this far outside of any place, it wouldn't make sense for anyone to be shaping out here. The fact there was someone out here, and there was the sense of shaping he'd detected, suggested there was something more taking place.

And then he saw it.

It was the dark robe of an Inquisitor.

Tolan's breath caught.

Why would an Inquisitor be all the way out here?

The disciples had the Inquisitor surrounded, power pulsing away from them, wrapping around the Inquisitor. They were squeezing. With enough power, they'd crush the Inquisitor. He could feel the power the Inquisitor used to resist, the way he pushed against the shaping, but would it be enough?

The Inquisitor glared at them, shifting his gaze to Tolan. "You are with them."

Tolan ignored him and frowned. There was something wrong—more than just what he detected.

"What is it?" his father asked.

"Why would he be all the way out here?"

His father shook his head. "He probably chased us."

That didn't make sense. There had been no sign of the Inquisitor. Had he chased them, he would have caught up to them by now. They had taken enough time at the waste for him to have caught them.

Tolan headed toward the Inquisitor. "What are you doing out here?"

"We are doing nothing but protecting Terndahl from those like yourself who would harm it. That is the purpose of the Inquisitors."

Tolan grunted. "It seems to me your purpose was to torment students at the Academy."

"Only those who are deserving."

Tolan couldn't take his gaze off him, and there was a

part of him that was troubled, bothered by all of this, and he couldn't help but think there was something more he wasn't understanding.

The Inquisitors had to be up to something.

They hadn't chased them all the way here. Tolan would have seen them by now.

He probed with earth. Using that shaping, he let it flow out from him, striking the ground near the Inquisitor.

In doing so, there came a surge of energy, a reflection of something familiar. The more Tolan pushed on it, the more certain he was of what he was feeling.

Something was off.

"Tolan," his father said, grabbing for him.

Tolan shook him away. He had lived on his own for long enough, away from his parents for long enough, he no longer needed his father's approval for anything, certainly not for this. In this case, he was determined to understand what was taking place here.

If he was going to go with the disciples, he wanted to know whether there was some reason for the Inquisitors to be out here before he went.

And Aela had attacked the Grand Master. She had attacked him.

That was not serving the Academy.

"What are you doing out here?" Tolan asked, leaning close to the Inquisitor.

"You of all people should know the Inquisitors ask the questions."

"You might ask the questions during an Inquisition, but I'm asking them now."

The man glared at him and a shaping began to build, as if he was trying to resist the hold upon him. With enough pressure, he might be able to escape. He was powerful. Tolan could feel the energy he was using, the nature of the shaping and how it struggled against his captivity. Would the disciples be able to hold him as well as they intended? Someone this powerful might be able to overwhelm their shaping.

This was an Inquisitor, after all. This was someone accustomed to dealing with incredible power outside of the Academy.

And he had no idea what the disciples were capable of.

Then again, they did have bondars. With those bondars, they should be able to withstand anything thrown their way. Using that power and strength, there should be no trouble for the disciples to hold an Inquisitor.

"There's something wrong here," Tolan said, turning to his father and motioning to the space around him. "It's more than just the fact he's out here."

"There are Inquisitors all throughout Terndahl," his father said.

"Everywhere?"

Having not traveled that extensively throughout Terndahl, Tolan didn't know how many Inquisitors there were, and he had no idea whether or not this was unusual, but he couldn't help but feel as if it was. They had never encountered the Inquisitors in Ephra before the Selection—unless he'd been spirit-shaped to forget. It struck him as something he would have remembered.

There still seemed to be something about this that was off, though the more he focused, the more he felt the power around him, the harder it was to know whether there was anything he needed to be concerned by.

"Perhaps not quite everywhere, but we encounter them often enough that this is not unusual."

"Look at this place," Tolan said, waving his hands around him. They were far from any place of significance within Terndahl. "Why would they be out here? What would the Inquisitors think to find out here?" That was what Tolan had to come up with. His father not seeing how strange this was posed a danger.

He pushed out with a sense of earth again, letting that sense fill him. As he did, he could tell there was something off and unusual, but not what it was or where it came from.

Adding fire to the earth sensing, Tolan searched for anything else that might be noticeable, but as he focused on it, he wasn't able to come across anything more than what he already had.

That sense was there. As he drew upon what he detected, holding onto that power, he struggled to find whether there was anything within his sensing that might provide him with the answers. He needed to learn how to pick up on what he was detecting.

And yet, there was the ongoing strangeness.

Of *any*thing, that was what troubled him the most. The strangeness mattered.

"Let us deal with him," his father said.

"Deal with him?" Tolan asked, tearing his gaze away from the ground. "What do you mean by that?"

"We have experience with the Inquisitors, Tolan. We will take care of him."

The comment sent a shiver through him. Was this what he was getting into? After everything, he was now going to be drawn into something like this?

Before he had the opportunity to say anything more or to argue with his father, another sense of shaping built. And then another. And then another.

They came from all around, blooming nearby.

The disciples looked over before turning their attention to the Inquisitor.

The man stood, smiling. "Did you think I was just biding my time?"

"He signaled them," one of the other disciples said.

"Then we need to take care of—"

Tolan's father didn't have a chance to finish. A burst of power exploded, slamming into where he was standing. When it did, he was tossed off his feet. The shaping confining the Inquisitor suddenly released, and the man began to pull upon power.

Tolan's father grabbed him, and with a burst of wind, they went streaking into the air.

There was a level of control to the shaping that impressed him, though he knew it probably should not. His father had already proven he had shaping ability beyond what Tolan had known.

Another sense of shaping came near the waste.

"Are they all Inquisitors?" Tolan asked.

"Enough of them are," he said.

"What now?"

"Now we have to backtrack."

"Why backtrack?"

"We can't lead them where we're going. If they find out where we have been, then we will—"

His father didn't have the opportunity to finish. Another shaping thundered near him, striking the space where they had been. The air seemed to shake, wind whipping around, and water lashed at them from above. The power within the shaping was incredible.

His father grunted.

He held onto the power of the shaping and used that as he drew them higher into the sky.

Tolan wanted to help but didn't think there was anything he'd be able to do. This shaping was beyond him.

"How do they signal to each other?"

"We haven't detected that. There's some shaping they use."

"Spirit?" Tolan asked.

His father glanced at him, building another shaping which sent them streaking deeper into Amitan, away from the border of the waste. "Probably spirit, though there aren't many of us who have the ability to utilize spirit."

The fact there *weren't many* suggested there were some.

And with the continual buildup of pressure, the ongoing surge of energy, Tolan understood why his father was running. There were too many Inquisitors.

"You can leave me behind," Tolan said.

"I'm not leaving you. We just found you."

He thought about the way his father and the others had talked about the Inquisitors. The cold way they had seemed willing—almost eager—to dispatch them. With that point of view, he wasn't even sure he wanted to go with them. He wanted to know his father, and he wanted to know why his parents had abandoned him to the Draasin Lord, but he wasn't sure he wanted to go with someone that willing to harm. How was that any different than the Inquisitors?

Then again, if he went back to the Academy, and back to where the Inquisitors were, he would be heading back toward someone else who had proven themselves willing to harm.

There was no good answer. Everything seemed to force him into making a difficult choice, the kind of choice he didn't want to make. He had no idea if there was any way to do anything else.

"We can—"

His father didn't have a chance to finish. Another shaping caught them, throwing them violently off to the south before his father managed to gain control again. It was closer.

As it thundered, Tolan looked over, noticing several dark-cloaked Inquisitors.

"Where are you guiding us?"

"I'm guiding us to the only way we can escape this."

"Where is that?"

Another explosion of shaping struck and his father

gritted his teeth, clenching his jaw, and they surged forward, gliding on that shaping, streaking forward.

And in the distance, Tolan caught sight of the translucent form of the Shapers Path.

That was where his father was headed.

They might be able to shape quickly, they might be able to use that shaping to carry them, but there were limits to how far and how long they could travel. On the Shapers Path, there wouldn't be those same limitations. They would be able to travel faster.

But would they be able to outrun the Inquisitors?

When they reached the Shapers Path, his father landed and they surged forward. Power continued to build behind them, and then Tolan noticed it in front of them. His father stopped, looking all around.

"I'm sorry, Tolan. I thought we were going to be able to keep you from all of this."

"Keep me from you fighting Terndahl?"

"You don't understand. Not yet, but if you come with us, I will make sure you do."

A shaping built from his father, and it slammed into one of the nearby Inquisitors. A disciple suddenly appeared, wrapping another shaping around that Inquisitor. The Inquisitor dropped, twitching, before falling still.

Tolan could only stare.

Was this what he wanted?

Power slammed into him again and again. As it did, he didn't know. Maybe there would be no answer. He'd not wanted to make a choice. He'd not wanted to leave the Academy. Had there not been the attack and the Inquisitors assaulting him, Tolan wasn't sure he even would have left. The Inquisition had been terrible, but he'd survived. And now in the hours since he had left, running along the Shapers Path, gliding with the disciples and with his father, he no longer knew if that was even what he wanted.

Master Minden had wanted him to leave, but she had done so in order to protect him. He thought that the only reason.

And yet, if the Inquisitors were doing something, if they had attacked the Academy and were plotting something outside of the Academy near the border, shouldn't he return and warn others?

Master Minden might not be the right person for that. Tolan would need to find the Grand Master. He believed the Grand Master would have to come around; he believed there would have to be some way of finding him, helping him. If he didn't and couldn't, who was he? What did he believe in?

Another explosion of power came near him. And then another. With each one, Tolan didn't know how to respond. Worse, there might not be any choice in the matter. It was either be destroyed by the Inquisitors or go with the disciples.

As he looked over at his father, he couldn't help but feel as if neither choice was right.

3

Shapings erupted all around Tolan, blast after blast surging through him. None of them were his shaping, but all of them were power he could feel as it rolled through him, an overwhelming sense as each element was thrown behind him. As much as he wanted to pay attention to the shapings themselves, he struggled to make sense of what was taking place around him. He ran, racing along the Shapers Path, using a surge of wind and fire as he went. It carried him faster than he would have expected and he neared Amitan.

Another blast exploded behind him. It was fire and earth, the two of them mingling together, and Tolan was pushed forward along the Shapers Path.

"You need to keep moving. We're doing all we can to hold them at bay." His father placed a gentle hand on his back. He hadn't even realized his father had stayed with him but was thankful he had. The gesture reminded Tolan of when he was younger, times when they'd been venturing out of Ephra as a family, their way of trying to help him reach his ability to shape—and continuing to fail. It was a memory Tolan had not expected.

"Why?"

It was the only thing that came to him. He needed to know why he should go with his father. He still wasn't certain. Leaving the Academy, going with him, meant he was admitting to others that he served the Draasin Lord.

"We came to help you, Tolan, but we can't help if you aren't willing."

He and his father weren't alone as they ran. There were three others, all dressed in clothing of the disciples of the Draasin Lord, three men who had powerful shapings they used to impressive effect. As they fought, blasting backward behind them toward the shapers of the Academy, Tolan had no idea how many people were injured. Would others from the Academy be harmed because of this? The idea they would, that it would be because of him, troubled him.

There were people he knew in the Academy. People he cared about. Friends.

His father pushed, guiding him away, and Tolan allowed himself to be nudged along the path, though with each step, he found a growing trepidation within him.

"Watch out," his father said. He pushed down on Tolan's back, forcing him down. Tolan rolled to the side and caught sight of a black-cloaked shaper streaking toward them. A shaping built from his father, a swirl of power reminding Tolan of how he reached for the elementals. It burst from him, heading toward the shaper.

Not just a shaper. An Inquisitor.

They deflected the shaping and shifted, landing on an intersecting Shapers Path in front of them. Tolan's father lunged forward, shaping after shaping erupting from him.

This was a man he had believed not capable of shaping? Growing up, he'd never known his father had any capacity to shape, but then, he would never have known his parents had the ability to make bondars.

The Inquisitor deflected each shaping.

Tolan didn't recognize the man but suspected he was one of the Inquisitors who'd chased him when he had last been in Amitan. He watched as his father confronted the Inquisitor, power after power bursting, the shapings that emerged nothing like Tolan had been taught at the Academy. As he focused, he recognized a sense of something else, not just the power of the shaping, but also a sense of elemental energy.

That had to be imagined, didn't it?

The Inquisitor managed to deflect each attack. He stood with his hands out, a shaping building between them. It was growing with incredible power. Heat and a surge of wind gusted between his hands, and Tolan could tell it was going to strike his father.

He raised his hand and pushed out flame. It streaked from him, a shaping of fire that came out uncontrolled, and with it, an image of saa burst from him. The elemental formed within the flame, twisting toward the Inquisitor. When it struck the Inquisitor, the man fell backward, tumbling off the Shapers Path.

His father glanced behind him, starting to smile, but then his face tightened in a frown. "Move."

He jumped over Tolan, another shaping rising.

Tolan realized two Inquisitors were behind him, both trying to reach his father, starting their attack. As they did, he debated whether he should help or not. Helping the last time had been more instinctive than intentional, and it was possible the Inquisitor wouldn't even know Tolan had been involved. If he continued to help, he was pitting himself against the Academy.

Was that what he wanted?

Yet, it seemed as if the *Inquisitors* had pitted themselves against the Academy.

Maybe not all of them. It was possible it was only Aela and a subset and not all of them.

Leaving meant he left his friends—people he cared about—to whatever fate the Inquisitors would push upon them.

That as much as anything motivated him.

Tolan spun around, looking to see where more of the fighting was taking place. He could feel the surging energy of the shapings as they flowed, blasting all around him. Many of them came from the disciples, and their particular style of shaping was unique enough that he could detect it. It was different than what the Inquisitors used. That style of shaping was more like what Tolan had been taught.

Why would he be aware of such differences?

When he had faced the disciples before, he hadn't been aware of any difference between their shaping and his, but then, at that time, his capacity to shape was different, limited. Since then, he'd grown with his skill. Perhaps that was all there was to it.

Another shaping started to build behind him.

Spinning, Tolan prepared to shape when he realized there was an Inquisitor.

"You are with the Draasin Lord," the Inquisitor said.

Tolan didn't recognize the man, but he recognized his voice. There was something to it he'd heard before.

"I'm not with the Draasin Lord."

"Yet they came for you?" The Inquisitor started to shape, spirit building from him.

Tolan recognized it only as a type of shaping he was not familiar with. He resisted, pushing against it, and changed his focus, turning toward a shaping of fire, inverting it. As the spirit shaping struck him, it split off to either side of him, drifting away. It had been an effective shaping against the Grand Inquisitor, so he suspected it would be effective on this man.

His face twisted in a sneer. "Only disciples know that shaping."

"What about you?" Tolan stood, looking around. The fighting had moved farther along the Shapers Path. He would have to deal with this Inquisitor on his own, and yet, he wasn't sure if he could withstand this type of attack for much longer. The Inquisitors were some of the most skilled shapers at the Academy. They had the ability to shape each of the elements, along with spirit, and were incredibly powerful. "I saw what you did to the Grand Master."

"The Grand Master deserves whatever fate befalls him. He made a mistake of thinking he could step outside of his place."

"His place?" The idea the Inquisitor would try to overthrow the Grand Master angered him. "What do you claim the Grand Master's place is?"

"He thinks the Academy stands outside the law."

That wasn't Tolan's experience with the Grand Master at all. He viewed his role as one of service to the Academy, but also in service of shaping. He might not view the elementals the same way as Tolan, but Tolan was beginning to understand that very few people did. Most feared them, but he had to believe that fear came from the unknown, not at all from an understanding of how the elementals really could be used. Most believed the elementals were meant to serve the shapers, but not Tolan. He didn't see them as servants. He saw them as wanting to be freed.

"You will return and face your punishment."

"Another Inquisition? I've withstood one already."

The Inquisitor glared at him and took a step toward him. As he did, shaping built, and Tolan resisted its effect, wrapping his own—a mixture of fire and earth—internally, inverting it so he protected himself. When the Inquisitor reached him, the Shaping struck his barrier and bounced off, deflected so Tolan felt it as little more than a minor push.

"A challenge. Consider me impressed," the Inquisitor said.

If he continued to banter with the Inquisitor, Tolan had little doubt he would be overpowered. He didn't think he could withstand someone like this indefinitely. It meant he needed to end it, and he needed to do so quickly.

And it meant he would have to decide about what he was going to do.

Yet, he already knew what he was going to do. The Inquisitor had made his feelings about the Grand Master known. If the Inquisitors took control of the Academy, his friends would suffer.

Tolan still wasn't entirely sure how he felt about everyone at the Academy, but there were those friends. Despite the Inquisition, there had been those who cared about him.

He needed to attack in a way that involved using his shaping—his unique shaping. It meant a combination of using the element bond along with elementals.

Which one could he use?

Fire. That was the one that always came to mind, and partly because he had known it best through using the furios. In this case, he didn't have the furios. However, he had not only his connection to the element bonds but could use a twisting of saa, or perhaps even esalash. Either way, if he combined the two elementals, he could work them together. In doing so, he thought he could mix it in such a way to overpower this shaper.

Esalash first.

Tolan began his shaping, focusing on what he wanted

from the elemental, the shape of it, and smoke began to build. The Inquisitor tried to resist, sending wind swirling around, but Tolan struck, adding a hint of saa, twisting that flame elemental at him. It struck the Inquisitor, and though he met some resistance, Tolan managed to blast him. He shifted his focus, and in doing so, he added earth, slamming that into him.

The combined shaping left the Inquisitor lying on the Shapers Path.

Slowly, the shaping dissipated. The Inquisitor lay motionless. He breathed, but slowly. His chest rose and fell steadily. Looking around, Tolan could still feel the effect of other shapings, the ongoing attacks from the disciples of the Draasin Lord as they fought with Inquisitors.

Tolan was conflicted. Which side was he supposed to work with? Who should he side with?

He didn't know. All he knew was he was not about to allow the Inquisitors to harm him.

Focusing on the nearest shaping, he headed toward it.

It was probably a mistake to be heading directly toward the shaping. At first, he had no idea who he was detecting, but the sense of it was that of an Inquisitor and not one of the disciples of the Draasin Lord. Would it make a difference?

He lost sight of his father and the other disciples, and though he knew they were still there, he couldn't determine where. He followed the sense of the shapings, and as he approached, he recognized there was considerable power wrapped within it. It was not just a single element bond shaping, but one using multiple bonds, and spirit was mixed within it.

A dangerous shaping.

He had to act. He had to do something in order to stop it.

As he ran, he focused on his sense of fire and earth, wrapping the shaping around him, holding it twisted and inverted within him so he could defend himself from spirit-shaping most of all. It might not deflect other shapings, but others were nearly as dangerous as spirit could be.

It struck.

Tolan staggered. The strength of the shaping was impressive, and it slammed against his barrier, forcing him back. As much as he tried to ignore it, he didn't know he could.

Ducking down, Tolan pulled on his sense of power, shaping as much as he could. He focused on one of the elementals, using a combination of fire and wind, letting that surge from him. As it did, he pushed it forward, letting it hit the sense he had in front of him. He wanted it to strike, and to do so with vigor.

Tolan had no idea where the shaping would go, but he let it lash out, sweeping away. It struck something but was met with resistance.

He scrambled to his feet, lurching forward. As he did, he saw a figure cloaked in the black of the Inquisitors, her hair streaming behind her, standing a dozen feet from him, watching him. Amusement shone in her eyes.

"I knew you sided with the Draasin Lord," Aela said.

"And I told you I don't."

"You've proven yourself. You can no longer deny you're in service of the Draasin Lord."

Tolan realized what she was doing. She was shaping as she spoke, raising her voice, sending it out away from her.

Could he contain it?

A shaping of wind.

No. Not a shaping, but a request to the wind elemental. It would be difficult and the chances were good that it wouldn't even work, but he thought he had to try.

"Ara, please keep her from broadcasting her voice," he whispered, sending out a wind shaping.

Wind started to swirl around him, growing with increasing intensity. He didn't know if it was effective, but it seemed as if it was.

"And you have proven you are willing to attack the Academy," he said. "I saw what you did to the Grand Master."

"The Grand Master was merely neutralized while we eliminated his mistake."

"What mistake was that?"

"You."

Tolan frowned. "The Grand Master hadn't done anything with me."

"No, which is part of the problem. He should have removed you as a threat long ago. If only he acted with more resiliency, perhaps we wouldn't have this situation."

There came the sense of shapings around him, some of them from the disciples, the particular way they were able to bury the elementals within the shapings. Mixed within his sense was that of other shapings, those coming from the Inquisitors.

"I'm not going to allow you to attack the Academy."

"Do you believe you are responsible for defending the Academy now? You really have an arrogance for someone who had no ability to shape before they came here."

She sent a shaping at him and Tolan reacted barely in time, twisting off to the side as he did, pushing outward with a blast of earth. He tried to use it to disrupt the Shapers Path, to knock her free, but she smoothed it quickly. He wasn't sure if he was going to be able to overwhelm her. Aela was a powerful shaper, not just an Inquisitor.

"You are untrained. You have some potential, which I admit is surprising given your background, but your inexperience will be your downfall."

Tolan pushed out with fire, then wind and earth and finally water, striking with shaping after shaping. He could feel his strength beginning to wane. As it did, he realized what her strategy was. She had wanted him to get weakened and had wanted to force him to use more of his power than he was accustomed to doing. She would wait it out.

Did it have to be his?

He had his connection to the elementals. If he could use that, he might be able to force her back.

Only if they responded.

In this place, within Amitan, without having a proximity to the Keystone, he wasn't sure he would have enough strength in order to draw the elementals out.

Perhaps not here.

There was a place where he knew the elementals responded.

He jumped.

He fell to the earth, crashing with his speed, the wind whistling around him, and he landed on a cushioned shaping already running through the city. He headed to the outskirts of Amitan, focusing on whether Aela followed him, and could feel her shaping trailing after him. All he had to do was stay a step ahead of her.

A shaping streaked past him.

Aela was carried on her shaping of wind and fire, and she hovered in the air. It was a powerful shaping, the kind he wondered if he could even re-create, but now wasn't the time to experiment with shapings like that.

He ran. Reaching the forest was the first step. If he could do that, he could disappear within the trees and he thought he could reach the park where the Keystone had been.

Aela traveled past him, sliding on a shaping of air that moved her far more rapidly than he could keep up with. Tolan turned off to the left, darting down a side street. He tried to stay between buildings, hiding himself. If he'd had better control over his shaping, he might have been able to grab it while he was running, but he found it difficult to do. Instead, he had to stay focused on avoiding Aela.

A shaping built behind him and Tolan ducked, darting off into an alleyway.

From here, he worried he was going to get squeezed and there would be nowhere else to go. He focused on what he could control, making his way rapidly through the alley. There was no one out. He wasn't surprised by that. Many people within Amitan were sensers and would be aware of shaping used around them. If they detected as much power as was thrown around now, anyone with any sense would stay clear.

Power built behind him and Tolan spun, focusing briefly on the way the fire rolled through him, detecting the steady sense of it. It flowed from his hand, and as he had done before, he twisted it, sending a spiral of saa through it. The shaping twisted like an elemental and spiraled away.

Using a shaping like that didn't take quite as much energy. Tolan didn't know if it had something to do with the nature of his connection to the elementals or from a familiarity. He certainly had practiced these shapings far more than he'd practiced others.

Spinning back around, he squeezed along through the alley and was thankful when it emerged on the opposite street. He continued running, twisting and turning as he navigated through the streets. A small grouping of people in the distance caught his attention, and he feared for a moment they might be Inquisitors, but they were not.

Tolan skirted around them, disappearing into the throng, and when he had, he glanced back.

There was no sign of the Inquisitor.

He needed her to know where he was, if only so he could draw her away.

Focusing on a shaping, he directed it straight overhead. He hesitated for a moment, letting wind and water spin, and then raced onward.

Her shaping reacted almost instantaneously. She caught up to him and did so just as he saw the forest.

"If only you were better trained, you might have made this chase a little more interesting."

"If only you better understood how I shaped, you might have been able to capture me," he said.

With that, Tolan focused on earth, letting it rumble through him. He used an image of jinnar, the dangerous earth elemental he had some experience with, and it surged upward, crashing toward her, and disrupted her long enough for him to race toward the forest.

He reached the edge of the trees as she blasted through his shaping. For a moment, Tolan worried he had actually called an elemental she had destroyed, but he didn't have a sense of that. If there had been an elemental called, he thought he would have connected to it and would've been aware of it, but there was nothing like that.

Once in the trees, he focused on earth, using that to try to conceal himself. He didn't need to stay hidden for long and had needed only to mask himself so she couldn't track him easily.

He had been through here often enough that he knew the way. Still, as he went, he left a trail, not bothering to mask where he was going, willing to reveal it to her, let her know he was passing through here. She needed to know where the Keystone had been, if only so he could find some way of stopping her.

The forest began to fade and, in the distance, he saw the clearing, the park where he knew the Keystone to have been. If he could reach it, then...

A shaping slammed into him.

It sent him staggering forward.

Tolan rolled, everything in his body hurting. Had she broken something? A water shaping could restore him, but he needed to get to a water shaper in order to do so. As that thought hit him, another followed.

It was a mistake coming here. He should have stayed near the city, near other people, and should have drawn her toward the Academy where other shapers would be and could help.

Now he was isolated.

There was no one here who even knew he would be out here. He had run from his father and the help the disciples might be able to offer.

Aela stalked toward him, and loomed close. "*That* was more interesting," she said.

Shaping built. Spirit shaping.

Immediately, Tolan reached for fire, wrapping it inward, protecting himself. The power of her shaping slammed into him, splitting off to either side, but she left it pouring into him, an unrelenting sense, and he continued to grow increasingly tired.

"How long can you hold on? You aren't quite as strong as I was led to believe, though I suspect you've been using bondars the entire time you shaped. Do you think you are the only one who knows how to use a bondar?"

That explained her strength, and as it continued to

flood into him, overwhelming him, he realized he would not be able to withstand her spirit shaping. Looking up at her, he knew he'd already lost.

4

As Tolan lay there, staring up at Aela as she continued to build a shaping growing increasingly potent the longer she stood over him, he couldn't help but wonder what sort of bondar she used. Even as he wondered, he knew. There were spirit bondars, and he had seen how they could be used.

He didn't have any of his bondars.

Or did he?

He still had the necklace, and he slipped his hand forward, grabbing it, and attempted a shaping through it.

It was a different sort of shaping than attempting it through the furios or the other bondars. In this case, he needed to focus more intently, but found himself struggling to relax and find that emptiness he knew would grant him an ability to reach through the bondar. If it was spirit, then he needed to use spirit through it.

A shaping built, growing increasingly potent.

Tolan pushed it out through the ring, forcing the shaping away from him, through the bondar. As it built, he exploded it toward Aela.

She was tossed off him and he scrambled to his feet, racing toward the clearing.

What was he thinking?

What he should be doing was returning to the city—to the Academy. There had to be master shapers there who could help. The only problem was, he didn't know how many of the master shapers were still under the influence of the Inquisitors. How many remained who would side with Aela?

The stone wall loomed in front of him, and Tolan jumped for it.

He pushed off with a hint of a wind shaping, letting it carry him forward, clearing the top of the wall. He landed, rolling forward. When he was done, he paused, looking around.

There was always something peaceful about this place. Partly, it came from the fact the Keystone had been here. Power existed here. The other part of it came from the fact this was where he first had really begun to understand the elementals and how to shape them, regardless of what method he used. This was his place.

It was the only thing he could think of to escape from Aela. If he could use the power of the clearing, even without the Keystone, he thought he might be able to stop her.

When that was done, he would have to figure out what to do next. He still had to deal with the fact his father and the disciples of the Draasin Lord had come for him, though he still wasn't certain whether he had any interest in going with them. It might be better to return to the Academy if he was able to stop the Inquisitors.

A shaping started to build on the other side of the wall.

Tolan ignored it. He focused instead on his shaping, thinking about the various elementals. He worked through all of them, adding earth by drawing jinnar, fire with saa and esalash, wind with ara and lowei, along with water through washir and udilm. They were the easiest for him to summon at short notice, and he focused on one after another, letting the power of those elementals—elementals that could take a more physical form—begin to appear.

Power exploded.

Tolan knew he was imagining it and knew he had experienced these elementals when he'd been here before, drawing them out of the bond. And in doing so, he was able to release power. If he could do that again, he might be able to use the elementals to stop Aela.

"Help me," he whispered.

Speaking to the elementals should be easy. It should be nothing more than talking. As he had experience speaking to them, he knew they could answer if they wanted.

Aela landed on the top of the wall surrounding the park. She stared at him, and as she looked past him, she smiled. "You have just proven everything we've said about you."

"What have I proven?"

"You have proven your interest in working with the Draasin Lord."

"I have done nothing other than shape."

"Nothing?" She swept her hand around and attempted to push on a powerful shaping, though he couldn't detect which element bond she used. Possibly all of them. "You released elementals."

"These are shapings. How would I have released an elemental?"

She frowned. She wouldn't have a good answer to that. If she claimed he'd done it, it would be saying he knew somehow to release elementals faster than even those who'd been fully trained at the Academy.

"Help me," he whispered, pushing it out on a shaping of wind.

Her shaping slammed into the elementals but did nothing.

That wasn't quite true. It enraged them.

Power burst from the elementals, and they all converged, turning toward Aela.

The shaping building from her was not quite what he would've expected. He thought she might turn and run, or might try to attack them, choosing the elementals to try and overpower, as if to force them back into the elemental bond, but she didn't do that at all.

Instead, she sent a shaping out from her. It wasn't the kind of shaping he expected. It burst forward, streaking upward, and exploded high above the park.

A calling.

It was the only thing it could be, but what kind of calling was she using?

Whatever it was, it was designed to draw more of the Inquisitors here.

If the others appeared, he wouldn't be able to withstand them.

Tolan attempted a shaping of his own, but he was tired. The effort of trying to shape, not only through the bondar, but of trying to withstand her, had been more than he could handle. He was exhausted. If he'd managed to have a bondar, earth or fire, he might not have struggled nearly as much, but he had been drawing from his own stores. There were limits to how much he could do.

A shaping built overhead, and an Inquisitor dropped from the sky. Then another. Then another. Within moments, there were a dozen Inquisitors.

They all surrounded Aela.

They ignored him, focusing on the elementals. They sent shapings toward each of the elementals, shapings designed to force the elemental back into the bond, pushing upon them, driving them away from this world.

Maybe he could add another elemental? If he could summon more, then perhaps he could overwhelm their ability.

Which elemental would he focus on?

If summoned a draasin, he thought he might be able to distract them. They would be forced to focus all their attention on the draasin and use more power than they currently were in order to stop them.

The draasin was one elemental he rarely attempted. Doing so was dangerous, but he had to try.

Taking a deep breath, he imagined the draasin. He thought of fire. He summoned flame, drawing it through him, through this place, through the power that had once been here and where a lingering amount of it remained. When the Keystone had been here, he had been able to summon the draasin, and he thought he could again.

It started slowly, flames spreading outward as if to form arms. A body elongated and gradually grew. It was different than what he remembered of the draasin depicted in the books in the Academy. With it, there came power, but it was the kind of power he felt was coming more from him than from the actual elemental.

Tolan continued to feed the draasin, giving more and more of himself to the shaping. As he did, he felt it growing, emerging. At the same time, it didn't feel nearly as potent as he detected from the other elementals he had summoned. Either this wasn't the same type of elemental, or what he was drawing forth wasn't a draasin.

Maybe this was a mistake, attempting the draasin? He'd never done so, and in order to use it effectively, he thought he needed to find an elemental that could be powerful.

Hyza.

For some reason, he'd felt connected to hyza ever since he'd experienced it. There was power that came from his connection to that elemental, and he was aware of fire—but also earth.

Focusing on it, he shifted his shaping, and the draasin

wings that had elongated began to curl downward, turning into legs, and through that, he continued to pull upon hyza, letting more and more power come.

This time, there was a sense of independence. He detected the overwhelming change, the drawing of the elemental.

"Help me," he whispered.

The elemental separated from the bond.

Tolan *felt* it as it did. It was a popping, as if the elemental had been there and then was not. Through it, he was able to detect the way it manifested.

There came a hissing, a painful sound like steam burning off, and the elemental darted forward, slamming into the nearest of the Inquisitors.

Tolan turned toward the Inquisitors. The effect of the shaping had been enough that he could no longer shape anymore. He had sapped his strength, but perhaps it was unnecessary to do anything more. As he turned to the others, he saw most of the elementals had been suppressed.

The Inquisitors had done that?

Tolan had barely detected it. When he had done something similar before, he had been acutely aware of when the elementals were forced back into the bond, and this time, he was not.

Was it a matter of his distraction? He had been so focused on the draasin—and then hyza—that he hadn't been thinking about the other elementals. Without those other elementals, he didn't have the same support. It wouldn't be long before the Inquisitors managed to overpower hyza, forcing it back into the bond.

Yet, there was something different about hyza than the other elementals.

Hyza felt *real*. The others hadn't popped out of the bond quite the way he felt hyza had. With hyza, he felt a strange connection, an awareness of the elemental, and there was a ferocity, a rage that boiled within it. Tolan latched onto that, letting the elemental know he was there with it and for it.

He turned toward the Inquisitors. There might not be anything he could do, but he wasn't going to go down without a fight.

Aela approached. Shaping swirled around her, keeping hyza at bay. The other Inquisitors worked to suppress the remaining elementals—or whatever they were. Two of the Inquisitors were down, their bodies broken, their proximity to hyza suggesting it had been responsible for what had happened. Tolan had a hard time finding any remorse.

"I think you have quite a few answers we would like." She turned her gaze upon the field before it settled on hyza. "Here I have long thought the Draasin Lord was wrong, but perhaps there is some power to controlling the elementals. With an untrained shaper nearly able to hold us back, I can't deny I'm curious to know what someone with actual training might be able to do." She motioned to the others, who fanned out around her.

Tolan remained fixed in place and hyza stayed near him, practically guarding him.

"Go," he whispered.

The elemental cocked his head to the side, almost as if it understood what he was saying.

"Don't stay. I don't want you to be caught up in this. You don't need to be here with me."

Aela grinned at him. "Are you trying to speak to it? I find it amusing you would think you could have a conversation with an elemental."

He ignored her taunting. There would be no escaping. Nothing he could do to prevent her from reaching it, but he still wanted to fight. There had to be some way of stopping her, but perhaps that time was beyond him.

She continued toward him. The shaping building from her was incredible, and he couldn't imagine how she was able to hold onto such power despite having used shaping for as long as she had. At this point, Tolan had nothing left, everything within him overwhelmed.

She smiled as she approached. "I think your last Inquisition was not nearly long enough. This time, you will remain with us until we have the answers we seek."

Tolan could only shake his head.

A shaping was building, but it was not nearby.

Did she have more Inquisitors coming?

It didn't seem like the shaping he had detected from the disciples, so whoever was using it was not near enough to be of much help. He ignored that he was isolated. There was nothing to do about it anyway. He was trapped, and once the Inquisitors captured him, there would be no escaping.

Another shaping built. This one was nearer.

He detected something familiar within it, though why would that be?

This shaping caught Aela's attention. She looked up. As she did, Tolan brought his eyes up to the sky and realized there were three shapers approaching.

He blinked, half unable to believe what he was saying. "Grand Master?"

Aela shifted the focus of her shaping, angling it upward. As she did, it blasted against an unseen barrier the Grand Master held. It wasn't just the Grand Master. The Grand Inquisitor was with him, and she created a shaping, this one of spirit, and it flooded downward, swirling toward him, an alarming kind of power.

Tolan turned his attention to hyza. "You need to go. There's nothing you can do here other than get forced back into the bond."

The elemental looked at him, a flicker of understanding crossing its eyes, and he thought he heard a whisper of something in the back of his mind, but then it was gone.

The elemental darted off, loping toward the forest before clearing the wall with a powerful jump. When the elemental was gone, two of the Inquisitors grabbed Tolan.

"Take him. I will catch up with you," Aela said.

With a blast of shaping, they took to the air. Tolan tried to resist, attempting to fight, but he was exhausted. The Inquisitors held onto him easily, carrying him as if he was a child. Compared to them, his shaping ability was childlike.

In the air, they headed south, away from Amitan.

"Where are you taking me?" His voice was weak, and he wished he had more strength in the questioning, but he simply did not.

One of them started to answer, but a strange shaping near him built and slammed into one of the Inquisitors. The man went spinning off, spiraling away and dropping to the ground. It left only one of the Inquisitors holding onto Tolan.

He barely had time to register that the attack had come from one of the disciples. The nature of it was similar to their attack, powerful, flowing from them, but the kind of attack reminding him of the way he shaped, a similar sort of energy to what he drew upon when pulling on the elementals.

That no longer seemed to be a coincidence.

Maybe the disciples of the Draasin Lord were more like him than he realized.

His father served the disciples, so perhaps that was why.

The other Inquisitor wrapped Tolan in a shaping of earth, squeezing him. He added wind, forcing Tolan with him, and together they streaked higher and higher into the sky. Tolan could no longer keep track of where they were. For a moment, he thought he felt the effect of their shaping and keep track of where he was being taken, but he lost it.

He needed to fight.

If he could call upon ara, perhaps the wind elemental would give him a little bit of strength, enough that he'd be able to escape his capture. He focused on nothing more than the sense of wind. He ignored everything else. The pain. His fatigue. The fear he felt at what was taking place. Through it all, he focused instead on wind and nothing more.

The elemental whistled past him, and he drew upon it. Ara began to appear.

"Help me," he whispered. It felt like he was asking the elementals to help an awful lot, and yet, despite that, they still answered.

This time, it twisted, unwinding him from the Inquisitor, and Tolan dropped.

He streaked toward the ground, moving far more rapidly than he could control. He focused on wind, on earth—thinking he'd be able to buffer his landing on water to try to cushion the blow, and even on fire, though he had no idea what using fire would even do. Perhaps nothing at this point.

As he continued to drop, he felt himself slowing.

Only, it wasn't anything he was doing.

He searched for signs of the elemental, something that would tell him why he was slowing, but he could come up with nothing.

Then he landed.

The suddenness of it took away his breath and he spun around, looking for anything able to help him understand who had guided him to the ground. It wasn't likely to be the Inquisitors. They would have no reason to have helped him like that. Maybe it was one of the disciples.

Tolan looked up, and as he did, he saw two disciples

facing the Inquisitor. Neither of them was his father. Where was his father?

If he were involved, he would have to be nearby.

Tolan searched for evidence of him, looking around the clearing, but there was nothing. He started toward the tree and a figure appeared.

Tolan tried to prepare a shaping, readying to wrap himself in it, but it didn't come to him nearly as quickly as he needed it to.

He slipped his hand around the bondar. If nothing else, he was going to fight however he could, and if that meant using power of the bondar—however weak it might be at this point—he was going to do that.

As the figure appeared, Tolan's hand dropped to his side. "Ferrah?"

5

Ferrah started toward him, her hand clutched around something and her eyes darting around, scanning the forest all about them. Her chin was jutted forward, her jaw set, and as soon as she felt confident there wasn't anyone else in the vicinity, she went running toward him.

"Ferrah, you shouldn't be here."

"*You* shouldn't be here."

"The Inquisitors—"

"I know what happened with the Inquisitors. We saw the effect of it."

"You know?"

"The Grand Master has secured the Academy. I was barely able to escape."

"Why would you have wanted to escape?"

"I knew you weren't in the Academy, which meant this somehow involved you." She arched a brow at him, grabbing for his arm. "This always seems to involve you."

"Ferrah, this time, I don't know that you should be here. There are disciples of the Draasin Lord."

"I'm aware. I saw them in the city."

"It's more than that. It's my father."

"What about your father?"

He needed to tell her. When it came to Ferrah, he didn't like lying to her about anything. She deserved the truth, if only because she had helped him so much and had been such a part of everything he had done. Yet telling her the truth about this was terrifying. It meant admitting he was everything people had always said him to be. For so long, he had fought that. Tolan had avoided those rumors, ignoring them, and yet, despite everything, it turned out the rumors were true.

"He's… He's with them."

It was difficult to say, and incredibly difficult to admit, and yet, telling Ferrah wasn't as hard as he thought it would be.

She looked at him with sadness marking her deep blue eyes. "Tolan, I am sorry."

"We can talk about it somewhere else. I don't know that I want to be here when the disciples show up." After what he'd seen, the violence within them and his father's eagerness to attack, how could he? That wasn't what he wanted for himself.

"Where would you go?"

"Back to the Academy, if I can."

"Why do you think you can't?"

At first, he had intended to run, thinking he had no choice. If it were no longer necessary, did he have to run?

Now the truth about the Inquisitors was out, it was possible he wouldn't need to. He *could* return to the Academy.

And if he did, then he would never know anything about his father.

Considering the fact his parents had left him behind, he wasn't sure if that even bothered him. He needed to go, to learn what had happened and why they had abandoned him, and yet, if he left now, there were other answers he'd never have.

He looked around, and as he did, he knew he wouldn't be able to shape his way back. "Do you think you could help?"

"We aren't that far from the Shapers Path," she said.

"I don't know that I can reach the Shapers Path. After what I've gone through, it might be more than I can shape."

She slipped her arm around his waist. "Hold on."

With that, she shaped, bursting from the ground with a hint of wind. She added a touch of fire to it, just a little bit, and the combined effect carried them soaring into the air. Even as tired as he was, Tolan was well aware of the way she used her shaping, and more than that, he recognized how much power she had in it. Ferrah didn't need to use bondars—yet it seemed she was doing.

"How did you know where to find me?" he asked.

"I followed the Grand Master," she said, flushing so her pale cheeks seemed to match her red hair.

"If he learned you did…"

"Then he'd better not learn what I did," she said, shooting him a hard-eyed stare.

They reached the Shapers Path. From here, he was able to walk, and she released him, allowing him to make his way along the Shapers Path unaided. In the distance, the sense of shaping continued to build, the occasional burst of power exploding nearby enough to cause him to stop and look, to see if he could pick up on what triggered the shaping, and yet he was unable to do so. Every so often, he would detect a sense of shaping coming from the disciples. Each time he did, Tolan paused, looking to see if there was anything within that shaping that he could determine, but there wasn't anything other than that strange sense triggering an awareness, a memory of the elementals, leaving him believing the disciples must use a shaping similar to his.

"You were able to make it all the way out here after the Grand Master?" He'd seen the type of shaping the Grand Master could use and the way he was able to travel. Ferrah shouldn't be able to follow so easily.

"I'm not without shaping strength, Tolan," she said. "It's easy enough to use earth and wind to track you and your shapings."

"You were willing to risk yourself against disciples of the Draasin Lord?"

"Don't make it sound like I did something heroic. I didn't know they would be here."

"But you were willing to come here for me?"

"Tolan, we're friends."

As he looked at her, noticing the way she watched him,

he recognized a hesitation within her. "Is that all we are?"

She turned and looked at him. Jonas had teased him about having an interest in Ferrah. For a while, Tolan hadn't believed he had interest in her like that. She was his friend and attempting to change that friendship into something else was a surefire way of losing that friend.

"Is this the time?"

Tolan looked around. "Would you rather we talk about it back at the Academy?"

"In the dorms? No. I just didn't think talking about something like this after running from disciples of the Draasin Lord along with the Inquisitors was the right thing to do, either." She looked around and turned toward him, smiling. "If this is where you want to have the conversation, then let's do it. What are you thinking?"

"I…" he stammered

She smiled. "Always so shy when it comes to this, and yet you're probably the most confident person I know. But let me make it easy for you."

She leaned toward him, kissing him gently on the lips. He kissed back, and…

A shaping struck him, throwing him off the Shapers Path.

Tolan cried out and attempted to reach for a shaping, but he was unable to do so. He fell, the ground looming toward him too quickly to react.

And then wind caught him, holding him.

He looked over to see Ferrah dropping down next to him. Shaping wrapped around her, her face caught in a tight concentration.

"See? I told you now wasn't a good time."

"I can't shape anything right now," he said.

"Use this," she said, handing him a bondar. It was a withering, the bondar for wind, and the markings along the surface of it told him she had taken it from the Academy.

"I thought you didn't want me to take the bondars from the Academy."

"Only because you tend to draw the wrong kind of attention."

"And this doesn't?"

"Not quite as much as you. Are you going to use it or what?"

Taking the bondar, Tolan tried to draw wind through it, and it came slowly, but at least with a shaping of wind, he was able to protect himself a little bit. He looked up, searching for where the attack had come from, but saw nothing. "I didn't even detect a shaping."

"It targeted you."

If it was targeting him, then it meant it was one of the Inquisitors. The disciples—and his father—would not have targeted him. Had any of them been left to recover? There had been nearly a dozen of the Inquisitors, and that wasn't saying anything about Aela.

Tolan focused, searching through the sky for a sense of shaping, but there wasn't anything.

"That's strange," he whispered.

"That you were attacked or that it hasn't returned?"

"Mostly that it hasn't returned." He'd grown far too accustomed to being attacked since coming to the Academy. He had gone through his share and more of shaped attacks on himself or on those around him.

Another shaping built and he looked up, preparing to push away with wind, ready to swirl it through the withering, perhaps to add a sense of ara to it in order to prevent anyone from reaching him, but there was no need.

The Grand Master lowered himself in front of them. He glanced from Tolan to Ferrah. "Shaper Changen. I didn't realize you were outside the Academy."

Ferrah flushed again, this time more deeply than she had before. "I'm sorry, Grand Master, it's just that—"

The Grand Master waved his hand dismissively. "You don't need to explain. I understand you and Shaper Ethar have a unique friendship."

This time, it was Tolan's turn to flush. Warmth worked up his cheeks. "Grand Master, I don't know what to tell you about the attack, but Master Aela—"

"I know all about Aela. She thought she could distract me with an attack, but unfortunately for her, spirit shapings don't work quite as effectively on those who can shape spirit." He glanced from Tolan to Ferrah. "You did well managing to avoid her attack for as long as you did."

"I think I got lucky," Tolan said.

"Luck or skill?"

Tolan thought about everything he'd done. "Perhaps a bit of both."

He wasn't sure whether there had been some skill to it, but the more he thought about it, the more he thought it was both, as he had said. He would like to have skill, and in the time he'd been in the Academy, his knowledge had continued to grow and develop, but he still wasn't where he could be if he'd remained there.

"It was interesting you decided to bring her there."

Tolan turned away from the Grand Master, looking around the park. "I wanted to get her away from the city."

The Grand Master watched Tolan knowingly for a moment. "Ah. Then you did well, Shaper Ethar. It did take us a little bit longer to reach you, but perhaps you prevented others from experiencing the danger of a shaper attack upon Amitan."

"What happened to Aela?" he asked.

"She has escaped."

"Escaped?"

"It seems she and the others with her had a very different approach to shaping. Unfortunately, it has weakened the Inquisitors."

"I'm sorry, Grand Master."

"Why would you be sorry? You helped ensure they weren't successful. I think they saw an opportunity and decided to use that opportunity to maneuver for power. Fortunately for us, they were unsuccessful and they underestimated not just me, but you."

The sound of the forest around him caught his attention, and Tolan looked around. Every so often, he thought he had a sense of shaping near him and he began to worry the disciples would appear. If they did, he might have to reveal to the Grand Master the role he had, and he had no interest in doing that.

"I think we should be heading back to the Academy," the Grand Master said.

"Are you worried about another attack?" Ferrah asked.

The Grand Master nodded. "There's always the possibility of another attack. Unfortunately, when it comes to what we've experienced, they will see this as a sign of weakness. Where they see weakness, they will think they need to press."

A shaping built from the Grand Master, powerful and swift, and Tolan was acutely aware of how he used spirit, pushing it out, sweeping in a sharp arc radiating away from him. When it cleared, the Grand Master nodded, looking from Tolan to Ferrah.

"Do you think you can make it back on your own?" he asked.

"You aren't going to guide us back?" Ferrah asked.

"I don't know that it's necessary," he said.

She nodded, and when she did, the Grand Master pushed off with a shaping, taking to the air, and disappeared. It wasn't so much that he ascended to the Shapers Path high overhead, it was simply that he disappeared.

"I'd like to learn how to shape like that," Ferrah said longingly.

"It was a mixture of each element bond," Tolan said.

She glanced over at him. "How do you know?"

"I could feel it."

"You could *feel* the shaping the Grand Master used?"

Tolan nodded.

"Are you always able to detect shapings like that?"

"Most of the time, but usually it's a matter of knowing

when someone is shaping, and lately it's a matter of being able to determine what element bonds are used."

"You do realize how valuable that is, don't you?"

"From the way you say it, I imagine it's quite valuable?" She laughed. "Quite."

"Well, the Grand Master wanted us to return to the Academy."

As much as he might want to continue his conversation with Ferrah, he also didn't want to linger out here any longer. They should disappear before the Inquisitors returned.

Ferrah eyed him for a moment before nodding.

With that, she shaped, heading to the Shapers Path. Tolan held onto the withering, squeezing it and sending a shaping of wind through it. It wasn't controlled, and he blasted upward, coming to land next to Ferrah on the Path. His strength was gradually returning, and he hoped by the time he reached the Academy, it would be back enough that he wouldn't be quite so weakened.

They started back along the Shapers Path, neither of them speaking. In the distance, the city began to loom into view. As they neared, the distant sense of a shaping caught his attention, though it wasn't in the city at all. It was behind them. As he approached, Tolan hesitated, glancing back, worried the shaping was close.

Ferrah glanced in his direction. "What is it?"

Turning toward the shaping, he focused on the nature of it. Behind him stretched much of the forest. In the distance, he could vaguely make out the edge of the clearing where the Keystone had been, where he had been attacked by the Inquisitors, and yet, that wasn't where he detected the power. The shaping came from somewhere else, farther from the city, in a place he couldn't quite understand.

It was far enough from him that he wondered if perhaps he was even detecting it correctly. And maybe he was not.

When the shaping came to him again, Tolan was certain of what he was feeling.

Buried within the shaping was a sense of the elementals. It was the same sort of shaping he used, the same way he grasped at power. As it surged, it resonated within him.

His father.

He was still out there, and what was more, he was near enough that Tolan could detect his shaping.

"Tolan?" Ferrah said.

Tolan squeezed his eyes shut. He wanted those answers, and he wanted to know why his father had suddenly appeared, but more than that, he wanted to know where his father had gone, but not like this. Not after what he'd seen of them.

Instead, he turned away, heading back toward Amitan and the Academy.

When the shaping came again, he tried to ignore it, but every so often, he glanced back, thinking he might catch a glimpse of his father. Each time the shaping returned, he stiffened, and it wasn't until they crossed over the border into Amitan and neared the Academy that the sense of the shaping finally began to fade to nothing.

6

LIFE BACK AT THE ACADEMY WAS NO DIFFERENT THAN IT had been before. Tolan had expected to be greeted with scorn and derision, but there was none of that. It was almost as if the others at the Academy didn't know what had taken place. Most of the students had been sequestered in the dormitories, though some had been outside the Academy, locked away. When the uprising had begun, they hadn't known it was Inquisitors versus the Academy. All they thought was that the disciples had attacked. Most within the Academy had enough sense to run when that took place, which was why no one had made note of his absence.

The student dormitory for the second levels was awash with activity. Most of the students sat in the common area, and they did so in groupings of friends, chattering loudly, some playing games while others sat and read, but for the most part, all were oblivious to the Inquisitor uprising.

Ferrah patted his arm. "It's okay. No one knows what happened," she said.

Tolan's gaze swept around the room. No one knew about what had just happened, but they all still knew about the Inquisition. They all still viewed him as a servant of the Draasin Lord. Now he knew the truth of his father, how could he be anything but what they'd always believed him to be?

He looked around, shaking his head. "I don't know that I want to be here."

"Jonas will want to see you."

"Will he?" After the Inquisition, he was no longer certain how Jonas viewed him. They had been friends, but when he had begun to shape more easily, Jonas had been suspicious of him—and rightly so. Tolan had been secretive about how he'd been shaping. Tolan should talk with Jonas, at least to smooth things over.

"You know he will."

"I think… I think I need to stop in the library."

She frowned as she looked at him. "The library? Why would you need to go there?"

"Master Minden saw me when I was chased by the Inquisitors." She had done more than that. She had seemed to know who he was and why the Inquisitors were after him, but she also had helped escort him to a place where he could escape. He had questions about her, and didn't know if she would even be there to answer them.

"If you want, I can go with you."

"I'd like that."

They looked around for a moment, and when they did, his eyes settled on Jonas.

He was sitting near the far wall, talking to Gray and Tara, but when he locked eyes with Tolan, he sat upright.

"I guess I'm not going to the library quite yet," Tolan said.

If he turned around now, it would be abandoning his friend and basically throwing away any friendship they had. And Master Minden would be at the library when he finally returned. He didn't need to go to her now in order to talk with her about her role in all of this. He could find her another time. Besides, if he waited, he might have a better understanding as to what had taken place and *his* role within it, not just hers.

Starting toward Jonas, Ferrah stayed with him, her hand resting on his arm. He held onto it, comforted by her presence. As he approached, Jonas glanced from him to her.

A hint of a smile started to twist his lips. "Well?"

"Well what?" Ferrah said.

Jonas grinned. "It's about time the two of you…"

Ferrah looked down, almost as if realizing she had her hand resting on Tolan. Her face flushed, putting more color into her pale and freckled cheeks, but she didn't remove her hand.

"Where have you been? The Academy has been on lockdown."

"So we've heard. We were in the library," Ferrah said.

"Always in the library." Glancing at Gray, a slender man who had never really aligned himself with any group, Jonas smirked. "I think they have someplace in the library that they sneak away to." Turning his attention back to them, he asked, "Do you know why we were on lockdown?"

"I don't," Tolan said quickly.

"Some are saying there was another elemental attack. The Great Mother knows we've had enough over the time we've been here."

That might be a better thing to believe than the truth. He should have asked the Grand Master what story they were going to let out, but he hadn't. What sort of things would the Academy want known about the Inquisitors? With Aela a part of it, and the likelihood there would be no further lessons on spirit shaping, he suspected the Grand Master would try to keep it quiet.

"Maybe it was an elemental attack," Ferrah said.

Tolan clenched his jaw. It was increasingly difficult to refrain from saying anything. He didn't want others to know he was as partial to the elementals as he was, but he also didn't like the idea that others blamed the elementals for various attacks. That sort of behavior led to fear, and with fear, there was a greater willingness to shove the elementals back into the bond.

"I bet Ethar here was a part of it," a deep and drawling voice said.

Tolan turned to see Draln heading toward him. He was dressed in his formal cloak, and the sneer on his face reminded Tolan of the Inquisitors. It wouldn't surprise him to learn Draln had some spirit-shaping ability, and it wouldn't surprise him to learn they'd tried to recruit Draln.

"After all, the Inquisitors did find reason to hold him as long as they did."

"And they released him," Ferrah said.

Draln turned to her, shrugging. "They may have released him, but they held him long enough. They don't do that unless there's reason to do so. He's guilty of something."

"You're guilty of being an ass."

"Why won't you let Ethar defend himself?"

Tolan didn't say anything, and Draln continued to smirk.

"See? He can't defend himself. Because I'm telling the truth."

"Or he doesn't say anything because there's no reason to," Ferrah said.

"I think it's cute you feel the need to defend him like that. What are you going to do when he's taken away for his next Inquisition? Are you going to go to the Inquisitors, tell them they have it wrong, and be surprised when they drag you away to the Inquisition? I can assure you, I've seen what happens when people think they can influence the Inquisitors."

That was part of Tolan's fear. He didn't want people he cared about getting drawn into it, and certainly didn't want Ferrah to get pulled into an Inquisition. She had a brighter future at the Academy than that. With people like

Draln, he knew he needed to speak up, and if he didn't, Draln would continue to taunt him, abusing him.

At the same time, he didn't trust himself. Now he knew the truth of his father, he didn't know if there was anything to say. He was everything they'd always accused him of being.

The image of his father standing with the other disciples of the Draasin Lord flashed back into his mind. With it came the sense of power he had from them. The same power that resonated within him. That couldn't be a coincidence. It was almost as if he should have gone with them. Perhaps if he had, he would better understand his brand of shaping. There were lessons he could learn at the Academy, but no one had been able to teach him how to use shaping the way he did, to involve the image of the elementals in it, to make his power greater the way he did.

"What are you going to say to the Grand Master?" Ferrah asked when Tolan had said nothing.

"The Grand Master knows I'm not involved in any of this. Besides, some of us report what we see," Draln said.

"Yeah? And what are you reporting?"

"Only that we know exactly what Ethar here is up to."

Ferrah gave him a searching look, practically begging for him to say something, but there wasn't anything for Tolan to say.

"I'm sure the Grand Master appreciates your support," he said.

With that, Tolan pushed his way past the other man, heading to the back rooms and the quarters he shared with Jonas and Ferrah. His bed looked far too inviting, and being as tired as he was after the attack, he wanted nothing more than to sink into it, to drift off to sleep, but if he did that, he wasn't sure he'd be able to get back up.

Ferrah followed him into the room. "You can't let him keep pushing you like that."

"I don't think it matters," Tolan said, taking a seat on his bed.

"It matters. You know it matters to someone like him. He's going to use your unwillingness to fight back against you."

"I've dealt with people like Draln my whole life."

"Your whole life?"

"Well, ever since my parents left."

Ferrah took a seat on the bed next to him, glancing at the doorway. A shaping built from her, wind and earth, and with it, she created a barrier that swirled around them. It muted the sounds from the great room, isolating them. "This isn't quite the way I'm sure you wanted to have a conversation, but this might be the only way we can."

Tolan stared down at his hands. "I told you everyone had always accused me of serving the Draasin Lord."

"Because your parents were abducted."

He looked up, meeting her eyes. "Apparently not abducted."

"You don't know that. If the Draasin Lord can spirit-shape, then they could have been forced to serve. You know what happened when I was spirit-shaped."

Tolan took a deep breath. "What if they can't be spirit-shaped?"

"Anyone could be spirit-shaped."

He shook his head. "I haven't been spirit-shaped. They've tried, and I think that with enough force, they might be able to push past my natural barriers, but when they have attempted to spirit-shape me, they've failed."

"Because you have the ability to shape spirit."

"Apparently. But it's more than that. There are techniques you can use to avoid spirit-shaping."

"There are?"

"I use fire. I think other elements would work just as well, but it's the one that's come easiest to me, probably because I had the furios for as long as I did, getting a chance to be familiar with fire."

"How do you use fire?"

"It's a shaping I wrap around myself. Nothing more than that, and I don't even wrap it around my entire body, just my mind. When I place it, I twist it inward, inverting it."

Heat began to wash through him as he said it. He realized how foolish it was to be trying to explain a shaping to Ferrah—one of the strongest shapers in their level.

"I don't understand how you would invert it. Are you shaping yourself? You know how dangerous that can be."

"I don't think I'm shaping myself, though it's possible I am a little bit." Then again, he didn't think he was. If he was shaping himself, the nature of the shaping would be a little bit different. There was never a time when he'd pushed on himself. It was always a matter of this shaping simply being held above the surface of his mind, the connection to fire allowing him to know how to do so, and when he inverted it, he twisted it in a way that it angled toward him, but it also shielded itself from the other shapers knowing what he was doing. The Grand Inquisitor had seemed surprised when he'd done it.

"Can you show me?"

"Maybe when I have more strength back."

"I'm sorry. I should have known."

"No. I want to show you." Tolan took her hand, squeezing it before letting his hands fall off to the side. "I just don't know that I can do it right now. With as much as we've done, I don't know that I have the strength to shape. If I use it and do something uncontrolled, I run the risk of…"

The thing was, he didn't know what he ran the risk of. Possibly losing control of the shaping. When it came to his shaping, that was the biggest danger.

"Can you tell me more about your parents?"

"I don't know what there is to say. If my father is a disciple," he said, lowering his voice, turning his attention toward the door. He didn't need anyone out there knowing that was his fear. If Draln were to discover it, he could easily imagine the endless and unrelenting taunting the other man would give him. "Everything I thought growing up would be wrong. I defended them for so long, thinking they couldn't be disciples of the Draasin Lord. Why would I ever believe they could be?"

"I think everyone wants to believe the best of their parents."

"You don't have an experience like that."

"I don't, but my parents had a different obsession."

"The same one you have?"

"It's not an obsession. It's a matter of trying to understand the nature of places of power."

"Like the Convergence you're convinced is in your homeland."

She took a deep breath, her gaze drifting to the other side of the room. Tolan followed it to see her books rested there. "That's part of what I hope to learn here. I was thinking if I could uncover anything, I might be able to understand the nature of why Par is what it is, and I never expected to find a similar sort of power here in Amitan."

"It makes sense that there would be," he said.

"It does. Which is why I should have considered that before."

"Maybe you've been spirit-shaped before."

He said it with a smile, but as he did, a look of horror dawned across her face. "What if I have?"

"I don't know that we would even know."

That was one of the dangers of a spirit-shaping. It could be done with such skill that no trace of it remained. When his friends had been spirit-shaped to forget about the place of Convergence, they had been no different than before. They had no memory of that time, almost as if the events leading up to their finding the Convergence had been wiped from their minds. Everything else remained. The level of control required for shaping like that had to be incredible, and Tolan couldn't help but think if they could better understand how that shaping had taken place, they might be able to discover if they'd been shaped before.

"What makes you think you can't experience a spirit-shaping?" Ferrah asked after a while.

"When the Grand Inquisitor tried to shape me, she failed."

"What if she didn't want you to be spirit-shaped?" Ferrah looked up, meeting his eyes. "I mean, what if it was never her intention to take those memories from you?"

"Why would she want me to keep them, but not you and Jonas?"

"I don't know."

He thought about his experience with the Grand Inquisitor when he had been in the Inquisition. There'd been a strange sense of familiarity with her. She had seemed to know him, but why would that be?

Then again, she was a powerful spirit shaper, and with that power, she would be able to reach deep inside his mind, drawing away all traces of information, and in doing so, she could reach for secrets he had intended to keep. Perhaps she had uncovered something about his parents. Maybe she had used a memory—a memory like the one he'd had while in the Inquisition—to get a better understanding of who he was and where he came from. And with knowledge like that, he could see her trying to use that against him.

He needed to be careful. The other Inquisitors might be gone, but the Grand Inquisitor remained. She was powerful, and she might pose as much of a threat as any.

"What if we're wrong about the Draasin Lord?"

Ferrah frowned at him. "Why would you say that?"

"I don't know. It's just…"

"You think that because your parents went to serve the Draasin Lord, we're suddenly wrong? Think about what we've seen. What *you've* seen. The Great Mother knows that you of all people at the Academy have as much experience as any student. You've seen the way the Draasin Lord's disciples are willing to attack, and the violence they are all too eager to inflict. And you've seen the way the rogue elementals attack. They're dangerous."

Tolan was probably alone in feeling the elementals weren't as dangerous as most believed. And he'd already shared with Ferrah that he doubted they were what most believed.

"It's good you were rescued from the disciples," she said.

"You mean my father."

"The disciples," she said. Ferrah glanced at the door, then at Tolan. "I imagine you're tired after everything that took place. You can rest, and I'll do a little bit of reading."

"Thanks. That would be nice."

"If you want, I could sit by you?"

He met her eyes and smiled. "That would be even nicer."

She gathered her books, coming to take a seat next to him. As he settled onto the bed, resting his head near her, a mixture of emotions flowed through him. He was thrilled by the idea of the closeness with Ferrah, and yet there was a part of him that remained uncertain. He couldn't help but feel as if some part of him was different, wrong, and because of his belief about the elementals, he worried he would never fully fit in at the Academy. As he drifted to sleep, the memory of his father and the shaping pulled at him, a promise of power, but it was also a question that rolled through him.

What if he was meant to be somewhere else? What if he was meant to learn somewhere else?

As he drifted off, a sense of shaping came to him distantly, reminding him of his power, a twisting of the elemental energy within the shaping, and his heart skipped a beat before he drifted off to sleep.

7

Sitting in the fire tower was a strange experience. Tolan sat near the back of the room, longing for the furios, wishing he had the bondar as he had ever since coming to the Academy. He felt naked without it, empty, and almost as if he would be helpless, yet he knew he wouldn't be. He no longer was quite so dependent upon it, so he needn't be concerned about not having it. At the same time, it was something he'd grown accustomed to having with him. Its absence left him uncomfortable, unsettled, as if he wouldn't be able to perform the shapings he needed in order to satisfy Master Sartan.

Ferrah joined him at the back of the room, and he smiled at her. "You don't have to sit back here with me."

"That's okay," she said.

"It's not. I know you like to sit toward the front."

"I thought I should get a better sense of what it's like to see the tower from this perspective."

"You mean back here with me? You don't need that perspective."

She smiled at him. "It's not that I need that perspective, but I thought you could use the company."

Looking around the room, Tolan wondered if Jonas would sit by them. In the days leading up to his Inquisition, Jonas had been avoiding him after an argument they'd had. He had done so as his way of protecting himself to avoid conflict, but Tolan needed his friends. Losing Jonas had made the Inquisition all the harder.

Master Sartan came into the room from an area in the back, and swept his gaze around the students. "It seems some have decided not to attend class today."

There were fewer students than usual, and Tolan didn't know if it was because of what had recently happened, or if there was something else.

"Perhaps others decided they knew enough about fire shaping, and they don't need to attend my lectures any longer."

Near the front of the class, Draln snickered. Tolan wasn't surprised to see he was here, and even less surprised he was surrounded by his usual cadre of people, all of them looking to try to get in his good graces.

"Today, we are going to talk about the use of fire on oneself."

Tolan frowned. The timing couldn't be coincidental, could it? He resisted the urge to glance over at Ferrah, but could feel her stiffen. Had she gone to Master Sartan and asked? It wouldn't surprise him that she would. She would probably think it was her way of trying to protect him, and in doing so, she would think she was finding out information useful to Tolan when he was performing his shaping. Instead, he felt as if it was setting him up for questions he didn't want to answer.

He didn't feel any danger using the shaping the way he had, and though he knew Ferrah worried about it and didn't like that he had placed a fire shaping around his mind—

inverting it in a way to protect himself from spirit—he knew it wasn't dangerous.

"There was a time when shapers experimented with their abilities. It was a dangerous time, and too often, people would become far too confident with how they used shapings, thinking they could manage the power. Rarely were they able to manage it in any way that gave them control. When it comes to shaping, particularly when shaping upon oneself, control is an illusion."

Master Sartan began a shaping of fire that swirled in front of him. It created a sphere, a circle of power, and he held it in place. The control that Master Sartan used amazed Tolan. He knew just how much power it took to hold a shaping like that and understood just how difficult it was to keep it from collapsing in on itself. It was the kind of shaping he wished he was better able to do.

"Fire can be dangerous. Fire is both constructive and destructive. It is what makes fire unique among all of the elements, and perhaps the most powerful." Master Sartan smiled, releasing his hold on the ball of flame. "I imagine you will hear the same from the other master shapers.

When it comes to water, they will claim it gives life, and that without water, there would be no healing. The earth shapers will claim that earth is the most powerful of the elements, and that one must have earth for food and that we spring forth from the earth. The wind shapers will claim that without wind, there would be no breath and without breath, there would be no life. I would argue all are true, and yet, through them all, fire burned the brightest. Without heat, we would die. Without fire, there would be no growth, no crops to feed us. Without the flames, there would be no… Yes, Shaper Changen?"

Tolan glanced over and realized Ferrah had her hand in the air. He hadn't realized she was sitting there like that, but she leaned forward, and when Master Sartan called on her, she flashed a smile.

"What about spirit?"

"Yes, well, spirit is different from the other elements."

"Is it not equally powerful?"

"Spirit is powerful, and much can be done with it, but scholars over the years have viewed spirit as something of a higher-level element. It isn't quite necessary for life, not the way that other elements are."

"What you mean by higher level?"

"Do you intend to continue to question me during my lecture, Shaper Changen, or do you intend to allow me to have my time? You can speak to me after the lecture if you have additional questions."

Ferrah leaned back, pressing her lips together in a tight frown. He could sense the irritation radiating off her.

"You shouldn't push him like that," Tolan said to her.

"I was asking a question. I'm not pushing at all."

"Maybe you shouldn't ask him so many questions."

She frowned at him but made a point of looking away, as if making a show of ignoring him. If she wasn't careful, she'd return to her usual location at the front of the class, and he enjoyed having her near him like this.

"Ages ago, there were shapers who sought to try to become closer to power. Given the nature of fire, an attempt was made to use this element to help them gain a greater understanding of it," Master Sartan went on. "A shaping was used, power poured upon the shaper, and they did so with the intent of trying to gain an increased sense and understanding of fire. What we know of it tells us that it was a dangerous and destructive type of shaping, but more than that, it changed the nature of the shaper. No longer did they have the same ability to shape."

"What did they have?" someone near the front asked.

Master Sartan smiled, as if he had been hoping someone would question him like that. "We have lost their records. All we know is that a shaping like that twists the individual, turns them into something different."

"Did it work?" This came from Jason, one of the shapers who hung around Draln. He leaned forward, and Tolan could almost imagine him calculating how to use a shaping like that in order to gain access to increased power.

"The reports are that those who did commit themselves to fire became more powerful, yet there was a cost.

With fire, there's always a cost. You see, with fire, it is essential to maintain control of the shaping." Once again, Master Sartan held onto a shaping of fire, a ball that glowed in front of him. It twisted, spiraling slowly before he released it. "If you lose control, the shaping can consume you. That is the nature of fire. It wants to be released. It longs for that. If you can maintain your hold over it, you can use it, manipulate it, but you must always maintain that connection. It's why we have spent so much time focusing on small shapings in the time we've worked together. You build upon each shaping, gaining increased ability along with increased control."

He fell into a silence, and no one spoke.

What would someone be like if they committed themselves to fire the way Master Sartan was describing? That wasn't what he was doing when using fire on himself, regardless of what Ferrah might think. He was using it as a shield, and though he inverted it, he wasn't shaping himself. They had been warned that attempting to shape oneself was dangerous, and he had no interest in risking himself, as he was not nearly as powerful a shaper as he needed to be in order to control it.

"What we understand is that those who attempted this shaping lost control. In doing so, they lost themselves. Records, as I have said, are sparse, making it difficult for us to know whether other attempts were successful, but we have enough records of the time that tell us the creatures they became were horrible and far too connected to fire, letting it rage out of control within them." Master

Sartan paused, sending his gaze sweeping around the classroom. "This is why we caution you against using shapings on yourself. Doing so poses dangers. Not only could you destroy yourself, but you could lose yourself. That is perhaps a worse fate than death."

He looked around the room again, and smiled. "Today, I would like you to practice this shaping." He held onto the ball of fire, letting it twist around him as it spiraled. A shaping like that wouldn't have much use other than in an attack, but it would allow a level of control, and in his case, Tolan thought having an increased level of control wouldn't be a bad thing. "Working with the shaping like this will require that you have a level of control. If you lose control of it, you will find fire unforgiving. It's best you attempt this shaping here rather than someplace else where you won't have the same opportunity for protection."

Tolan glanced over at Ferrah. She was already beginning to shape, using fire as it began to build, the heat of it rising more and more. Her circle of fire was small and compact, and the flames glowed with an orange intensity. She held onto it, twisting it from side to side much like Master Sartan had done, and as she did, she stared at it, focusing on the power. Tolan watched her, noticing how she was pulling on the power within the shaping, and wondered whether he would be able to do something similar. He had never had the same level of control as Ferrah, even when using the furios.

"Now see if you can make it larger," Master Sartan said to her.

She released her shaping, the ball of flame disappearing. She looked up at him. "I'm not sure I can control it quite as well."

"You won't know how well you can control it until you begin to push yourself." Master Sartan glanced over at Tolan. "What about you, Shaper Ethar?"

Tolan took a deep breath, focusing on fire. As he did, he created a small ball of flame. It was compact, no larger than his fist, the heat glowing from it radiating with a powerful force. It threatened to overwhelm him even in such a small shape, but Tolan squeezed down on it, trying to force it toward himself. He attempted to spin it the same way Ferrah did, but it began to pull apart, the flames tearing away from him.

Tolan stopped the spinning, holding onto his focus, trying to restrict the ball of flame so it didn't manage to burst free.

"You will find that fire wants to live. It tries to get free. And when it does, unless it's controlled, it will be destructive." Master Sartan stood across from him, watching him, and Tolan felt the weight of his gaze upon him. He didn't want to fail with Master Sartan so close.

Worse, he could feel the gaze of the others, all looking at him. They likely wondered if he had some shaping ability they didn't understand because he was somehow tied to the Draasin Lord.

Tolan held onto that connection to shaping, twisting it. It worked slowly, spiraling in place, and as it did, he maintained his connection to it, not letting the flames drift away. That was the challenge. With this shaping, it was more about holding it steady, keeping it confined, and preventing it from escaping. Understanding that it was all about control gave him an increased power over it. He was able to restrict how high the flames leaped, wrapping them tightly, and he let the ball of flame grow just a little bit. This time, he twisted it, spinning it in place, and continued to feed it, letting power flow into it and yet he still held onto the flame.

"Good. Now I would like you to practice summoning and dismissing the flame."

With that, Master Sartan departed, leaving Tolan and Ferrah alone at the table. He breathed out, looking around the room. No one else had been watching him. It was all in his imagination. The only person who would have been watching him had been Master Sartan—and Ferrah.

"That was good," she said.

"It's harder than I thought it would be."

"Shaping?"

"Most of the time while I've been at the Academy, I haven't been able to perform the shapings the master shapers want me to. It's different when I can actually accomplish what they ask."

"This one is a good shaping. I think Master Sartan is right. It's about holding power over the element bond, keeping it constricted as you shape it. I'm impressed you were able to let it grow under control."

Tolan glanced at her. "Why?"

"When I tried to do that, it started to increase in size but I could already feel it was trying to escape my ability to hold onto it. I had to dismiss the ball of fire and summon a new one with less power flowing in it."

That hadn't been what he had done it all. He had summoned a ball of fire, but had increased its size by pushing more power into it. What other way was there?

Tolan sat back, looking around the room. Everyone was attempting the same shaping, and there were varying degrees of success. Every so often, there would be a burst of heat and an explosion of power, but Master Sartan was there, dismissing the flames that tried to escape. Several people were working with furios, and as they used those devices, they were able to summon the fire, but they didn't have the same control those who shaped without them were able to exert.

"What do you think you'd be able to do if we had a furios?" he asked.

"It's hard to say. When I use them, I find there's almost too much power available. It's easier if I attempt to shape without it."

"I think the power would allow better control."

"Possibly, but it's a crutch. If you can learn control without the furios, you don't need a crutch."

Tolan wasn't sure how he felt about that. Having the furios had allowed him to understand what it was like to shape, and without it, he wasn't sure he would have known the level of control necessary with each of the other elements. While the furios had certainly helped, it hadn't restricted him from learning. In his mind, it was the exact opposite. Having the furios had allowed him to understand the nature of shaping even better.

"I wonder if Master Sartan would let me use the furios."

"Tolan, you can already shape without it."

"That's not the point. Even though I can shape without it, I…" It was hard to explain what it was like not having the bondar any longer. In the days since the Inquisitors' uprising, and in the time since he had returned to the Academy, Tolan had considered heading into the spirit tower in order to see if Aela had left behind his bondars, and yet he was hesitant to do so. The last time he was there, he had been attacked by the spirit shapers, and that memory was far too acute still. He didn't think anyone would attack him, but since he'd returned, he'd seen no sign of the Inquisitors—including the Grand Inquisitor.

"I think you need to stop using a crutch when you shape. You have talent, Tolan. I've seen it."

He sat back, focusing on shaping the ball of fire again. As before, he started small, spinning it in place, and gradually beginning to increase it in size. As he did, he maintained his focus and control over it. It was easier this time and took a drawing of power in order to make it work, but far less than it once would have required.

He still couldn't shake the sense he would have been better able to shape the sphere with the furios. He would've had far more control over it, but he thought what Ferrah said was true. Having the furios *had* been a crutch. He was using it rather than focusing on mastering his connection to shaping without it. Now he no longer had it, it was better to shape on his own, to practice and work with each of the elements so he had a similar mastery.

The only part he wished he had was a way to summon elementals. The furios had been responsible for helping him do that, and though he had managed to do it while in the park by the old Keystone, outside of there, he doubted he would be able to re-create that.

"See?" Ferrah said, smiling at him. "You can shape quite well without it."

"I still miss having it."

"You missed the power you had with it."

"Is that so different?"

"Power is temptation," she said. "You know it can be dangerous. That way leads to the…"

Tolan tensed.

"I'm sorry. That's not what I was meaning."

He shook his head. "It's okay. I understand. And you're right. If I am not careful, that way will lead toward something I don't want." He looked around. No one was listening, at least not that they could tell, but there were enough people in the classroom that he didn't want anyone to hear the nature of their conversation. "And it's not about power."

"Then what is it?"

He took a deep breath, looking around the room, thinking of how he would answer but knowing there wasn't an answer to give. Not that Ferrah would understand. She probably wouldn't want him to be drawing upon the power of the elementals either, yet Tolan didn't have any reason to fear the elementals as so many others did.

"I don't know what it is, but it's not power," he said.

He focused again on his shaping. If nothing else, he was going to master what Master Sartan wanted. And if he had the opportunity, he was going to find his bondars, even if it meant returning to the spirit tower.

8

THE PARK OUTSIDE THE ACADEMY WAS QUIET AT THIS TIME of day, leaving Tolan the only one sitting there, staring at the flat surface of the water, trying to find meaning and understanding that did not come. It had been a week since the uprising. A week since he had seen his father, and a week since he had learned his parents served the Draasin Lord.

In that time, Tolan still didn't know quite what to make of it. He'd gone through the motions, attending his classes, practicing his shaping without any bondars for assistance, and had returned to his room. He still had not gone to the library and was a little bit concerned about doing so. He didn't know what sort of reception he might get from Master Minden.

The park was as good a place as any to practice shaping, to flow from one form to another, using what he knew to see if there was a way to draw upon the elementals. It was isolated, and yet at the same time, there was a sense of power here. Perhaps not as much as was in the place of the Convergence, but there still was some power.

Focusing on water, he created a spiral within it, using his connection to shape the water in a steady pattern. It happened far more easily than it had before, and he held that connection, twisting it around and around before releasing his shaping. They had worked on similar shapings in class, and while Tolan had managed to do them, there had been a sense he still was missing something.

He had yet to try pushing the sense of the elementals into his shaping. While in the Academy and undergoing his classes, he was hesitant. Without the bondar, there was less of a risk he would lose control of the shaping, and more of a risk he would simply fail. With the bondar, he could explain ignorance and claim he was drawing upon power that he didn't really understand. Without it, it was far more difficult to do so.

Focusing on the elemental, Tolan thought about waya, an elemental that swirled within water, leaping above the waves. What he was shaping did not create significant waves, but he thought he could use that power to send a steady current through the water, and if he could do that, then he thought he might be able to find the elemental within the wave he formed.

It would be easier with the bondar. At least with the bondar, the type of shaping he would be capable of doing would be more significant, and he thought he could generate a real wave, enough he might be able to pull waya out of the bond.

Tolan sat back, shaking his head. What was he thinking?

He had taken to shaping like this, to thinking about elementals in such a way that he no longer viewed them the same way that others within Terndahl did. Was it even wise to see them like that? It was dangerous. He knew what the elementals were capable of doing, and he knew just how challenging it could be when he lost control of the shaping. If he allowed an elemental to escape, it would be his fault.

"There you are."

Tolan turned and looked up at Jonas. There was a hint of a smile on his face, his gaze darting toward the water.

"You came out here to practice?" Jonas asked.

Tolan sighed. "I needed to get outside the walls of the Academy."

"Why?"

He had to be careful with what he said. Jonas didn't understand what he'd gone through and having not shared with him about the Inquisitors' uprising, it wasn't anything he could understand. He didn't want to bring Jonas in on it, either. The other man didn't need that sort of distraction, and Tolan wasn't sure he should be the one to share anyway.

"I thought maybe a change in scenery might give me an opportunity to better understand my shapings."

Jonas threw himself on the ground next to him. "Ever since you got back, you've been much better at shaping. I know I accused you of using a bondar when you worked, but…"

"But I was," Tolan said.

Jonas blinked, watching him for a moment. "What about now?"

"Ever since the Inquisition, I haven't had the same need for bondars. It's like I had the opportunity to focus. As much as I hate to admit it, I actually benefited from the Inquisition."

Jonas chuckled, turning his attention to water and creating a funnel that spiraled out before dropping back into the pond with a splash. Jonas had incredible control over water. "Don't let the Inquisitors know about that. Otherwise they might decide all students need an Inquisition like that."

"Hopefully, the Grand Master will decide otherwise."

"Was he involved in the Inquisition?"

"I think he was trying to intervene on my behalf, but when it comes to the Inquisitions, the Grand Inquisitor is in charge."

Jonas shook his head. "In Velminth, we had someone dragged away for an Inquisition. It was probably five years ago, and I remember it like it was just yesterday. They came in, searching for someone they believed responsible for a couple of elemental releases that had happened recently, and dragged him off to a building somewhere near the center of town. No one heard anything, but when they left, he was gone, departing with them."

"I don't have the same experience with Inquisitions. I'd never seen one before we came here. The only time I'd ever even seen an Inquisitor was when they came to the village for the Selection." Even that was nothing like Jonas mentioned. "I have a sense my Inquisition was different than most."

"Other than the fact that students rarely face the Inquisition? I was talking to some of the older students, and they can't remember the last time anyone faced an Inquisition."

Tolan grunted. "That's not how I want to be noticed."

Jonas chuckled again. "You might not want to be, but the good news is that you were released. There was no consequence."

"That's not quite true."

"Why?"

"It's complicated. And not something I'm able to talk about."

"But you can talk about it with Ferrah?" Jonas held his gaze, and while he smiled, there was a hint of a hurt expression hiding behind his eyes. "I see the two of you talking at night. She sealed off the room, blocking everyone else out, and it's not until she lowers that shaping that we can even get into the room. Now, if she had closed the door as well, we might question what was going on in there," Jonas said, grinning a little bit, "but she leaves the door open. Which tells me whatever you're talking about in there is something she doesn't feel can be shared with anyone else."

Tolan needed the help of his friend. Jonas had been there for him and with him ever since he'd come to the Academy. He couldn't risk alienating Jonas the way he had with Tanner in Ephra. "When was the last time you saw Master Aela?"

"I don't know. We haven't had a spirit class in quite a while."

"Have you seen her in the halls of the Academy?"

"What are you getting at, Tolan?"

Tolan looked around, and on a whim, decided to wrap wind around himself and Tanner. He didn't have nearly the same strength that Ferrah did with a similar shaping, but had enough control over it that he was able to seal off the possibility that others could listen in. When the shaping took hold, the soft sounds of insects chirping in the park faded. The occasional calling from the birds disappeared. The burbling sound within the pond was gone. There was nothing but silence.

"Master Aela attacked me, Jonas."

Jonas had been looking around, almost as if trying to understand the shaping that Tolan had placed, and he jerked his head around. "She *what?*"

"It was after the Inquisition. I came across her and asked her what sort of lessons I might have missed, and she offered to show me some of the things I needed to learn." That should have been a warning, but he'd never experienced any of the master shapers posing a threat to him, and of all of them, he'd not expected Master Aela to be the dangerous one. "She used a spirit shaping on me. At least, she tried."

"What do you mean, she tried?"

"While I was in the Inquisition, getting a better handle on my ability to shape wasn't the only thing I did. I learned how to protect myself from spirit shaping." That was as good an answer as any, and prevented him from trying to explain to Jonas that he had the ability to use spirit. That was one piece of information he intended to keep to himself, at least for now. "There's a trick to it, and I've shown Ferrah, which is why I think Master Sartan gave us our talk on shaping oneself."

Jonas blinked. "I don't know which of these to be most upset about. That you told Ferrah how to do it or that it involves shaping yourself."

For a moment, Tolan thought he saw a flicker of movement, but it disappeared. Maybe it was nothing more than imagined. "It's not a shaping that I used on myself, at least not the same way Master Sartan described it. It's not even a shaping upon myself. It's more like, it's *around* myself."

"I don't know that that makes it any better."

"It's like a barrier, sort of like how I'm using wind now."

"About that. You never were that powerful before." Jonas looked around before his gaze settled back on Tolan. "I mean, it's one thing to discover you can shape, but this is something more than just shaping. This is a control and power you never had before."

"I'm just copying what I've seen Ferrah doing."

"That's all? I guess that's better than what I thought you were doing."

"And what did you think I was doing?"

"I don't know, maybe using a bondar and lying to me?"

Tolan shook his head. "No bondars. When Aela attacked me, she took my bondars."

"Why don't you go and get them back?" Jonas watched him for a moment. "I see. You don't want to go back there."

"I don't think the Inquisitors are there anymore. The Grand Master knew about the attack, and he helped keep them from hurting me, but the idea of going back there, the way she very nearly controlled me, the awareness I had as she was trying to force herself into my mind…" Tolan shivered. Even now, it was difficult. The idea of it pained him and left him feeling helpless.

That might be the worst part of it. He hated the idea of being helpless, especially when it came to shaping and others more powerful than he was. For his whole life, he had been around others who were far more powerful, much more capable with not only shaping, but even sensing. When he'd been living in Ephra, he had never been much of a skilled sensor, something that had always shamed him.

"Was it just her?" Jonas asked.

"It was more than Master Aela, but I don't know who the other Inquisitors were."

"That explains why we haven't seen nearly as many."

"There aren't usually all that many Inquisitors found in the Academy."

"Not usually, but ever since they took you and began your Inquisition, there had been a steady presence of Inquisitors within the Academy. And now there are none." Jonas shrugged. "Most people just thought they'd gotten what they needed from you and departed, but this makes a little bit more sense."

"As far as I know, Aela escaped."

"Why would the Inquisitors attack you and then run from the Academy?"

It didn't make all that much sense. She'd made it seem like it was all about trying to uncover information about the Draasin Lord, but he didn't think that was quite the case. It became almost personal, about her finding some way to defeat him, of convincing herself he truly did serve the Draasin Lord, even though at the time, Tolan had not thought he had. "I don't really know."

"Have you gone to the Grand Master about it?"

"Not yet. I think I need to, but I…"

"You're nervous to do that, too."

Tolan shrugged.

"You did change during Inquisition."

"What's that supposed to mean?"

"It just means that even though you might have gained power, you're a little bit more uncertain than before. Not that I blame you. Anyone who's gone through an Inquisition would have to change, wouldn't they? I can't imagine what it was like and what you went through."

Tolan grunted. "Other than the cell, it wasn't painful." There had been the constant questioning, the fear for himself and his friends, and eventually, the vision he had, but pain wasn't a part of it.

Could it be that way for others? He didn't really know what an Inquisition was like if used upon other shapers, only what it had been like for him.

"I think you're lucky."

"You know, I didn't feel so lucky when I faced that sort

of thing," he said.

"You survived. I think of everything you went through, and how bad it could have been, but you came through it. Yet again, Tolan Ethar was in the middle of an attack on the Academy."

"You do realize I have no interest in being a part of that."

"That, you tell us. Somehow, you always end up in the middle of them, though."

Tolan shook his head. It was a terrible thing to be caught up in the middle of every attack that had taken place at the Academy ever since he had come here, and if he could avoid it, he certainly would. "This time wasn't my fault."

"You're saying the other times were your fault?"

"Not necessarily, but I was more a part of them."

Jonas chuckled, leaning back and staring out at the water. "I think you need to figure out what the Inquisitors were after, Tolan."

"I don't want to get involved in it."

"That's not the Tolan Ethar I know."

"This Tolan Ethar will be able to stay at the Academy and continue to learn."

"How much more do you think you have to learn?"

"I don't know. Considering I don't have the same control as even one of the master shapers, there's still quite a bit."

It was more than just what he had to learn. It was the opportunities the Academy offered. And there was something else, something he didn't want to share with Jonas just yet. He needed to be prepared for whether his father would come for him again. He didn't want to deal with the disciples while untrained. It motivated him, and because of that, and because of what had happened and the way the Inquisitors had tried to attack him, Tolan felt as if he had to work with an increased intensity.

"We all have quite a bit to learn, but eventually, the Academy will spit us out and ask us to serve. I just hope I have a chance to do something useful."

"You don't think you will?" Tolan asked.

"Maybe now more than I did before. When I first came here, able to shape wind and water, I think I was just hoping I'd be able to stay."

"You were never in danger of not making it past the first test."

"I don't know about that, Tolan. You'd be surprised how many shapers who have what you think are reasonable skills are sent home after the first test."

"The only shapers we had in Ephra made it through those."

"The only shapers?"

Tolan frowned. "Maybe not the only ones. There were other shapers, but most of them didn't even get an opportunity to train at the Academy."

They weren't considered master shapers. They were still shapers, and still able to instruct at the shaping school, but only those who served at the Academy and had reached a certain level within it were able to be called master shapers.

When Tolan was done, by the time he made it through

another level here, he might even be able to be considered a master shaper. It was something he hadn't given much thought to. It was difficult to comprehend he would one day be considered a master shaper.

"In Velminth, we had quite a few shapers who didn't make it past the first test. Maybe the ones in Ephra were like that. Selected to learn at the Academy but not able to continue on through it."

"I thought if you were Selected, you had to stay and serve here?"

"I think you do, but you also commit to serving wherever the Academy needs you."

He hadn't considered where the Academy would need him. When all of this was over, when he finally finished with his time at the Academy, where would they ask him to serve? He didn't really want to go back to Ephra, and didn't want to stay in Amitan, either. His strange and compelling desire to understand the elementals made things difficult. Perhaps he would never fit in.

Tolan released his wind shaping, letting it relax, and as it did, he looked around, but there was still no one else near them. Every so often, he thought he felt a flicker of movement, and the sense of shapings was nearby, but they were faint and muted, the kind that made it difficult to know who and what was shaping.

"Thanks for coming and talking to me," he said to Jonas.

"You know, this would've been easier had you been willing to come to me."

"I didn't know how much you wanted me to."

"You thought I'd be upset with you?"

"Are you?"

"Maybe a little, but partly it's because of how quickly you've improved. I've made progress while here, but it's not been anything like what you have done."

"I had the most to learn. Everybody else had some ability. Unlike me."

They sat there and Jonas used a shaping on the water, sending it spiraling one way and then the other. Tolan watched, focusing on the power that he used, and began to work on wind, testing to see whether he could twist it and use it in a similar way to how Jonas was using water. He added wind into the water, and the funnel rose higher into the air. As it did, he felt as if he belonged, if only for a moment.

The distant sense of a shaping came to him. It caught him off guard, causing him to lose control of the wind. Tolan looked up, staring into the distance.

"What is it?"

He frowned, pushing away the sense of shaping. That couldn't have been a shaping like his, could it? There would be no reason for his father to have remained here—or one of the disciples of the Draasin Lord.

Only, he still had no idea where they'd gone or if they had even left. They had been chased from the Academy, but that didn't mean they were gone. And if there were disciples of the Draasin Lord still in the city, the Academy wasn't safe, regardless of whether his father was with them.

The shaping didn't come again, and Tolan turned back

to focus on how Jonas was shaping the water, trying to ignore the unsettled feeling within himself, but he couldn't shake it. If his father was out there, and if he were going to try to come for him again, then Tolan wasn't safe. Neither were his friends. Or the Academy.

"Tolan?"

He looked up, forcing a smile. "Hmm?"

"You look like you have something on your mind again."

"I was just thinking."

"That could be dangerous."

Tolan smiled.

"You better not let Ferrah learn that you were thinking. She might like you less."

"Ferrah likes me just fine, thank you very much."

"I'm well aware of how much Ferrah likes you, Tolan."

There was hurt in the words, hurt he didn't hide all that well. It wasn't as if he wanted to hurt his friend, but at the same time, he knew Ferrah had no interest in Jonas, whereas his interest in her was reciprocated.

The only problem was that if he were to act on it, he would potentially drag her into whatever issues he was caught up in. It was more than about just him. It was about his family and their service to the Draasin Lord and whatever that might mean.

"There you go again," Jonas said.

Tolan turned back to the water, determined to focus on it and try to find some way of ignoring the troubled thoughts rolling through his mind. It was difficult to do, but in this moment, he would find a way.

9

It was late in the day, the sun having long since set, and Tolan had taken a reprieve from Jonas, leaving the park and making his way into the main part of the Academy. He wandered the halls, debating what he would do next. Speaking with Jonas had left him determined he needed to do something, though he remained uncertain what that something should be.

On the one hand, he *did* need to go to the Grand Master and find out more about the Inquisitors. As he had been involved in it, he needed to better understand what had taken place. Not only whether there was more to be worried about when it came to the Inquisitors, but he needed to better understand why the uprising had taken place. The Inquisitors should serve the Academy—and Terndahl.

The other thing he needed to do was visit the library. He'd been avoiding it, concerned about the way Master

Minden would receive him, yet knew she would welcome him. She had been the most welcoming of the master shapers at the Academy.

Understanding the Inquisitors seemed to be the most important. Tolan headed toward the Grand Master's rooms, finding the hall outside his quarters empty. He stopped, hesitating a moment before knocking. He put a hint of an earth shaping into the knock, wanting to be loud enough so the other man could hear him, but not so powerful that he would destroy the door—if he even could. Tolan didn't even know if his earth shaping was strong enough to overcome whatever protections the Grand Master might have on his rooms. It was possible the Grand Master had layered protections over the door, and those protections might be enough that even his earth shaping wouldn't be able to knock it down. Not that Tolan was a particularly strong earth shaper, but…

He pushed away those thoughts. He was nervous, and with his nervousness came uncertainty.

There was no answer.

It might mean the Grand Master just didn't want to visit with him, though Tolan had never had the sense from the Grand Master that he avoided shapers. And he had been always willing to speak with him before.

More likely than not, the Grand Master simply wasn't here. If he wasn't, then knocking again and again, regardless of how much of an earth shaping he put into it, wouldn't make a difference.

Tolan decided to try one more time, waiting, but when there was no answer, he turned and headed back down the hallway. He caught sight of Draln with several of the older students, but ignored the man. Since the Inquisition, Draln had been even more aggressive with his taunts, but they had been more about him serving the Draasin Lord and less about his inability to shape. In many ways, those taunts were even worse. At least when Draln went on about his shaping, it was a criticism of skill rather than of him.

Turning the corner, Tolan started toward the library, staring at the tile as he made his way, and nearly ran into a group of shapers.

"Excuse me," he said, looking up.

When he did, his stomach sank. Velthan.

It was bad enough that he'd had to deal with Velthan in Ephra, but now he was here, Velthan used knowledge of Tolan's past to torment him in a way that was far more personal than any others. Velthan had found Tolan's Inquisition all too interesting, and there had been nothing Tolan had been able to do to avoid his brand of torment.

The other man grinned. "Tolan Ethar. I'm surprised you're still here after the Inquisition." He raised his voice, making a point of emphasizing *Inquisition*.

Two of the girls trailing after him snickered, and Tolan resisted the urge to snap back at him. There was no need to empower him in that way. Tolan was the senior shaper, and he no longer was quite as overmatched as he once had been when it came to Velthan. In fact, he might even be a more powerful shaper than Velthan.

"You mean the Inquisition where nothing was uncovered despite the Inquisitors' insistence that I was guilty?"

Tolan leaned toward Velthan, smiling dangerously. "Do you think you could withstand a month of Inquisition? I'm sure the Grand Master would be encouraged to know of your interest." If nothing else, the fact it was known he was friendly with the Grand Master was beneficial for Tolan.

"I doubt they'd be interested in me, as I don't serve the Draasin Lord."

"Are you sure? Perhaps my taint extends to you. You know," Tolan started, raising his voice so the others with Velthan could hear, "we are from the same city. As far as anyone else is concerned, you and I are both influenced by the Draasin Lord."

Two of Velthan's followers slipped off to the side, trying to distance themselves even a little. Tolan smiled to himself. It was probably more than he needed to do and were it not for the fact that Velthan had been awful to him for more than just his time in the Academy, he might not have said anything.

"I don't serve the Draasin Lord," Velthan spat. "Unlike you." With that, he stormed off, leaving Tolan standing in the middle of the hall, his heart fluttering. He took a deep breath, steadying himself, knowing it didn't matter what Velthan might say. He didn't know what Tolan had been through, and didn't have any idea that he feared the connection to the Draasin Lord and what it might mean. It was luck on Velthan's part, his way of trying to torment Tolan the way he'd always tried to.

When the sounds of their footsteps had faded, he took another deep breath and headed down the hall.

The library would be quiet at this time of day. There wouldn't be much activity, and he thought that made a good time to visit. There was no guarantee that Master Minden would be there, but he could check with one of the other master librarians, and if she wasn't there, he thought he could get word to her.

At the door to the library, Tolan paused for a moment before heading inside. As he often did, he detected a faint sense of power, a shaping that slithered over him, and then it passed. It was meant to prevent shaping inside the library, and yet he'd detected others shaping here before. Most of the time, he suspected it came from Master Minden, but he wasn't sure if there were others who might have an ability as well.

Still in the doorway, he looked around. Unsurprisingly, Ferrah sat at one of the front tables near the dais, a stack of books in front of her. She had her head down, her red hair draped on either side of her, and even from here, Tolan could tell she clenched her jaw the way she did when she was focused on her task. There was only one other student in the library. Wallace sat alone, leaning back, his legs resting on a chair opposite him. He looked up when Tolan entered.

Nodding to the other man, Tolan headed toward the front of the library. The two librarians on duty were both friendly to him. Master Jensen had often provided him plenty of research in the time that he had come, and Master Luna was one he didn't know quite as well as some, but he had spent some time working with her, trying to find specific books. She was friendly with him the same way most of the master librarians were. Considering the nature of the work they did, such friendliness was not necessary, and yet they were always more than happy to help students find the works they needed.

"What are you researching?" he whispered.

"Tolan," Ferrah said, looking up and smiling. She slipped her arm over the book she had folded out in front of her.

He reached for it, but he wasn't fast enough.

She pulled it away from him, keeping him from being able to tell what she was looking into. "Where have you been?"

"Practicing in the park. I had a conversation with Jonas."

"What did you tell him?"

"I told him about the uprising," he said, keeping his voice low. Then again, in the library, he always kept his voice low. Anything else would be sure to draw the ire of the librarians. "I've kept enough from him as it is."

"It's probably good you shared. I imagine that made him happy."

"I don't know if *happy* is quite the right way to put it."

"Why not?"

"He's still upset that I kept things from him for as long as I did."

"Can you blame him?"

Taking a seat, Tolan glanced at her stack of books for a moment before shaking his head. "No. That's why I told him what I did. I didn't want to keep anything from him anymore."

Besides, sharing with Jonas felt good. He liked the idea that there weren't secrets from his friend, and he might have him there to support him if it came down to another fight.

Nodding to the stack of books, Tolan smiled. "Are you really going to try to keep all that from me?"

"You don't need to know anything about what I'm looking at."

"And here I thought you'd been the one to tell me I shouldn't keep things from my friends."

"You won't like what I'm looking into."

"Why?" He tried to glance at the book, but her arm blocked him from being able to see what she was hiding.

"Fine, but don't get mad at me."

It was a strange thing for her to say, but Tolan nodded.

When she pushed book toward him, he glanced down at it and realized right away why she'd said what she did. There was a section on shaping, and a series of grotesque images, all of them demonstrating what it looked like when someone turned a shaping upon themselves.

"Really?"

"I said, don't get mad at me."

"And I've told you I didn't shape myself."

"I believe you."

"So much so, you went and talked to Master Sartan."

"I didn't talk about you and how you shape the barrier over your mind. I went to ask him what would actually happen if someone shaped themselves."

He looked at the page. On it was a depiction of a man as he slowly evolved into a horrible-looking creature. It was intricately drawn, almost as if flames consumed him, matching the way Master Sartan had described it.

"I went to find out if there was in any danger in the way you'd been shaping, and he took it the wrong way."

Tolan shook his head. "And because of what he described, you decided to research more about it?"

"I was curious."

"If he finds out what you're doing, he's going to think you intend to try this."

Ferrah glanced down at the book, grabbing it and pulling it toward her. "That's just the thing. Everything I can tell suggests those who did this were not necessarily trying to shape themselves so they could have more power."

"Why would they have done it to themselves?"

"I don't really know. It's difficult to read. The language is dead, and while a couple of the librarians might still be able to read it, I'm stuck trying to decipher it."

"You can decipher a dead language?"

"Not really," Ferrah said, smiling at him. "I was mostly looking at the pictures."

Tolan blinked before laughing and realized he was too loud. He clapped his hand over his mouth and shook his head. "What can you tell from this?"

"Mostly, they seem to be doing it in service to fire." She flipped a few pages and there was a picture of a man kneeling in front of the sun, hands stretched up to the sky. It was drawn in such a way as to show flames around the man, and it seemed as if he was calling upon them. "If you look at how they worshipped fire, it seemed as if they welcomed that power, but I don't know if they were welcoming it because they wanted power or if there was something more to it. The ancient shapers were different than us."

"Some think they were more ignorant than us."

"Maybe in some ways, but in others, they might have known power differently. They lived in a time when the elementals were still free. I think there are things we could learn from the elementals, if only we were willing to do so."

Tolan frowned. That was the first time he had heard her make a comment like that.

"I'd be careful making comments like that," he said.

"Why? There's no harm in commenting on how the elementals grant a very different type of understanding of power. And it's not like it's untrue."

Tolan reached for the book, and Ferrah let him take it. He flipped through the pages, and though he couldn't read anything written there, the images were enough for him to grasp what she was saying. It was almost as if whoever had written this had known there would come a time when the language would be gone and the images would need to carry part of the story. On each page, there were depictions of shapers—and they had to be shapers with the way the flames were drawn around them, swirling as if to gain more and more power. On some pages, the flames surrounded the man—or woman. On others, the flames were off in the distance, as if something they were searching for. On almost all pages, there seemed to be a reverence for fire.

"I think they were worshiping fire."

Ferrah nodded. "That was my thought, too, but it's such a strange thing to believe. Do you think there are stories of others who worship water or earth or wind the same way they worshipped fire?"

"I don't know. Is that why you have the stack of books?" Reaching for the books she had at the corner of the table, he sorted through them, but none of them seemed to be the same as this book. He closed the book on fire, looking at the cover. It was plain. It seemed to be made of a thick, almost black leather, and a symbol had been stamped into the surface, though he couldn't decipher whether it was one of the runes for fire or not.

"These are a little different. I thought I'd look into various ways of protecting oneself."

"How did you justify that with the librarian?"

"With Master Jensen, it's pretty easy. He knows I have an interest in this sort of thing."

Tolan glanced up at the master librarian sitting at the dais. He had barely looked up when Tolan entered and kept his gaze focused on his work. As far as Tolan knew, most of the master librarians had things they researched, and he always saw them working while they were here. He had yet to figure out what they worked on, or what they did with their research.

"Did you uncover anything?"

"Not yet. I've found there are others who've done shapings like the one you described, wrapping one around themselves to protect from spirit."

"See?"

"None of them has reportedly been successful."

"It worked, Ferrah."

"I believe it worked, but the question is why? And if it worked, we must wonder if it causes any danger to you. We don't know. Which is part of the reason we need to be careful."

"I practiced with it while in the Inquisition, and knew it wasn't going to cause any harm to me."

"You knew? Come on, Tolan. You probably wished you had your furios with you in order to make it even stronger."

"Well…"

She shook her head. "I'm glad you haven't made a big deal about them."

"Jonas thinks I should return to the spirit tower to reclaim them."

"That's if they're even still there," she said, turning her attention back to the book.

"Why wouldn't they still be there?" He'd dropped them during the chaos, when Aela had chased him from the spirit tower, which suggested they would still be there—but then again, it had been over a week, long enough that they might not be. If the Grand Master—or the Grand Inquisitor—went to the spirit tower to try to understand what had happened with Aela, they might've uncovered the bondars and taken them for themselves.

He was as concerned about the furios as he was about the golan that he had found in Ephra and believed his parents had made. That was one that he thought he could use to help him understand the making of bondars.

"If she knew what they were, the chances are good she'd have grabbed them, wouldn't she? When she attacked you, wasn't she more powerful than you remembered?"

"She was," he said, thinking back to that day. "And if she used my bondars against me…"

"They're not *your* bondars."

"They are more mine than they were hers."

"Tolan…"

He shook his head and knew he wasn't going to convince Ferrah of that. It didn't really matter anyway.

"I don't really want to go back to the tower to see."

"You don't have to go alone."

"You'd be willing to go with me?"

She glanced up, smiling briefly. "Didn't you tell me Jonas thought you should go after them?"

Tolan leaned back on the hard wooden chair, staring at the table for a moment. "Jonas said something else that made sense."

"If you keep talking like that, you're going to make me reevaluate my opinion of him."

He chuckled. "He thinks I should go to the Grand Master and figure out what's going on with the Inquisitors."

Ferrah looked up, cupping her hands on top of the book. "I don't know if that's a good idea."

"Why?"

"Because it will pull you into it more deeply."

"I'm already pulled into it as deeply as I can be. I mean,

they came after me and attacked me—and this was after they held me for an Inquisition!"

He realized his voice was starting to get too loud, and he looked up to see Master Jensen looking at him. He shook his head slightly and Tolan mouthed "Sorry" to him. There was something else he could do so he didn't upset the master librarians, and he reached for wind, wrapping it around him and Ferrah as he had at the park.

"What did you do?" Ferrah asked.

"I shaped a barrier around us."

"In the *library*?"

"That is where we are."

"You shouldn't be able to shape here at all."

"I know they say we shouldn't be able to shape here, but it's less impossible than they would have us believe."

Ferrah leaned toward him, her jaw clenched for a moment. "I've tried, Tolan. Ever since we first came to the Academy, I've tried to shape here, and I've never been able to do so. What's the trick?"

"No trick. I just shaped."

"Just like that?"

He nodded.

"Do you have a withering?"

"Do *you* still have the withering?"

She flushed. "No. I returned it so I didn't upset Master Rorn. She said I could borrow it but seeing as how I can shape well enough without it, I didn't want to have it outside of the Academy."

"And you accused me of having a crutch."

"That crutch helped me save you."

"And I thank you."

"You really don't have a withering?"

"I've already told you I don't have any bondars. I'm shaping on my own." That wasn't entirely true. He still had the bondar he'd found in his parents' home, but the ring that allowed him to more easily reach spirit wasn't all that useful for things like this. It might be a spirit bondar, but it still required a fair amount of strength on his part.

"You still shouldn't be able to shape in the library. It's sealed off, separating us from the bonds."

"What if I don't shape by accessing the element bonds?"

Ferrah looked at him, amusement shining in her eyes. "Tolan—everyone shapes by using the element bonds. That's how it's done."

He hadn't had this conversation with her before and hadn't talked with her about the unique way he felt he shaped. And now he was here with her, he thought he owed it to her to tell her he didn't think his shaping was the same as others'. "Everyone else might, but when it comes to shaping, I've begun to wonder if perhaps my shaping technique is different."

"How would yours be different?"

"From what I can tell from books Master Jensen's lent me, the old shapers used to connect to the elements directly." And one of those books had been written by her ancestor, so he wondered if she suspected.

"And you think you have a way of shaping that's more like the old shapers?"

"I don't know. I—"

Ferrah cut him off with a laugh. "Of course, you do."

"Why do I get the sense you're making fun of me?"

"I'm not making fun of you. I'm just trying to get a sense of what you think you can do."

"I can shape differently than you."

She glanced at him. "I guess that's true."

"You guess? I'm holding onto a shaping of wind right now. I'm shaping in the library—a place you seem to believe it's impossible to do so."

"Fine. You've made your point."

"Good. And I'd like you to tell me that I'm right."

"You want me to tell you what?"

He smiled at her, leaning forward. "I'd like you tell me that I'm right."

"You had better be careful."

"Why? Maybe you should be careful. Otherwise I might shape—"

Ferrah reached toward him and Tolan sat back, letting the shaping dissipate. When he did, he glanced up at Master Jensen and had the sense that the master librarian was keeping an eye on him, even though he seemed to be looking down at his book. Maybe he was aware that Tolan was shaping.

He was prepared to say something more when he caught sight of a librarian on the upper level. Glancing up, he saw Master Minden, but she never came down.

Tolan turned his attention back to Master Jensen. "I'm going to talk with him for a moment."

"Don't say anything that's going to upset him."

"When have you ever known me to say something that might upset the librarians?"

"Maybe not the librarians, but you don't seem to have any filters."

"I don't know if I should be offended by that or not."

"Not. Very much not."

Tolan got to his feet, made his way toward the master librarian, and approached the dais slowly, carefully. The master librarian was watching him. He was old like so many and had thinning hair. His librarian robe, a marker of station as much as any, was worn and tattered. As Tolan neared, he closed the book he was working on and slid it back.

"Shaper Ethar, to what do I owe this pleasure? Is there anything I can help you find?"

"Not a book this time, Master Jensen."

"If not a book, then what do you think I can help you find? I am a master librarian, after all."

"I was looking for Master Minden."

"Is there a reason?"

"The two of us were working on a project, and—"

Master Jensen cut him off by raising his hand. "I'm sorry. If the two of you were working on a project, I cannot interfere."

"I just wanted to know where she went. I haven't seen her in a few days."

Then again, he hadn't tried to see her for a few days. He wasn't about to tell Master Jensen that, though.

"I will share your concern with her. She can come and

find you when she is ready to resume work on the project."

"Master Jensen—"

The master frowned at him. "If there's anything else?"

Tolan stared at him for a moment before shaking his head.

Master Jensen opened his book, looking down at it. "Good."

With that, Tolan debated how hard to push, but knew pressing one of the master librarians would only cause trouble. They had been helpful to him over the time he'd been here and he didn't want to upset them, particularly not Master Jensen, who could be fickle. He wanted access to the library and didn't want to ruin that.

"If you could pass on the word," he said.

Master Jensen nodded and said nothing else.

Tolan stopped at Ferrah's table and leaned down. "I think I'm going to return to the rooms."

"I'll read a bit more before I return," Ferrah said.

"Find me when you return?"

"You won't find me?"

"I've always wanted to find you."

She met his gaze, holding it for a moment, and then smiled. "I'll find you."

With that, Tolan headed out of the library, meandering toward the back, nodding to Wallace as he left. He paused at the main door and decided he wanted to try to find the Grand Master one more time. Even if he wasn't there, Tolan was determined to attempt to reach him.

As he started, a flurry of movement at the opposite end

of the hallway caught his attention. Tolan turned and could swear he saw Master Minden making her way along the hallway.

Hesitating, he debated where he should go first. Did he go to the Grand Master or did he try to reach Master Minden?

He had already attempted the Grand Master and seeing as how he wasn't there even a little bit ago, he didn't think that it mattered if he were to go and try to find him. But following Master Minden, finding out what had happened with her, had more value.

Tolan hurried down the hall and hoped he wouldn't upset her by trailing after her.

10

HE RACED THROUGH THE HALLWAY AFTER MASTER MINDEN. The halls in this section of the Academy were quiet, the walls mostly bare other than the occasional painting, and there were a few lanterns giving off enough light by which to see. There wasn't much more than that.

He was surprised by just how fast she was able to make her way through the hallway. As he went, he found she was taking turn after turn, almost as if she was trying to evade him.

Tolan told himself if she decided to head down, as if to go beneath the tower, he would turn away. He wasn't about to end up following her to the bowels of the earth and didn't want to risk getting captured again. Instead, she continued to turn.

As he went, he started to question whether this was Master Minden at all? It was possible he was following nothing more than a shadow.

He paused, pulling on a shaping, using the earth to detect whether anyone had come through here. An earth sensing was enough to alert him to the fact that he hadn't been making this up. There was someone here, and though the sensing was unable to tell him who, there was enough of a recent feel to it that he knew he wasn't wrong.

Stairs headed up. This was a section of the Academy that he rarely entered. The students stuck to a few major parts of the building. There were the five major towers, each one representing the elements, and each with a teaching section, but also the instructors stayed there. There were some students who would stay in the tower and study with each of the instructors if they found they favored one element bond over another. Most were graduates of the Academy, and would study within the tower while trying to decide what to do next.

The main part of the Academy was only a few stories high, and it consisted of the Grand Master's quarters along with the library, but he hadn't seen much else within it. It sat in the middle of the towers, surrounded by the five different element towers, and deep beneath it was the Convergence. As he followed Master Minden—or whoever it was he was following—he couldn't help but wonder if there was something more up here that he was missing.

Tolan continued up the stairs. He paused at one point, holding onto a slick wooden railing, focusing on earth and adding a hint of wind. If he could use the wind to help him determine whether there was someone up there, then perhaps he wouldn't be surprised by someone coming through here. That was his fear. He didn't want to be caught off-guard.

At the next landing, he paused. Looking around, he found it looked nothing like the lower landing. Whereas on the main level, everything was all decorative, an expanse of marble and smooth stone depicting the Academy's prestige and age, this had narrower walls. There were paintings lining the hallway, and they looked incredibly old. Some looked to be fading, so old the paint was disappearing from the canvas, and despite knowing he should turn back, Tolan found himself standing in front of one of the paintings, staring at it.

There was something strange about it. It was more than the fact that it was fading as much as it was, but the man looking back at him had dark eyes, a square jaw, and long brown hair. There was a sense of power and purpose that the artist had managed to capture. Behind him, in the distance of the background, flames swept across the page. The paint had faded, leaving nothing but a residual, and he could tell someone had shaped the canvas in order to preserve it as long as possible.

"Did you come to examine the portrait gallery?"

Tolan jumped, cursing to himself and turning to see Master Minden. Somehow, she'd managed to sneak up on him. He shouldn't be surprised, but she was old, frail, and with her milky white eyes, he didn't think that she saw much—while at the same time, she always managed to see everything.

"I was just trying to find you."

"Yes, so I have heard."

Tolan cocked his head to the side. "You heard?"

"My eyes might not be as strong as they once had been, but my hearing is just fine, Shaper Ethar."

There was a soft rebuke in it, and yet there was something more. Could she have heard through his windshaping barrier?

He hadn't said anything to Ferrah that he needed to conceal, but the idea she would be able to listen through the shaping surprised him.

Should it? He'd already learned that Master Minden was more than she appeared. She had power and knowledge, and a skill with shaping that he thought she hid from others, as if she wanted to prevent them from knowing just how powerful she was.

"The last time I saw you, I was—"

"Getting chased by the Inquisitors. I recall that."

"You knew others were coming for me."

She turned slowly, nodding down the hallway. A shaping built from her, sweeping in either direction. As it did, he realized she'd sealed off the hallway. Not just one section of it, but the entire hallway. The power of the shaping was unlike anything he'd felt from any shaper other than the Grand Master.

Not for the first time, he found himself wondering who Master Minden was. How was it that she had as much power as she seemed to possess?

"This is not quite the place for such conversations."

"Why not?"

"Do know where you are?"

"I'm above the main level of the Academy."

She *tsk*ed. "A basic answer for someone who is anything but basic. Yes, you are above the main level of the Academy, and in that you are quite right, but the answer is a bit more complicated, as I suspect you already know."

"Where are we?"

"There are many things from the past that we can learn."

"That's why you study the books."

"That's why we study the past, Shaper Ethar. The more we can learn, the better equipped we are for avoiding the same mistakes made before us. We aren't the first shapers, and it's unlikely we'll be the last."

Tolan glanced over at her. She stood in front of one of the paintings—the same one that he had been staring at, he realized. She looked at it, though he wondered just how much she would be able to see.

"Unlikely?"

She nodded. "It is possible we destroy shaping."

"I didn't think there was any risk of destroying shaping."

"Perhaps not quite the way you think I mean. The element bonds are intact, which means they hold the elementals within them, but there is something else we must be concerned about."

"What?"

She glanced over at him. "We have talked in the past about how you reach for shaping in a different way."

He tensed. It was like the conversation he'd started to

have with Ferrah. "We haven't talked all that much about it."

"Because you have failed to ask the right questions."

"And what questions are those?"

"Questions about how. Why. And if you are the first."

She smiled at him, and when she did, she turned away, making him follow her as she headed down the hallway. She didn't go very far, pausing in front of another painting. When she did, she studied it much like she had the last. Tolan found himself studying it with her. There was something different about this than the last. For one, it seemed even older, if such a thing were possible. The last had been ancient, the paint at risk of fading, were it not for the shaping around it. This one had faded too, and that was even though he could feel the shaping upon it. There was nothing more than a blur of soft colors.

"What do you see on this canvas?" she asked.

"I don't see much of anything."

"No? Perhaps it's only my memory, then."

"What do you see?"

"I see the draasin. Three of them, flying overhead, with a shaper below." She smiled, and it was almost as if she could see it.

Tolan had never questioned her mind before, and probably shouldn't now, but the way she looked at the canvas, the way she stared at it, left him questioning whether she was all there. "How old is this one?"

"Old," she said softly.

"As old as all of them?"

She took a deep breath, raising her hand to the painting. She motioned to it, and he looked at where she pointed. "If you track the colors, you might be able to catch sight of the draasin, too. The artist depicts them as well as any has ever depicted them."

He stared, wondering if he might be able to make something out, but even as he did, he couldn't find anything in the painting that would help him see what Master Minden was seeing. There wasn't even a hint of the draasin on the page. It was little more than smears of brown and orange, though there were hints of red within it.

"I don't see it."

"Imagine a draasin, if you can."

Tolan fixed the image of the draasin in his mind. He had seen one near the Keystone one time. It had been made entirely of flames and looked powerful. It was the one elemental he was most terrified of summoning, though he had attempted to do so when back there with Aela.

"Are you imagining one?"

"As much as I can," he said.

"Good. Now imagine three. If you can, then perhaps you can make out the image on the page."

Tolan continued to stare, thinking that he needed to do so in order to satisfy Master Minden, but even as he did, there was nothing about the painting that he could discover. There was nothing there that would help him see the draasin like she saw them. Even if he did, imagining one draasin was one thing, but three? The idea there could be three of those creatures out in the world, unleashed and flying freely… terrified him, if he was truly honest with himself. There were times when he still questioned whether the bond made sense, and whether it served a purpose. When it came to the draasin, Tolan couldn't help but think that perhaps it *did* serve a purpose, only because the draasin were so powerful and terrifying.

"Are you able to imagine them?"

"I don't know that I want to."

Master Minden pulled her gaze away from the portrait and turned to him, shaking her head. "You fear the draasin."

"Should I not?"

"Why fear what we should honor and revere?"

"You would have us honor and revere the draasin?"

"I would have us honor and revere all the elementals, certainly more than we do these days."

"Master Minden?"

"Oh, Shaper Ethar, I'm sure others would accuse me of sympathizing with the elementals, but I can assure you I understand that in the current form, the elementals cannot be freed from the bond. I also recognize there is something about shaping that has changed for us. We're losing something of ourselves these days."

"What are we losing?"

"Shapers like you."

Tolan smiled, but realized she wasn't joking. "What do you mean?"

"I detected your shaping in the library, Shaper Ethar."

Tolan felt a flush working up, starting in his neck. "I

wasn't trying to do anything that would damage the library," he said quickly.

"Of course, you weren't. I would have acted differently had I detected anything like that. You used wind, and created a bit of a barrier around yourself and your friend. Your conversation was quite interesting."

"You *did* hear it."

"There's not much that takes place in the library that I don't hear."

"How?"

Tolan looked around. As earlier, he felt the presence of her shaping, the barrier that she sent up and down the hallway, the sheer power of it. It didn't even appear as if Master Minden was straining. Was she using a withering? That would explain how she was able to draw more power than he would've expected, but he didn't see her holding onto anything. Both of her hands were clasped in front of her, smoothing down the long black robe that marked her as one of the Master librarians.

Was there a way of using a bondar without holding onto it? It had been Tolan's experience that he had to hold one of the bondars in order to effectively utilize it, but maybe that wasn't necessary.

"As I said, my understanding of shaping is a little bit different. All of the master librarians' understanding of shaping is different."

She motioned along the hallway.

"This is the master librarian section of the Academy, isn't it?"

She nodded. "It is. It's designed to be difficult to find,

and only those who can shape in a specific fashion are able to uncover it."

"I didn't shape in any sort of fashion."

"No? And then what was it that I felt you doing as you trailed me? Were you not using earth and wind?"

Tolan stared at her. How had she known?

"How powerful are you?" he whispered.

"Always with the wrong questions. That's quite different for you, Shaper Ethar."

"What are the right questions?"

She turned away from him, making her way along the hallway. Tolan could do nothing but follow. There was something he thought he might learn here, though he had no idea what it would be. She left him feeling unsettled, partly by the fact that she seemed so powerful, but partly by the fact there were things she knew and understood yet she was not sharing with him, but they were things he thought she *would* share with him if he were only willing to ask the right questions.

She stopped in front of another painting. This one had a bit more color in it, but the edges were charred, it started to curl down. The shaping holding it in place was incredible. It was a mixture of earth and water, of all things. As he focused on the shaping, he realized water was used in order to try to heal the canvas.

"Why would water be used on a canvas?"

She glanced over at him before turning her attention back to the page. "There aren't many who even recognize water is utilized on this canvas."

"I thought you said there weren't many who came here."

"The master librarians. And the Grand Master, along with some of the master shapers, have been brought here, but it's doubtful they would be able to find it on their own."

"The Grand Master couldn't find this place on his own?"

"I suspect the Grand Master could, as he is a bit more powerful than he lets on. He hid the fact he could shape spirit for years; his way of avoiding becoming an Inquisitor." A hint of a smile tugged at the corners of her lips. "Not that I could blame him. Knowing the Inquisitors as we do now, I think had he gone to them, there might have been a very different outcome."

"I doubt the Grand Master would have done the same thing that Aela did."

"Just what do you think Master Aela did?"

"She turned the Inquisitors against the Academy."

"No. She intended to try to find information about the Draasin Lord. Nothing more than that."

"If it was nothing more than that, why would the Grand Master have gone after her?"

"She made the mistake of attacking him, and then she made the secondary mistake of trying to reach for power she shouldn't have. As far as the Inquisitors are concerned, she did nothing wrong."

"I was there, Master Minden."

"I'm well aware you were there. You could have been elsewhere."

Tolan glanced behind him again, looking along the length of the hallway. Was anyone here who could listen? He believed that Master Minden had sealed off the hall, but what if there was someone here who could listen to them? Maybe this wasn't the right place for this conversation.

"Did you know?"

"Did I know what?"

"About my father."

"There are many things I can't see, Shaper Ethar."

"You knew they were coming for me."

"I know those who call themselves the disciples of the Draasin Lord aren't quite what others within the Academy would have us believe."

"And what are they?"

"There's only one way for you to gain that knowledge."

"By going with them?"

She shrugged. "That would be the way."

Tolan shook his head. "I thought I wanted to go with them but doing so means I abandon the Academy. I'm not ready for that." He said nothing about the hesitation he felt over how they attacked and the violence they had shown.

"Even if it means you will gain an understanding?"

"Not if it means I betray the Academy."

"And what exactly do you think the Academy is?"

"The Academy serves Terndahl."

"The Academy trains shapers for Terndahl. The people of Terndahl have decided that means that our shapers protect them, but that hasn't always been the case. Much like it hasn't always been the case that the elementals have been spirited away, hidden from the rest of the world."

She pointed to the portrait. As she did, shaping streamed out from the end of her fingers, smoothing back the curled edges of the page.

"What do you see?"

"There's a little bit more color on this one than the last one, but I think it's too faded."

"Perhaps you're right, Shaper Ethar. It's a shame. There was a time when these portraits were magnificent."

"What does this one depict?"

"The elementals."

"Do all of these depict the elementals?" He glanced back down the hall, looking toward the one portrait that he had seen, that of the man who had seemed to look at him with a bright intensity burning within his eyes. There was a purpose to him, the same kind of purpose Tolan wished he could find.

"Not all. Many of them are portraits of the earliest librarians at the Academy. We are as vain as any, wanting to ensure we have ourselves preserved for the future."

"Is there a portrait of you?"

"Unfortunately."

"And all of the master librarians?"

"As I said, unfortunately. Not all of them make it into this hallway, but each of us has our likeness depicted by an artist of considerable skill once we are promoted to master librarian. Many are simply in storage. If you ask me, that is for the best."

Tolan found himself laughing. It was always so easy to

be with Master Minden. There was an affability to her, and despite the fact she knew so much about him, and that he felt as if he didn't know much about himself, being around Master Minden seemed to make everything easier.

"What does this portrait depict of the elementals?"

"In this case, it is one of the earth elementals."

"How did it get burned?"

"As you undoubtedly know from your lessons, fire and earth don't always get along."

"What does that have to do with why it's burned?"

"One of the fire elementals was angry earth was depicted in the light it was."

"And what light was that?"

"As more important than fire." She smiled as she said it, and softly. "The elementals can be as foolish and petty as us, Shaper Ethar. Despite what we know of them, and despite the fact they have their own unique type of power, they aren't above a little pettiness. Then again, neither are we. I suspect others would attempt to do the same as the so-called Draasin Lord has done, and would try to gain subjugation over the elementals, to see if they couldn't use that sort of power."

"Why do you call him the *so-called* Draasin Lord?"

"There has been the threat of a Draasin Lord for far longer than there could exist a Draasin Lord."

"What does that mean?"

"It means you must find those answers on your own, Shaper Ethar."

She continued down the hallway, and when she stopped in front of another portrait, she smiled at it. This one had wisps of lines, but nothing more. It was better preserved than most of them had been, and as he looked at it, he thought it might be newer. Then again, if it were newer, why would it have basically nothing on it?

"What do you see on this one?" she asked.

Tolan looked at the painting, staring at it as he tried to come up with an answer, but there wasn't much of anything on it that made any sense to him. It was little more than faint lines scrolled across the page.

"Not much of anything. Is there something I'm supposed to see? It looks almost like someone had started their artwork but then never finished."

"It is difficult to depict wind," she said.

"This is meant to depict wind?"

"I'll admit, it is a difficult thing for one to see and visualize, but when you do, you start to understand what the artist was trying to show. In your time working with your shapings, have you not seen the wind elemental?"

It was a more direct question than he was accustomed to when it came to Master Minden. Most of the time, she was more round-about with her approach, not quite so direct, but she said it so matter-of-factly, he suspected she knew the answer even though she asked.

"I've seen the wind elemental," he said.

"And how would you draw it?"

"I'm not much of an artist."

"One doesn't need to be an artist to know how they would depict such things, Shaper Ethar."

Tolan tried to think about how he would have depicted the wind and realized that there wasn't much to show.

Wind, when visible—which wasn't very often—was difficult to see. It was translucent. When he had a sense of it, it was vague, and he had a sense that it was supposed to be. It was the way wind lived. It wasn't easy to see, not the same way fire or earth were easy to see. When he shaped wind, the sense of it came from a place deep inside of him, a place that came out with each breath, an extension of himself. With wind, there was nothing—and everything.

"I suppose this is how I would do it, too," he said.

Master Minden nodded, as if there was never a debate. "The artist was considered one of the most skilled in his time."

"I'm surprised there are so many depictions of the elementals," Tolan said.

"You are only surprised because in this time, the elementals are viewed differently than they were long ago. There was a time when the elementals were viewed with far more welcome, and the artists wanted to depict them as accurately as possible, no differently than they wanted to depict the master shapers as accurately as possible."

She said it almost with a sense of knowledge, and though he doubted it was possible she could be old enough to remember, he looked at her for a moment, wondering if maybe…

Tolan shook away that thought. That was as impossible as anything.

"What are you trying to get at?" he asked.

"I'm trying to encourage you to open your mind, nothing more than that. It's the same thing we would ask anyone who has the potential to be a master librarian."

Tolan blinked. "You want me to be a master librarian?"

"You would refuse?"

"It's just…" It was what he suspected Ferrah wanted, but it wasn't what he had wanted. Then again, Tolan hadn't given much thought to what he did want. Eventually, he would have to figure out what role he would take on when he finished with the Academy—if he were able to finish with it at all. Until that time, he didn't know what it was he wanted to do.

"You don't have to feel as if you need to make a decision now, Shaper Ethar. I brought you here for you to know that the possibility exists."

"I didn't realize you brought me here at all." Hadn't he followed her?

"You would never have found this place had I not wanted you to," she said, smiling at him. "And now, I think it's time for you to return to your studies."

"That's it?"

"What more would you have?"

"I guess I thought you might know something more about why the disciples of the Draasin Lord were after me."

"Not the disciples of the Draasin Lord," she said. "Your father."

"Did you know him?"

She smiled again, meeting his eyes with her milky white ones. "Like I said, I can see many things."

With that, she turned, heading back down the hallway, and Tolan had no choice but to follow her. As he went, his gaze lingered along the portraits, searching for understanding about what she was showing him, but he didn't come up with anything. There were dozens upon dozens of portraits here, and all of them were difficult to make out. Toward the end of the hall, they came to the portraits of people. There was the man he had seen when he first came here, but there was a woman next to him that he hadn't noticed before. It seemed almost as if she was watching him. The sense of it left him unsettled.

He hurried after Master Minden, reaching her on the stairs, and when he did, he cast one last look along the hallway, wondering if he would be allowed to return here again if he didn't choose to become a master librarian.

"Come along, Shaper Ethar."

Tolan followed her down the stairs, away from the quarters of the master librarians, and for some reason, he couldn't help but feel as if he was leaving a place he was supposed to know.

11

WIND WHISTLED AROUND HIM, HIS SHAPING GROWING, power flowing through him as he summoned the wind as Master Rorn instructed. Tolan focused on it, determined to follow her instruction as closely as possible. He needed to better understand how to shape, and he needed the level of control the master shapers taught.

Much like the fire-shaping class, this class and the wind shaping were all about control. Master Rorn wanted them to focus on shaping as well as they could, using a level of control to ensure they managed to hold onto their shaping, avoiding wind slipping from their grasp. She didn't speak of wind the same way Master Sartan had, and there was no dire warning about the destructive nature of the wind if they were to lose control of it, but she did caution them that they needed to understand control.

Had it ever been any different?

His earliest experience with the classes hadn't been

productive enough to know whether she had issued the same warning or not. He had been far more focused on simply trying to reach the ability to shape. It was possible the master shapers always warned about control.

He looked around. Jonas was across from him, and his wind shaping built with skill, a spiral of wind lifting off the ground before retreating. Tolan was able to copy that, but he didn't have the same level of skill that Jonas managed, though the more he practiced, the more he felt as if he could eventually reach it.

"Very good, Shaper Golud. Now I would like to see if you can't tighten the spiral," Master Rorn said, taking a place next to Jonas.

Jonas nodded, and when she was gone, he lowered his voice and leaned toward Tolan. "Tighten it? It's about all I can do to keep this one as tightly controlled."

"She sees potential in you. She's probably going to want you to study with her in the wind tower," Ferrah said. She was on the other side of Tolan, and her tower of wind wasn't nearly as tall as Jonas's, but she held it more tightly-controlled than Jonas did. It was a narrow band of wind, no taller than her midsection, and spiraled right in front of her. "You just have to keep pushing yourself."

"This is pushing myself," Jonas said, shaking his head. "I'd like to see you extend your column of wind."

Ferrah made a face at him and her shaping expanded, the column of wind growing just like Jonas had wanted. It elongated, stretching taller than her and then doubling in size. The entire time, she held it in the same tight spiral.

Tolan smiled. She still had the wind bondar.

He waited to see if Jonas would realize what she was doing, but she collapsed the column of wind before he had a chance to question her. When it was done, he leaned over to Ferrah. "You were the one who warned me about using a crutch."

"It wasn't a crutch. It was my way of harassing Jonas. Besides, he knows I don't need the bondar in order to shape."

"I don't know. You've been giving me a hard time about using the bondar, and now you're not doing anything different."

"Fine."

She pulled her hands out of her pockets and focused on a wind shaping. As it built from her, the spiral grew, increasing in size and stretched outward, taller than her. It was tightly controlled, far more than Tolan was able to do, and as it stretched, she glanced over at him.

"Are you going to do the same?"

Tolan started on his wind shaping. It built slowly, and with an increasing speed. As it did, he focused on the nature of the shaping, drawing it out, trying to keep it tightly controlled as he did. He should be able to hold onto it, and he had enough experience with wind that it shouldn't escape his ability to hold it, but somehow, it started to unwind on him. The column of wind began to grow taller and taller, and his ability to hold it became strained. The more he tried, scrambling to hang onto the sense of the wind, the less he found he was able to do so.

And then he lost control.

Wind burst out from him, the overall sense of control

faded, and Tolan was thrown back under the force of his shaping.

He shook himself, getting back to his feet, looking around. Unsurprisingly, Draln had a tight control over his wind shaping, his column spinning in front of him, and he sneered at Tolan, laughing as he said something to one of the shapers near him.

Tolan got to his feet and Master Rorn joined him. "Shaper Ethar, you must hold onto your control before you expand the column. If you don't, you run the risk of… Well, this."

"I'm sorry, Master Rorn. I know."

"If you would like to use a bondar, you certainly may."

Tolan glanced at Ferrah. The reason he had lost control was because he was trying to show off for her, and he should have known better than to do so. "I think I'm okay."

"It hasn't been all that long that you have been able to reach the element bond on your own. Don't try to exceed your capabilities, Shaper Ethar."

With that, Master Rorn made her way through the line of students, pausing and speaking words of encouragement to Draln and the others around him before continuing onward.

"Do you want to use the bondar?" Ferrah whispered.

"You know I don't."

"You were more than eager to use the bondar at other times."

"I'm going to master this shaping if it's the last thing I do."

"Don't let it be the last thing you do," she said.

He smiled at her, then began to shape again, pulling on his sense of wind. He needed to master these shapings. The ones all about control were the ones he needed to master most of all. If he could get a handle on them, he should be able to deal with more complicated shapings. He was determined to get to the point where he could handle complex ones.

This time, he focused on the spiral of wind, keeping it confined in front of him, using a small shaping, barely enough to twist the wind in front of him. Rather than trying to grow a tall column, Tolan focused on a tight spiral of air. It reminded him somewhat of the wind elemental tornas. He focused on it, putting that image into the shaping, holding it tightly in place the way he would have done were he to have a bondar. That seemed to be the key. As he focused on the elemental, the shape of it held much better than it did otherwise, and gradually the form took hold.

This one spun rapidly. As it did, he began to stretch it outward, elongating it while also keeping it narrowly confined. There were ways a shaping like this could be useful, though for the most part, such a shaping was meant only to demonstrate his prowess. He needed to get to the point where he was getting to use shapings that were beneficial.

"How are you doing that?" Ferrah asked.

"Doing what?"

"That. It's barely wider than my fist."

"I started small."

"When I start small, it is not like that."

"I just tried a different approach."

Ferrah frowned. "Are you sure you aren't using a bondar?"

Tolan looked over at her. "If I was using a bondar, don't you think I would've had better control with the last one?"

"I guess. I just…"

Tolan continued to elongate the shaping, holding onto it in a way that continued to have the sense of tornas within it. It wasn't quite the elemental, but he used what he knew about the elemental, his experience in having drawn it out, to power the shaping.

When the column of wind was as tall as him, he paused. If he stretched too much more, he had a feeling he'd lose control. There was a stirring within it, almost a sense that he was nearly reaching into the wind bond. If he did that now, it was possible that he would free the elemental.

Not here. Doing that would be far too dangerous, not only for him but for the wind elemental. He didn't want to free the elemental, and he really didn't want to feel the pain from the elemental as it was forced back into the bond. Having that sensation once was enough. Tolan continued to squeeze it down, narrowing the column once again, waiting for it to compress. It happened slowly, gradually, and eventually he pressed it back into nothingness, little more than it had been before, and then he released the shaping.

When he was done, he breathed out. It had been far

more work than he had expected. He gathered himself, focusing on the wind shaping, and considered repeating it before changing his mind. It was possible he wouldn't have enough strength to control it the next time.

"I haven't seen a shaping like that before," Ferrah said.

"Maybe I have a talent with wind."

"You have a talent with something, alright."

"Release your shaping," Master Rorn said.

The students all along the top of the tower released their shapings, and Master Rorn headed to the center of the tower and swept her gaze around them all. Her long, flowing white robes gave her a look that suggested she served the wind. She was thin, like most who were prone to shaping the wind, and her sharp jawline jutted out as she looked at them.

"I would expect you will continue to practice these shapings. Your goal would be to have a column of wind twice your height by the time you reach your next testing. If you cannot do that, then wind will not be in your future."

"That's the only test?" someone near the front asked.

"That's not the only test, but it's one of them. As you will learn, many of these shapings will branch off this first. This is a complicated shaping designed to test your control. The others will test your connection to wind, and from there, you will continue to push yourself. As I said, practice will be essential."

"Do we need to worry about harming ourselves?"

"Not like with some of the other elements. Wind will be released, and as Shaper Ethar has so kindly demonstrated, it can be painful to lose control of the shaping, but it will not harm you, nor will it change you."

Heat worked up Tolan's cheeks and he could hear others near him chuckling, but he did his best to ignore it. It was difficult.

"That is all for the day."

Tolan headed toward the stairs leading back down out of the wind tower. He didn't wait for the others but Ferrah followed him, grabbing onto his arm.

"You don't need to be so sensitive about things like that. She was giving you no harder time than she has other students."

"I realize that, but it's more about what I've gone through to get here. Well, to stay here, really."

"I know what you've gone through but keep pushing yourself. Besides, you already demonstrated you have the kind of control she was trying to have us demonstrate. Sometimes with you, I get the sense it's not so much the shaping but it's how you approach it. You have the necessary strength, but you don't always have the same control."

When they reached the main part of the wind tower, Draln and a few of his friends shoved past Tolan, looking back at him. "Nice job back there, Ethar. Thanks for demonstrating how to avoid releasing your wind shaping."

"Anything for you, Draln."

Draln's friends glared at him before following Draln.

"What are you going to do with the rest of your day?" Ferrah asked.

It was early enough that they still had quite a bit of time left in the day, several hours before the evening meal.

He considered practicing shaping but holding onto the last one had taxed him more than he had expected. If he were to continue to practice, he would need to do so with some sort of assistance.

They reached the main part of the Academy, and he frowned. "You know, I still haven't gone back to the spirit tower to see if my bondars were there."

"You want to do that now?"

"I guess." He didn't, not really, but also thought he needed to face it. Jonas was right when he said that something about Tolan having changed ever since that day. He had become far more tentative. He was determined to push past it, to become the person he'd been before, to avoid that tentativeness. "If we have quite a bit of the afternoon left, what better time to do it than now?"

"We should see if Jonas—"

"We should see if Jonas would what?"

Tolan turned and Jonas jumped down the remaining few steps, landing on a cushion of wind. He flashed a smile.

"What are the two of you wanting to see if I would do?"

"Tolan is thinking about returning to the spirit tower."

"Now? Have you seen how beautiful the day is outside? We don't have anything for hours, and…" Jonas glanced from one of them to the other before shaking his head. "Fine. I'll go with you but let me lodge my dissatisfaction with it now."

"You don't have to go," Tolan said.

"Sure. I don't have to go, and if I don't, then you will go

off and have some crazy adventure again without me. No thanks. I don't like hearing about these adventures secondhand."

"Sometimes, secondhand is better than experiencing them directly."

"Says the guy who remembers everything."

Tolan shrugged, and they all started toward the spirit tower. They passed several others of their class; most were streaming out the main door rather than staying in the Academy building. Under different circumstances, Tolan would have wanted to be outside as well, anywhere but in here, but he needed to do this. It was well past time that he dealt with this issue.

Reaching the spirit tower involved going up a flight of stairs, and from there, he looked around, noting the markings on the wall and focusing on one in particular. The rune was one for spirit, and it wasn't one he knew all that well, but he knew it well enough to recognize the power within it. He had sat in the middle of something similar and had felt the way that a skilled spirit shaper had been able to use their control over it in order to confine him, trying to break into his mind.

A tap landed on his arm and he looked over. "Come on," Ferrah said.

He took a deep breath, focusing. He needed to move past this. It was unlikely they would find anything in the tower, but he needed to look, didn't he?

Looking toward the opening in the tower, Tolan focused on wind, adding a hint of fire, and shaped himself up.

It was easy to remember how difficult such a shaping was the first time he'd come here. The idea that he would be expected to have enough control to carry himself to the next level of the spirit tower had seemed a far-off goal. Without the furios, he wouldn't have been able to do so, and even with it, he'd barely been able to manage. His level of control had been such that he had exploded himself upward without any real control.

Landing on the ledge, he looked around the inside of the room. It wasn't much changed from the last time he was here, and though it had only been a few weeks, it had been long enough and so much had happened that it made it painful to look around.

"This is where they held you?" Ferrah asked.

Tolan headed to the center of the rune. He had to deal with it. He had to come to terms with the fact he was no longer captured, and not in any danger. Aela was gone. Most of the Inquisitors were gone. They wouldn't use this place against him again.

Motioning to the marking on the floor, he turned slowly in place. "Can you see it?"

"What are we supposed to see?" Jonas asked. His voice was hushed, and at least he was taking this far more seriously than before. Tolan was thankful for that.

"The rune. There is one set on the floor that matches the one on the wall. When I was here, Aela used the rune to overpower any defense that I might have."

"I don't really see anything," Jonas said. Tolan pointed and Jonas frowned while looking down at the floor. "Do you think all of the towers have markings like this?"

"I know the wind tower does," Ferrah said.

"It does?" Tolan asked. He looked up. "I don't remember seeing a marking like that on the tower."

"Because you're so focused on creating your strange spiral of wind, but if you were to pay attention to the floor, you would've seen there was a rune very much like this there."

If there was one in the wind tower that matched the one in the spirit tower, it likely meant there would be one in each of the towers. Maybe only the higher-level students, those who had committed themselves to a particular element bond, ever got to experience the power of the runes. Them and Tolan.

He focused on spirit. Reaching the shaping of it was difficult, and required that he abandon all control, to release himself and embrace a sense of emptiness, and to focus on the memory of the vision that had come to him. When he did, he could feel power flowing up from within him. It came from a deep place, buried, practically as if he had to force it out. As he did, he pushed it through the rune, wondering if he could use the power of it as well.

It surged for a moment, but then it faded. All control over it got lost.

Tolan shook his head. Either he wasn't strong enough or he was far too inexperienced to be able to manage a shaping like that.

"What did you do?" Ferrah asked.

"I tried to shape."

"What did you try to shape?"

"The ground," he said, smiling briefly.

"Do you really think that shaping here is going to work against spirit?" Jonas asked.

"Not really, but I thought I'd try to see if there was anything I could detect about the way they placed the pattern."

That was true enough, though he didn't really expect to be able to uncover anything.

"Did you?" Ferrah asked.

Tolan shook his head. "No."

He looked around the floor. It was easy to remember where he been forced, how he had been confined with the power within the rune, and he remembered where he had been lying when Aela had forced him down. The bondars should be nearby, but as he suspected, there was nothing.

"It looks like they took them," he said to Ferrah.

"Did you expect otherwise?"

"Not really, but I was hopeful I might be able to still have them."

"I think you should be thankful that you survived."

"You don't think that I am?"

"That's not what I'm saying."

Jonas grunted. "The two of you."

Tolan looked over at Jonas. "The two of us what?"

"Could the two of you stop bickering? You sound like my parents."

Tolan started to say something, thinking that he would smart off to Jonas, when a shaping began to build. It was powerful—and close.

He backed up, wrapping himself in a barrier of fire, inverting it immediately, protecting his mind. He readied a shaping and his heart hammered, fear coursing through him. There would be only one reason someone would come to the spirit tower, and he wasn't sure he was ready to confront the Inquisitors again.

Instead of Inquisitors, the Grand Master landed inside the spirit tower.

12

Tolan held onto his shaping, keeping his mind protected, still uncertain, regardless of the fact it was the Grand Master who had arrived. The other man looked around from Tolan to Ferrah and then to Jonas. It was difficult to know how the Grand Master would respond to the fact they were here. Would he be angry they had come to the spirit tower?

"The three of you aren't quite what I was expecting."

"I'm sorry, Grand Master, it's just that—"

"You were hoping to find your bondars."

Tolan blinked, nodding. "How did you know?"

The Grand Master smiled, looking around before turning his attention to the rune. A shaping built from him, soft and subtle, and it spread away from him, heading down into the rune. As it did, Tolan detected it, noting the way it reverberated against him.

Was the Grand Master shaping spirit?

Why would that be the first thing he did when he came to the spirit tower?

When he looked up, the Grand Master met Tolan's eyes. There was something within them that seemed almost knowing, as if the Grand Master understood what Tolan had done and the way he'd used spirit.

"There are many things I know, Tolan Ethar. Unfortunately, I suspect Aela took your bondars. She was far more capable than I would've expected when I confronted her, and the only reason for such competence from her would be the use of bondars to augment her strength. Now, the spirit tower has long been home to spirit bondars, but she didn't throw spirit at me but earth and fire, and I believe those are the two bondars you had?"

Tolan nodded. There was no point in denying it.

"As I thought. Unfortunately, it gave her a bit of an edge. Otherwise, we would have been able to restrain her and find some answers."

"Why did she attack you?"

"She was after you, Shaper Ethar, but unfortunately for her, she thought I would side with her in this. She lost track of the fact the Inquisitors and the Academy are separate entities."

"But the Grand Inquisitor—"

"The Grand Inquisitor serves at the Academy at my insistence. Irina and I are old friends, and in that regard, I trust her implicitly. It's why I invite her for all the Selections, and why I have allowed her to keep the Inquisitors involved in the Selections. I had thought in doing so I would be able to bridge the divide between the Academy and the Inquisitors, but..."

"I didn't realize there was a divide." Ferrah glanced from Tolan to the Grand Master. "We haven't seen anything like that in Par."

"Undoubtedly, you have not. Par is a unique place, filled with unique history. Much like Ephra."

"What does that have to do with anything?"

"There are quite a few questions I imagine you have, Shaper Changen, and do not worry about whether or not I will answer them. First, I would like to have a few words with Shaper Ethar, if you don't mind?"

Ferrah glanced at Tolan before nodding. She grabbed Jonas and they reached the ledge overlooking the drop back down to the main part of the spirit tower, and with a powerful shaping of wind, they disappeared.

When they were gone, the Grand Master turned to Tolan, smiling. He pressed outward, a flurry of power, and it took Tolan a moment to register that he used each of the elements, forming a barrier around them.

"Forgive the necessity of the barrier, but I fear there are eager ears these days."

"Ferrah and Jonas wouldn't try to listen in."

"Perhaps not them, but others might." The Grand Master walked to the center of the rune, looking down at it. "I wasn't expecting to detect such a skilled touch from you," he said. He looked up. "And know I mean no disrespect by that."

Tolan tensed. "What sort of touch?"

"With spirit." He smiled. "Don't worry, Shaper Ethar, I will keep your secret safe, the same secret the Grand Inquisitor is keeping."

"You knew I could use spirit?"

"When you were Selected, the Grand Inquisitor suspected you had potential for spirit. It would be the only explanation as to how you would pass the Selection without being able to shape any of the other traditional elements. It is rare enough for spirit to appear in isolation, but it has been reported to have occurred before."

"So, you knew about spirit before and didn't tell me."

"There's nothing to tell, Shaper Ethar. If you had failed to reach spirit, it would have done you no good to know why you had passed the Selection. And if you had believed you were destined to reach spirit, would you have tried so hard to reach the other elements?"

"Probably," he said.

The Grand Master watched him, smiling for a moment. "Perhaps you would have. Knowing you as I have over the last year, it is entirely possible you would have. Regardless, you proved yourself when she attempted to shape you. It would be far easier if we didn't have to worry about your knowledge of the Convergence, but considering your potential with spirit, that proved difficult. It would've required wiping away more memories than she felt comfortable doing."

"I thought I was safe from spirit because I could shape it."

"After your experience with Aela, did you still feel that way?"

"No, but I was here."

"As you were when you met with the Grand Master."

Tolan frowned. It was true enough, and in a place like this, so connected to spirit with the power of the spirit rune placed on the ground, he wasn't necessarily as protected as he would like to be. With this rune, she would have been able to do anything she wanted. Spirit might have protected him, but there would've been a limit to how much protection it would have provided. And given what he'd seen, he would have been disappointed to have lost everything.

"As you no doubt have come to realize, the spirit rune grants great power. The Grand Inquisitor thought she could remove only your memories of the Convergence, and I think she was surprised it failed. When I discovered it, I trusted you would not use that knowledge in a way that would damage the Academy. We both agreed to keep an eye on you, and you proved to be challenging to do just that."

"I'm sorry."

The Grand Master smiled. "There's no need for you to be sorry. You are an interesting young man, and have shown a tenacity that should not be surprising for someone so willing to submit themselves for Selection without any ability to shape." The Grand Master raised his hands, smiling. "And I know the reason you submitted yourself, but that changes nothing. Your friendship mattered to you, much like you have proven your friendships now matter to you. No doubt you will report to them everything we talk about."

"Unless you tell me I can't."

"Tell you or shape you?"

"How did you know we were here?"

"I placed a specific touch on the rune, enough that I would know whether it was being accessed. Typically, accessing a great rune like this requires someone to have far more skill in order to trigger it, and yet, you who have not trained with any spirit shapers, managed to do just that."

"Probably because I had one used on me."

The Grand Master smiled. "Perhaps that's all it is, or perhaps there is more to it. There is something quite natural about your shaping ability that is different than most."

Tolan swallowed. Now was the time he could tell the Grand Master about his ability to reach shaping without accessing the element bonds, but if he did that, then he opened himself to a different type of question.

Maybe there was a different approach he could try.

"Do you and the master librarians ever discuss the things students are researching?"

The Grand Master furrowed his brow. "That's an interesting question. Why would you ask that?"

"I was curious."

"An interesting thing for you to be curious about, Shaper Ethar. To answer your question—no. We don't routinely discuss research topics of the students. The master librarians are granted the freedom to monitor the use of the library, and there's no reason they should do otherwise."

Tolan nodded. If that were the case, it was possible that Master Minden hadn't shared with him.

"Then again, there are times when the master librarians find things that they bring to my attention." The Grand Master smiled, and something in his eyes seemed to twinkle. "I believe you and Master Minden have formed something of a friendship."

"She's helped me," he said carefully.

"There aren't many students who draw her notice. I can count on one hand the number who have over the years I've been here. Most of the time, she leaves the students alone, focusing on her research, allowing the other master librarians to interact with them."

Tolan waited for the Grand Master to say something more. Would he question Tolan about the types of things he'd been reading about? That would raise eyebrows, as would the fact that he continued to have such interest in elementals, though the Grand Master already knew that. He had been around Tolan enough that he understood the type of things that intrigued Tolan.

"She tells me you have potential to be a master librarian."

Tolan nodded.

"She has had that conversation with you, then. Interesting. Usually, the master librarians wait until a student has graduated to approach them about their potential to serve as a librarian."

"She showed me the hall of portraits."

He scratched his chin. "Did she? Then she must be quite eager to have you serve. The last student who showed such potential was Master Jensen, and even with him, she was far more reserved."

How long ago must that have been? Master Jensen was old now, incredibly old, and he imagined that it would've had to have been decades ago. And here he had thought Master Minden old. He would never have imagined she would have been responsible for drawing out Master Jensen.

"Did you see anything?"

"On the wall of portraits?"

The Grand Master nodded. "It's a test, you know."

"I didn't know. What sort of test?"

"If I told you that, the test wouldn't be useful."

"I saw several individuals, and she showed me the portraits of the elementals."

"Did she?"

"I wasn't able to see anything. I think she was hopeful I'd be able to make them out more, but the colors were subtle and the paintings were quite faded."

The Grand Master smiled to himself. "Sly, that one."

"Why?"

"You know what I see when I go to the wall of portraits?"

"The same, I would imagine."

"Now, but when I first went to them, there was one image I could see. One. The others are protected by a shaping, and that shaping is designed to help the master librarians determine who has potential. If you can see more than a few—and the number is kept by the master librarians, so don't ask me how many it is—then you have the necessary potential."

"Master Minden said you'd have the necessary potential to be a master librarian."

"I suspect that she's being kind. I have learned quite a bit throughout the years, and because of that, I've grown, which allows me the ability to see the portraits, but at the time, there was nothing."

"What does it matter if I can or can't see images in the portraits?"

"It's a marker of how you think," the Grand Master said. "To be honest, I'm probably not the best person to explain all of that. I know enough to be dangerous, but certainly not as much as someone like Asmane."

Tolan couldn't help but wonder what it meant that he had seen the images he had. Many of them were at least well enough depicted that he could make out details upon them, but toward the end of the line, he hadn't been able to see much of anything.

"There are certain images which carry greater weight than others. I suppose that's why Master Minden claimed that I have the potential—or would have had the potential —to have been a librarian."

"Which one?"

"The one with the first shaper. For the most part, there isn't anything in the other images I was able to make out. I could see details, faint lines that were a promise of something more, but when it came down to making out anything of use, that was not my strength."

"What sort of things do you mean by *of use*?"

"I mean there are images that depict the elementals. I'm sure she told you that."

"She did, but the one with the draasin, I couldn't see anything."

"Nothing?"

"Swirls of color. They were faint, but I couldn't make out the three draasin she claimed were there."

The Grand Master turned his attention back to the rune, and as he did, a shaping began to build. "When I went there, they were all blank. I remember thinking it was strange they would paint so many portraits like that, nothing but empty canvases, and yet that isn't at all what they did, as you know."

"Can you see the three draasin?"

"Not like Master Minden can." He pulled his gaze up, still not having released his shaping. "I think I understand why she wanted you to go, though I'm surprised she did."

"Why?"

"If you can even make out anything on that draasin portrait, it tells her you have the potential to truly understand the elementals."

"I don't understand how that test even would work."

"It's a shaping, no different than the Selection."

"Master Minden wanted me to leave the Academy."

The Grand Master tipped his head and studied him. Tolan wasn't sure if he should have shared that, but it seemed important, necessary to get out, and he feared if he didn't reveal it, he wouldn't learn the reason behind it. He wasn't hearing it from Master Minden, so he needed to find out from the Grand Master if there was something that would explain why she had wanted him to leave with the disciples of the Draasin Lord.

"When?"

"During the attack. She said I was summoned, and she was helping me escape."

The Grand Master started to laugh, at first softly, but then with more vigor. "Sometimes, she has plans she should share."

"What sort of plans?"

"Let's just say the Grand Master Librarian has not been the most concerned about the Draasin Lord's disciples."

"Even though they've attacked the city?"

"She views their attacks a bit differently than most, but then, that's probably why she is the librarian and I am the Grand Master. She's able to concern herself with things that involve thinking and planning, whereas I have to be involved in recognizing the dangers to our people."

"What sort of things does she think we should do?"

The Grand Master shrugged. "If it were up to her, we would invite the Draasin Lord's disciples to the Academy. Many of them studied here, so we would be basically welcoming them home."

"You disagree?"

"I disagree with the approach, not with the sentiment."

"What do you mean by that?"

"I think we have an opportunity to better understand

the disciples of the Draasin Lord." He looked up, meeting Tolan's gaze. His eyes bore into Tolan. "I'm sure you have no desire to leave the Academy, and yet at the same time, I suspect you question why the disciples came for you."

Tolan hesitated before nodding. "My father was with them."

"As you said."

Did he? "I want to know why they abandoned me."

"And I would like to know why they keep attacking in Amitan."

"We know why they keep attacking. They want to release the elementals and..." He almost said *control them*, but he didn't have that sense from the disciples when he had traveled with them. He didn't know what they were after, only that it didn't seem to be about controlling elementals. Had he stayed with his father, he might have learned, but staying with his father meant that he would be leaving the only place that had felt like he belonged.

"Perhaps, but what we need is someone on the inside. We've never been able to accomplish that, and if we could find some way to get someone inside the disciples of the Draasin Lord, we might be able to find not only where they hide, but to find some way to stop them for good."

Tolan thought about what the Grand Master was saying, and he realized what he was asking. He wanted Tolan to be that person. The only problem was, he didn't know that he could be. If he did, it meant he was betraying someone. If he went with them, did what the Grand Master asked of him, he would be betraying his father. If he went with his father and mother, then he was going against the Academy.

"I don't know if I can," he said.

"Just think about it."

Tolan nodded and turned away. What else could he do? There was no other choice but to at least consider it. And for the Grand Master, wouldn't he?

As much as he might want to avoid betraying both his friends and his family, he was going to be forced into deciding, and either choice he made would end up hurting someone.

"The Inquisitors are planning something," he said. In the time he'd been back, he'd forgotten about it, but now seemed to be the time to bring it back up. The Grand Master needed to know.

"What are they planning?"

He shook his head. "When I was with my father, they encountered an Inquisitor."

"They were chasing the disciples, Tolan. Nothing more nefarious than that."

"I'm not sure that's right. They're doing..." What, though? He had no idea, only that something had felt off when he'd been there.

The Grand Master offered him a hint of a smile, though it was little more than placating. "Perhaps you leave the spirit tower alone for a while."

"I will. If you hear anything of Aela..."

"I can't promise I will alert you. If it comes down to it, I would prefer to prevent her from harming any more within the Academy, but at the same time, she has served

Terndahl over the years, and I cannot overlook that service. Nor can you."

"What are you saying?"

"I'm saying if it comes down to it, Shaper Ethar, you might have to find it within yourself to forgive if it turns out she was acting on behalf of Terndahl."

With that, the Grand Master reached the edge of the spirit tower and disappeared with a shaping. He left Tolan alone, staring at the rune. There was something within the rune that held a trigger, a warning. Only the Grand Master would know if someone came here to shape, and he had to wonder if he could place something similar.

Doing so would be foolish, but at the same time, wouldn't he like to know if Aela returned?

Regardless of what the Grand Master might say, he couldn't trust the woman. She had already betrayed him—and others. She had told him exactly what she intended, and in doing so, had lost any credibility as to her service within Terndahl.

The only problem was that Tolan might be the only one who saw it that way.

More than that, he knew the Inquisitors were doing something, but not what that was. How could he uncover that secret?

Standing at the edge of the rune, he closed his eyes. For a moment, he squeezed his hand around the ring he'd claimed from his parents' home, the spirit bondar. As he did, he focused on spirit and pushed it out, letting it touch the rune but not trying to power it. Rather than that, he wanted nothing more than to leave a trace of a shaping.

He would like to know if someone else came here to attempt to use the rune.

With that being done, Tolan jumped, dropping back down out of the spirit tower and back into the rest of the Academy buildings.

13

Starlight twinkled overhead as Tolan rested on the Shapers Path, sitting with his legs crossed, focusing on the way the wind swirled around him. He'd stopped back after visiting with the Grand Master to find Ferrah and Jonas in the library, but didn't feel like staying. He needed to clear his mind, which brought him here.

At night, the city was quiet. No one was out, giving him an opportunity to be alone. He enjoyed the vantage, sitting above the city, getting an opportunity to look outward, to simply focus on everything around him.

The lights in the city cast a gentle glow, as many of them came from candles or lanterns, not shaped light at all. Those that were from shaped light were a purer light, orange or white, sometimes even a faint blue. They were easy to pick out, and all of them cast an additional glow throughout the night, almost like starlight on the ground.

He focused on his shaping, choosing wind to spin in a

tight spiral. He did so quickly, focusing on the column of wind before releasing it. Practicing like this would bring him closer to what the master shapers wanted from him, and he would need to have this practice if he were ever to achieve the skill that would allow him to pass on to the next level.

There was no one else around him. He was by himself, alone, and it was pleasant being like this. He enjoyed the solitude, the quiet, and the slight haze hanging in the air. Smells from the city drifted up to him. Most were pleasant, that of baking bread or the heat from a blacksmith forge that sent the metallic odor rising, and the smell of burning firewood. Those smells reminded him of Ephra, a familiar odor, one that seemed to be home, which surprised him considering how little he considered Ephra home these days.

Shapings throughout the city reverberated around him. They were steady, the rise and fall of specific beats of power, earth or fire or wind or air. Never spirit, though Tolan wasn't sure if he would be able to pick out the use of spirit if it came down to it. Often, the elements were mixed, and when they were, he suspected those shapers had much more skill. Typically, those shapings came from deeper within Amitan, near the Academy.

As his shaping column built and then collapsed, Tolan once again focused on the elemental. He added a hint of power, thinking about how the elemental had been, the way it granted him an additional connection to shaping and a focus to what he was able to do.

After a while, Tolan got to his feet. He needed to practice with the other elements, not just wind, but with earth and water. Fire was one he thought he could use reasonably well. He was less concerned about coming up with the necessary shaping that would be used in his test, and yet, he probably shouldn't be quite so confident with fire. It was a difficult element to master, and if he somehow lost control of it, if it somehow collapsed upon him, then he would find he would fail no differently than if he shaped one of the other elements incorrectly. Just because he had a familiarity with fire didn't mean he was guaranteed to pass through with it.

"I thought I would find you here."

Tolan looked up as Ferrah approached. She had a flowing cloak covering her, the hood thrown back, and the wind tousled her red hair. In the starlight, she was especially lovely.

"I'm not trying to hide from you, if that's what you think. I saw you in the library and I… I wanted some time out of the Academy."

Ferrah frowned at him. "Why would I think you were hiding from me?"

"I just didn't want you to jump to conclusions."

"Now I'm jumping to conclusions."

"That's not—"

Tolan cut off with her laughter, realizing she hadn't been implying anything.

"Why up here?" she asked.

"Up here is where the wind is," he said.

"You realize they are going to test us where the wind isn't."

He hadn't really given it much thought, but it made sense for them to do so. Why test them where it was easy to reach the wind? If they were supposed to be master shapers, they should be tested in a way that proved that.

"Then I should be practicing underground?"

"You'd be surprised at what exists underground."

"I don't know what to do," he said.

He had shared with Ferrah what the Grand Master had asked of him, and yet he hadn't shared with Jonas. There wasn't much reason to do so. Jonas wouldn't really understand the requirement the Grand Master asked of him, and if he did, he'd probably tell him to go ahead and do it.

Jonas didn't understand that if he did, if he went along with what the Grand Master wanted, he would be proving everyone right after all these years.

"It was a request, not a demand."

"I know, but it was request from the Grand Master."

"Which is basically the same?"

"What would you do?"

"I don't know," Ferrah said.

"You can see why I'm struggling."

"I knew why you were struggling," she said. "I would be as well. I'm just reminding you it was a request and not a command."

He smiled briefly. "I'm not even sure if I would be able to find him again."

"Do you think he left?"

"I don't know. I thought so, but every so often, I pick up the sense of a strange shaping." It had been like that ever since the uprising. There was the periodic sense there was something—or someone—out there, shaping in a way reminding him of his own power, and when they did, he couldn't help but question whether or not it was his father or other disciples of the Draasin Lord. Now he knew his father was with them, he didn't know if he should be more willing to go with them or more concerned about them as a whole.

"You want to know what happened to them, don't you?"

"I do, but…"

"But you fear they had a good reason for going."

Tolan looked over at her. "What if they did? What if *I* start to turn?"

"Tolan…"

"I know you don't want to think like that, but I didn't think my parents actually served the Draasin Lord, either. Now I don't have any choice in the matter."

"They probably had a good reason. Maybe they were acting like you."

"You think the Grand Master or someone else sent them to the Draasin Lord in order to find information?"

"It's possible," she said.

"I suppose."

Tolan stared out into the darkness. It would be better to believe that than to believe what he had seen.

"It's more than that, isn't it?"

Tolan nodded. "There's something to the elementals," he said.

"What do you think there is?"

"I don't really know, only that there is something I can

detect about the shaping that reminds me of how I shaped by focusing on the elementals first."

That had to be significant.

"There's even more reason for you to go, then."

"To find out about myself? I think the Academy would suggest that's why I'm here."

"Do you think you can learn about yourself at the Academy?"

Tolan took a deep breath. The answer was easy, and it came to him quickly, but it was painful. As much as he hated it, he didn't think he could learn what he wanted to know about himself. Not here. Not when it came to the elementals. And yet, if he went anywhere else, if he did what the Grand Master asked of him, it was possible he would find himself becoming something else.

"I don't know."

"The fact you can't answer that quickly and easily tells me all you need," Ferrah said.

"You think I should do it."

"I think you should consider it," she said softly.

"What about the Inquisitors?"

She shook her head. "We don't even know what they were after."

"The Grand Master thinks we should be open-minded about welcoming them back."

"Would you?"

Tolan took a deep breath. "How can I?"

If they did come back, there was no way he would be able to welcome them the way the Grand Master wanted, and he didn't even want to try.

Then again, for the good of the Academy, perhaps there was no choice in it.

"I can't be a spy," he said.

"I don't think they want you to be a spy. They want to know how to find the disciples of the Draasin Lord."

"Which means I would be a spy."

"That's not quite what that means."

"Fine, but—"

Tolan didn't get the opportunity to finish. Power bloomed near him, in several different places all at once. It was a steady pattern, and it was filled with multiple shapings, all of them overwhelming. He sat upright, looking out into the night, searching for the source.

"Is it the disciples?"

The fact that Ferrah no longer questioned how easily he detected shaping was probably good. There was no longer the need to justify what he was detecting, no longer a need for him to prove he was able to detect what he claimed he could.

"Not a shaping like that. There was a distinct signature to it, and this…"

It was spirit.

If there was spirit shaping, that meant Inquisitors.

"We should get back to the Academy," he said.

"Are you sure?"

Tolan focused on the sense of shapings all around him. What choice did he have but to return?

"I'm not going to be banished from the Academy because of the Inquisitors."

She helped him to his feet and they followed the

Shapers Path as they made their way back toward the main part of the city. When the Academy came into view, Tolan focused on the sense of shaping he had detected all around him. It bloomed continuously, a steady rhythmic sense, and he knew he wasn't imagining it. Not only was it there, and not only was it spirit shaping, but it continued to pulse, a rhythm.

A message.

"Can you tell what they're trying to shape?"

"Why would I be able to tell that?"

Tolan continued to stare at the Academy buildings, but he didn't have the sense the shaping came from within them. There was no sense of the shaping causing his connection to what he had placed around the spirit tower, either. If they were approaching that, they had done so quietly and not attempted to use power on the spirit rune.

"There's a message within their shaping. I can't quite make it all out, but it's definitely there."

"What sort of message?"

Tolan shook his head. "I can't tell. It's out of spirit, though, so I wasn't sure if I was somehow immune to it or not."

"If it's out of spirit, then maybe you're one of the only ones who can hear it."

Tolan hadn't considered that.

He stayed on the Shapers Path, letting the sense of the spirit shaping wash over him, the steady beating coming one after another, a tickle at the back of his mind.

Was there any way to open himself up to the message without being overwhelmed by it? He didn't think it was intending to spirit shape everyone in the city, and Ferrah's suggestion it could be a message only for spirit shapers had quite a bit of sense.

What if he spirit shaped?

Tolan began to pull on spirit, opening himself up to it. When he did so, it pulled on some distant part of him, requiring he open himself and give himself over, and as he did, he found he was able to gradually draw more and more power.

Spirit was finicky, different than his connection to the other elements, though possibly because he didn't know if there was an element bond. If there was, then the reason it was different was probably because there were no elementals forced within the bond. As far as anyone knew, there had never been a spirit elemental.

As he drew on the sense of the shaping, he didn't detect anything. It was there, regular and more powerful than he would've expected, but there wasn't anything else within it that he could detect.

"We need to go find the Grand Master," Tolan said.

"Tolan, I don't like you getting involved in this."

"I'm already involved," he said.

"That's not the point. I don't like you getting more involved in it."

"Then just come with me. We can tell the Grand Master, and then we can go back to the student quarters."

He had no intention of really going back to the dorms if there was a potential for attack. The dorms were isolated, and it would be all too easy for them to be caught within the dorms.

It was better to stay out in the open, and when it came down to it, it might be better to stay out in the city rather than risk going back to the Academy.

Ferrah watched him, seeming to calculate what he might do. He didn't even know what he might do.

Finally, she stretched out her hand, waiting for him to take it. When he did, he jumped, wrapping himself in a shaping of wind. All the practice had made it easier and he landed, using the spiraling column of air to hold him up, cushioning his landing.

They came to the ground in the courtyard outside the Academy entrance, and once they were there, Tolan hurried toward the door.

Students made their way through the halls in clusters of two or three, and the occasional single student. All seemed oblivious to the presence of the shaping Tolan so easily detected.

And why should he detect it?

What if that was the message?

Could he have been viewing it wrongly? He'd been looking at it as if they were trying to send a message to other spirit shapers and rather than that, what if they were trying to send a message to *him*, a notification they knew he was here?

That didn't seem right.

Tolan started down the hallway toward the Grand Master's rooms, ignoring other students, and when he reached the Grand Master's rooms, he knocked.

He worried for a moment that it would be like the last time he'd come here and that the Grand Master would be gone. Instead, the door came open with a flourish and the Grand Master stood on the other side, but he wasn't alone.

The Grand Inquisitor was with him.

"Shaper Ethar? Is there a reason for your visit at this time of night?"

"I…" Tolan wasn't quite sure how much he should say. Likely, the Grand Inquisitor had already learned he could detect spirit, and there was no questioning that the Grand Master knew about his ability. "I detected a shaping out in the city."

The Grand Master cocked his head to the side. "You did."

"I did. I feared it was a message from the Inquisitors." He said the last in a hurried way, glancing briefly down the hall in either direction, worried others might realize what he'd said. As he said it, he realized how foolish it sounded. Could he really believe he had to be the one to notify the Grand Master that the Inquisitors might be there?

"I'm afraid you have it wrong, Shaper Ethar," the Grand Master said.

"I do?" If so, he was relieved.

"It wasn't a message from the Inquisitors. It was a message *for* them."

"Why would you be sending a message to the Inquisitors?"

The Grand Master watched him for a moment before shaking his head. "Now is not really the time for this discussion, Shaper Ethar."

Tolan looked past the Grand Master, turning his attention to the Grand Inquisitor. What was he missing? If the rest of the Inquisitors returned, he had little doubt what would happen. They would come after him again.

"But what I saw—"

"Was their task. If they discovered the disciples, they would give chase."

Tolan stood motionless for a moment, feeling helpless. This was about more than just the disciples. And the Grand Master had already told him that. "Is this your way of restoring the Academy?"

"I'm afraid it's complicated."

"It doesn't have to be," Tolan said.

The Grand Master studied him, taking a deep breath, and he seemed to be preparing to say something, but he caught himself.

"Perhaps it would be best if you returned to your rooms," he said, glancing from Tolan to Ferrah.

Ferrah grabbed his arm, trying to pull him with her. Tolan didn't want to go. He didn't want to deal with this. He didn't want to have to wonder what sort of things the Inquisitors might do to him.

But then, the Grand Master had warned him, hadn't he?

The steady sense of the shaping continued to fill the air around him. It came from everywhere, a steadily building pressure he couldn't ignore.

So far, there had been no response, there had been nothing that would suggest the Inquisitors would respond to the summons, but Tolan had to believe they would. If this was a message for them, then it wouldn't be long before they responded.

He had a couple of choices. He could stay and be ready, or…

Tolan didn't want to think about the *or*.

"Come on, Tolan," Ferrah whispered.

He cast another look at the Grand Master before tearing his gaze away and following Ferrah down the hallway. The Grand Master's door closed behind him, shutting Tolan off from him.

"I can't believe they're welcoming them back."

"Why wouldn't they?" Ferrah said. "What did they do, really?"

"They attacked me!" He realized he was talking too loudly and lowered his voice. "You know what happened."

"I know what happened, and *they* know what happened, but this is for the good of the Academy. Is it for the good of the Academy to lose those who help with the Selection?"

"You sound like you're siding with them."

"It's not a matter of siding with them or not. It's a matter of understanding that things aren't straightforward. It's not neat and tidy."

"I never said it was." It seemed almost as if she didn't understand, and that troubled him as much as anything. Ferrah had always tried to understand.

"We should do as he suggests and get back to the dorms."

Tolan listened to the sound of the shaping. The steady rhythm of it hadn't changed, and as he focused on it, as he realized he could feel it but no others could, he debated what he should do—if anything.

"You go back. I'm going to stop in the library for a minute."

"Why the library?"

"There's just something I want to check on."

"Promise me you won't do anything too foolish?"

"You know me."

"Which means you can't make that promise."

He smiled at her. "That's not what it means. It just means I won't."

Ferrah hesitated, and he had a sense she might not leave him, and if she didn't, he would have to be more reserved in the questions he had for the librarians. He wanted to know if serving as a librarian would protect him from the Inquisitors.

Ferrah patted his arm and then continued down the hallway.

Tolan took a deep breath, letting it out with a shaky sigh. He stood in place for a moment, letting the sense of a shaping sweep over him. It was powerful and overwhelming, the kind of shaping he knew to fear. There was something buried within that shaping that suggested danger. Maybe it was nothing more than his imagination, but the longer he focused on it, aware of the sense of the shaping, the more certain he was that he detected it accurately.

As he watched the others around him, students making their way along the hallway, it was abundantly clear no one else detected the same thing Tolan did. And perhaps that was for the best. It was better for them to remain unaware of what was taking place, almost a peace in that.

It was at times like these that Tolan wondered how much easier it would have been to have remained blissfully unaware of everything he'd experienced. These students understood the danger of the Draasin Lord, but they also felt there was a real danger to the elementals, and they believed the way Tolan had once believed, that there was reason to fear the elementals. How much easier would it have been to have remained ignorant of the fact the elementals posed him no danger? He couldn't help but think it would be far better.

Reaching the library, Tolan paused at the doors. Were there answers in here?

No more than there were anywhere else. All of this left him feeling empty, hollow, and although it shouldn't, he still couldn't shake the fact the Grand Master welcomed the Inquisitors back, despite knowing what they had done to him.

Tolan pushed open the door, stepping inside. It would be better in the library, better not to be aware of the shaping, and at least within the library, he could cut himself off from shaping elsewhere. The only shaping he would be aware of here would be his own—and that of Master Minden.

The library was quiet.

There were a few students here, but not as many as there would have been earlier in the day. He looked around, searching for which of the master librarians were on duty, and was surprised Master Minden was here.

Next to her on the dais was another of the master librarians he didn't know all that well. Master Hevon was young, at least for a master librarian, and still had dark streaks within his hair rather than complete gray. He bent over the pad on the dais, writing with a furious sort of scrawl.

As he came into the library, Master Minden looked up. She barely hesitated before getting off the dais and beginning to wander along the edge of the library, looking at the shelves as if that was all she had ever intended to do.

Tolan joined her. "The Grand Master tells me they're calling back the Inquisitors."

"Shaper Ethar. I'm not sure that is much of your concern."

Tolan blinked. "Not my concern?"

"There are many things the Grand Master must consider."

"But you know what happened."

"I do, much as you know there are things you must ignore."

Tolan wasn't quite sure how to take that. What sort of things did he need to ignore? Was she trying to tell him he had to ignore the fact the Grand Master was calling back the very people who'd attacked him? She knew what he'd gone through, and she as much as anyone understood the way he had a connection to the elementals and that the Inquisitors would try to harm that in some way.

"What are you suggesting I do?" he asked.

"I believe the Grand Master has made that suggestion, too."

He frowned. "You think I need to leave."

"Does it have to be spelled out for you? You are bright, Shaper Ethar. Otherwise I wouldn't have suggested a path of study for you as I have."

"Why?"

"Because there are answers to be found outside of the Academy."

"What happens if they're not the answers we want?"

"How do we decide what answers we want?"

"I don't know."

"I suppose that's as good a response as any. We don't know, not until we go and search for those answers. In the case of what you have been through, and what fate you believe is out there for you, you can't know."

"But it means I—"

"Again, it means nothing other than you going in search of information."

"You want me to go. You always wanted me to go."

"Don't make this any harder than it needs to be," she said.

"Why?"

The master librarian tipped her head to the side. As she did, a soft shaping built from her. It was faint, barely more than enough to pick up the edges of, but it was there. When it dissipated, it rolled away from her, heading along the hallway and out into the main part of the Academy. It was spirit, at least as far as he could tell, though he wasn't sure how she used it or why such a shaping would be necessary now.

"Have you wondered at the nature of the shaping you detect?"

"It's a spirit summons."

"Is that all you think it is?"

"I don't know what else it might be."

"It is a spirit summons, and yet, there is more to it. When you are better trained, it's possible you will have a better sense of what exactly you are detecting within a shaping like this. For now, I would suggest you trust the Grand Master and others know what they are doing."

"Even if that means they're bringing back those who might be seeking power for themselves?"

"Again, I would suggest you trust the Grand Master. But even if you don't, there are answers you can find for yourself, but only if you're willing to look."

"Outside the city."

She bowed her head to him. "Unfortunately, when we look for answers, it often takes us to difficult places. In this case, you must take a dangerous journey. Only you can do it."

"I don't know I can provide the Grand Master with what he wants."

"How do you know unless you go?"

"Because it involves my parents."

"Are you so certain?"

He tipped his head, looking at her. "Are you saying it might not?"

"I'm saying the information you're after might not be quite as straightforward as you believe. There is bound to be more to it than you have uncovered."

"And if there's not?"

"If there's not, then you return."

"What if they try to—" Tolan lowered his voice, looking around, but the library was mostly empty other than the other librarian. One student sat alone in the corner of the room. Tolan noticed it was Wallace. He seemed to be in the library nearly as much as Tolan and Ferrah. Though they shared a room with him, they still didn't know all that much about him. He remained quiet, reserved, somewhat of an enigma. "What if they spirit-shape me to force me to do what they want?"

"What has your experience with spirit shaping been so far?"

"Not good," he said.

"How many shapers have managed to spirit-shape you?"

"Well, not all that many."

"You are touched by spirit, Tolan Ethar, and for someone who has been so touched, it grants a certain protection. If you had better control over it, you would not need to be as concerned, but even without control, even as you are, there is protection to you with spirit. Embrace that."

"How?"

"Do as you always have done."

"And what's that?"

"Let the shaping guide you."

14

FOR THE SECOND TIME THAT NIGHT, TOLAN FOUND HIMSELF outside, wind swirling around him, the sense of shapings all around. For the most part, it was spirit, the sense of the Grand Master and the Grand Inquisitor and whatever they were doing to call back the Inquisitors, but there were other shapings mixed in, some from within the Academy, but others outside in the main part of the city.

Amitan was a place of power, a place where shapers collected, and over the years, more and more shapers had remained, giving the city a certain sense of power that emanated from it. There weren't many other places within Terndahl quite as powerful as Amitan. It was the seat of the Academy, which made it special, but it was also the seat of Terndahl, the capital, and a place of much power.

Tolan focused on what he could detect all around him, letting those shapings swirl and flow over him and trying to work through what the master librarian had just suggested to him. It was the same as what the Grand Master had wanted, and in the case of Master Minden, he suspected there was more to it than she shared. He didn't know her well, but well enough to recognize she had some motive.

He should return to the dorms to give word to Ferrah, perhaps even Jonas, about what he was going to do, but maybe it was best to simply go. He didn't know if he would have the necessary stomach to do what was needed if he went back and told his friends. It was possible Ferrah —or even Jonas—would try to talk him out of it, and at this point, Tolan no longer thought he could—or should— be talked out of what needed to happen.

Leave the city.

Could he really be contemplating leaving?

More than that, he had to find out if there was some way to follow the shaping sense he suspected came from his father or the other disciples of the Draasin Lord. If he managed to find it, he would have to convince them he posed no threat if his father wasn't present.

All of it seemed far beyond what he as a student could do. It was more than he thought he *should* do.

Yet, his father was out there.

It was still hard to come to grips with the fact that his parents had left him, abandoning him so they could go in service of the Draasin Lord, and in doing so, they had abandoned him to a life of danger. Not only had he been put under the charge of Master Daniels, someone who he now understood served the Draasin Lord in a different and dangerous way, but he'd been subjected to the comments and rumors their disappearance had created. Life in Ephra had been hard.

Tolan tried to pick out individual shapings, but as he listened to them, there was nothing he could detect. There had to be some way to reach the disciples, but after spending the last few weeks feeling that strange shaping sense throughout the city, when he wanted to uncover it, he couldn't.

"Figures," he muttered.

There was something else he could do. If he couldn't find that, at least he could focus on the spirit shaping the Grand Master and Grand Inquisitor were using. As he focused on it, he detected the rhythm within it. There was something more, something he hadn't picked up on before. Perhaps he should have been aware of it sooner, but then, his connection to spirit wasn't nearly as profound as the ones who were shaping this.

They'd used the spirit rune.

How had he not noticed it before? Hadn't he left a hint of shaping overtop the spirit rune? The reason he had done it was so he would be able to detect anyone shaping, but then, if it was the Grand Master—and the Grand Inquisitor, he had to admit—their understanding of shaping spirit was so far above his, it would be easy for them to mask the fact they had done so. How did he expect to be able to uncover anything when they were shaping with it?

He should be pleased with the fact he was even aware of them shaping. Ferrah had not been. The other students within the Academy didn't seem as if they had been aware of it. It was one meant only for the Inquisitors.

Or perhaps not.

Tolan wished he had a better understanding of the nature of the shaping, but until he better understood spirit, he wasn't sure he'd be able to know what they were doing.

Using a burst of wind and fire, Tolan shaped himself up to the Shapers Path, landing on it. He wandered along it, veering toward the outer edges of the city, following it. He had traveled it enough that he was able to recognize its presence without seeing it. It was a surge of a presence pushing against his awareness, almost as if designed to do so.

Following the Shapers Path was faster than walking because there was something about the Shapers Path itself that helped speed travelers along it. It didn't take long for him to reach the outskirts of the city. From there, Tolan paused again, listening to the sense of the shaping. As before, it remained a steady presence, a building and rhythmic sense that tapped on his awareness. There was nothing new about it that he could pick up from here, though he wished he was better able to uncover the directionality to it. There was a source, but with so many shapings scattered all about the city, it seemed as if more than just the Grand Master and Grand Inquisitor were responsible for this shaping.

Standing here as he did, he was better able to detect other shapings. The Academy had its sense of shapings as it always did, and from here, he could ignore them. They were clustered, gathered together in a small sense within his mind, and he could ignore those as he focused on the rest of the city. Other shapings bloomed from time to time throughout the city, most of them without much power. Those would be from shapers who had perhaps trained at the Academy in the past, perhaps having never made it past the first testing, or perhaps those who lived in Amitan, descendants of powerful shapers. None of the shapings from them was sustained, and though some carried a bit of power, for the most part, they were not powerful.

Tolan looked around. The shaping sense he needed to find was along the edge here. The only time he had detected it closer into the city had been when they had come for him, but otherwise, it had remained outside, a rhythmic sort of sense reminding him a bit of the spirit shaping.

That was odd to think of, but it did fit with what he was detecting.

He couldn't find any evidence of that shaping.

Tolan continued along the Shapers Path, gliding around the city. Maybe regardless of what Master Minden and the Grand Master wanted, he wouldn't find any evidence of his father or the disciples. Perhaps this was a pointless exercise, a waste of his time, and perhaps he would end up back at the Academy anyway.

He reached the northern edge of the city. From here, the distant darkness of the forest spread beyond the borders of the city. Down within that forest, he had detected elementals before, some of them rogue, some of them he thought he'd freed from the bond. In the days since Master Aela had come after him, he hadn't detected the elementals quite the same way as before.

Could it be the loss of his bondars had taken away his connection to them? He didn't think so. When he had been shaping wind in particular, he still had felt some connection to the elementals, but it had been different than what he had known before. Perhaps weaker, but definitely changed.

Tolan breathed in the sense of the forest, letting that power swirl around him. Within that place, he was more acutely aware of earth and the earth bond, but he was also filled with hundreds of different senses through his connection to earth. It was more than just the trees; it was animals and the shape of the forest and the age, and so many different aspects to it.

In his classes with Master Shorav, they stayed in the Academy buildings for the most part, occasionally going out to the park nearby to work on their shapings, but they never went outside the Academy grounds like this. Tolan hadn't had the connection to earth quite like this before. It was more than just an earth sensing, and now he detected it, he felt the flowing power all around him, a sense that reminded him of the energy that was found outside the city, outside the Academy, and a reminder of how the elements filled everything.

Regardless of what Master Sartan might say, all the elements were life. In this place, standing here above the forest, Tolan was well aware of how earth was filled with life. It was more than just the element bond; it was a sense of everything existing out here. Not all of it was directly connected to the element bond, and yet the power of earth still touched it.

It wasn't only earth that he was able to detect. Wind blew between the trees, caressing the branches and the leaves, carrying the smells of the forest, that of decaying leaves and fresh pine, mixing with the occasional fragrance blowing off flowers that sprung to life. Earth and wind worked together to carry the overall sense of the forest.

More than just earth and wind were there, though.

Fire existed, though not the same way as a dancing flame. There was heat. It came from within the trees, within the animals scurrying along the trees or across the forest floor, and it came from deep within the earth itself. Regardless of how earth and fire countered each other, they coexisted, their powers and their energies lingering together in this place.

Lastly, but certainly not least, there was water. As he stood on the Shapers Path, focusing on everything within the forest, the sense of a stream burbling through, feeding the forest, giving the animals access to life-sustaining water, came to him. At night, he noticed the dew on the leaves, the dampness on the forest floor, and even a haze hanging in the air, suspended above the ground.

Tolan smiled to himself. It was strange he would have to come here to have such an understanding of the elements. None of them was tied to the element bonds. Despite that, there was still power that flowed through here.

Perhaps that was the message he needed. And maybe he needed to step away from the Academy more often in order to better understand the nature of power that rolled through the world. It wasn't just in this place. There were others just like it.

And despite that power, there had to be something missing.

What would it be like if the elementals roamed freely within the forest?

Everything he knew told him there had once been a time when the elementals had lived out in the world. Regardless of what the shapers of today might claim, the elementals hadn't been dangerous. Hadn't they added something to the world?

When he had freed them, they'd wandered, disappearing, heading off into… Where?

Tolan didn't know, and perhaps it didn't matter. What mattered was that the elementals needed to be freed.

As much as anything, he felt that truth.

It was unusual to be aware of that, and as he felt the sense of the forest, the power and energy that came from the presence of each of the elements within it, he wondered how much more powerful it would be were the elementals there.

The Academy would suppress the elementals, to hold them within the bond, but it wasn't necessary for shapers to have the elementals trapped within the bond to reach for power.

Tolan could shape without reaching the element

bonds. He felt certain of that. It was the reason he was able to shape in places others could not.

What did that mean?

What would it mean if the elementals were freed from the bonds? Would the bonds be destroyed? They were layers of energy, hidden and yet a part of the world, a source of power, but would they shatter if the elementals were freed?

Would the earth be torn apart if they were removed?

There had been a time before, when the elements had been separate from the elementals, where the bonds had been free of the elementals, and yet the world had turned.

Tolan found himself smiling, feeling a little bit foolish about the nature of his thoughts as he stood outside the city, floating along the Shapers Path. Strangely, he was no longer quite as aware of the spirit shaping that had hammered steadily ever since he had detected it with Ferrah.

With a start, Tolan turned back toward the Academy.

Why shouldn't he be aware of it?

Maybe the shaping had run its course.

No. It was still there, but was faint—certainly fainter than it had been before. He focused on it, listening for it, and searching for what he might be able to detect.

There wasn't much.

Tolan started back toward the Academy. It was well past time to do so, and he had been outside of the city long enough, enjoying his connection to the forest and to the various elements. But now he was out here, he needed to return. There had been no sign of his father and no sign of the disciples of the Draasin Lord, regardless of what the Grand Master or Master Minden might have wanted.

While starting toward the city, a sense of shaping came from behind him.

Tolan paused, looking back. It was outside the city.

He waited, hoping that it would come again.

Moments passed. Then more.

When the sense finally returned, it was distinct. Definitely a shaping, and it wasn't the kind of shaping that he expected. He had thought it might be from one of the disciples of the Draasin Lord, but that wasn't it at all. As he focused and listened to the sense of the shaping, he recognized a different kind of aspect to it, one far more dangerous to him.

One of the Inquisitors.

They had responded to the shaping.

Of course, they had. The Inquisitors would've had no reason not to respond to it. They would have known the Grand Master and the Grand Inquisitor had wanted them to come, and would have responded in kind, answering the call, and in doing so, putting Tolan at risk.

He froze, not willing or wanting to take a step anywhere. He had intended to return to the Academy, but now he detected that shaping, he wasn't so sure anymore.

The shaping came again, closer.

Tolan frowned to himself. Why did it seem to be coming toward *him*?

They shouldn't have been aware he was here. He hadn't been shaping, and there was no way for them to have identified his presence here, and yet, each time he detected the sense of the shaping, it came closer.

Tolan started along the Shapers Path, making his way more quickly as he ran, following the contours of the path, using his connection to earth sensing to ensure his safety as he followed it. It would be all too easy to tumble as he ran, and he had no interest in falling from the Shapers Path.

It was possible he'd already revealed himself in some way. Maybe his time standing at the edge of the forest, focusing on sensing the intricacies of the interconnectedness there, had revealed him. Could he have been shaping? He didn't think he had, but the way he had felt for the power within the forest certainly seemed possible.

Tolan continued to run, and the Academy loomed into view.

Shaping exploded near him.

Tolan stopped, looking around.

Another shaping exploded near him.

He turned, reaching for his connection to earth and wind, adding a hint of fire.

Another shaping exploded near him.

He had the sense these shapings were trying to circle him. That couldn't be a coincidence. What purpose would they have in circling him like that?

They were trying to cut him off somehow.

Did they think they could separate him from the shaping bond?

Perhaps they did, but the advantage he had was that he didn't need to have the element bonds in order to shape.

They couldn't know that, and yet, power continued to surge all around him.

He still saw no one.

If he lingered, he would open himself up to danger.

He couldn't stay here any longer.

Tolan focused on the Academy. He might have to drop to the ground, but if he did, he'd then have to run through the streets. Going that way would be far slower than traveling by the Shapers Path.

And there was the possibility he was simply imagining this. What if this wasn't the Inquisitors at all? What if this was nothing more than one of the master shapers out in the city?

He needed to be careful he didn't accuse someone of a shaping that wasn't theirs, and the fact he was on edge might mean he was envisioning something that simply didn't exist.

He continued to focus, and as he did, he couldn't help but feel the nature of the shaping. It had distinct elements to it that he recognized. He'd been attacked by it, and understood the nature of it.

There was no question in his mind. This came from an Inquisitor.

Tolan shifted the nature of his shaping, focusing on fire, pulling that inward, if only so he could protect his mind from the possibility of a spirit shaping attempted on him.

There came no sense of spirit, but perhaps they were waiting.

Another shaping exploded near him.

That couldn't be his imagination. Now he was even more certain that they were trying to control him in some way. What purpose did they hope to accomplish by trapping him like this?

Tolan pushed on fire, holding it inside him, and was able to protect himself, to protect his mind. He could hold onto it for a long time like this, but if it came down to it, he worried that he might need to fight, and he wasn't sure he could do that while trying to protect his mind at the same time.

Still there was no sign of whatever shapers were out there trying to reach him.

Where were they?

Unless they were right in front of him, hiding in plain sight, using some sort of earth shaping to hide themselves.

It was the kind of shaping he'd read about, but it wasn't the kind of shaping he knew how to create.

Tolan pushed on fire, holding onto it, and as he did, more and more of the sense of shaping continued to explode around him. It was there, powerful, and he made sure to hold onto his connection to the elements in order to keep the shaping.

Another surge of power, and this one definitely came from near him.

Tolan turned his attention toward it, maintaining his hold on fire as he focused it inwardly, and as he did, he also pushed outward, using a blast of fire and wind in order to attack where he had sensed the shaping.

It struck something, parting around it.

Another shaping, and Tolan turned, using his connection to power to detect it, and he spun, this time using earth, throwing it upward so it disrupted any shaping that might be there.

The earth exploded, the Shapers Path heaving for a moment before settling.

Not settling. Smoothed.

Whatever shaper was here, they had countered his attack, smoothing it out, keeping him from doing anything that would harm them.

This skill in smoothing the Shapers Path was incredible. It happened in a blink of an eye, his attempt at shaping countered so quickly as to be little more of a threat than a gnat biting at him.

Tolan held onto his connection to earth, but a shaping began to batter at it.

It started slowly, slithering against his shaping, but with increasing intensity, it began to work its way toward him, trying to slither underneath the protection he'd placed. If it succeeded, would they be able to shape him?

He didn't like the idea that they would be able to do anything to him. Worse, he didn't like the idea that he would have nothing that he could do to protect himself.

Taking a chance, he jumped.

And found he could not.

He remained on the Shapers Path, trapped. Whoever was around him, masked with earth shaping, held him confined.

Tolan turned his attention toward the shaping. He had to find some way of escaping. He had to break through whatever they were doing. He simply didn't have enough strength. If only he hadn't lost his bondars.

He'd had that sense more than once, and this time, it came with a feeling of frustration.

With everything he'd gone through, everything he'd survived so far, to be trapped like this, caught up after the Grand Master and the Grand Inquisitor had summoned the Inquisitors back to the Academy, left him feeling a certain sort of hollow emptiness.

Tolan pulled on each of his element bonds, but the connection to them failed.

He attempted to shape, and that still came, but strangely, it wasn't nearly as powerful as it normally was. Perhaps he was pulling on the element bonds far more than he had been aware of.

He continued to wrap himself in fire, turning it inward, but Master Sartan's warning flowed through him, a caution that he needed to be careful about using fire too closely to himself, not wanting to use it in a way that would damage himself.

Tolan instead focused on adding other elements to the shaping. Water and wind, earth. He even pushed on spirit, though pulling upon that was difficult.

Spirit was the only element that he had a bondar for, and he grabbed it, squeezing his fist around it, hoping he could find some way to use the bondar in order to draw enough power. With everything he could detect around him, he doubted the bondar would be enough to protect him.

Without any protection, hope faded.

The Inquisitors would finally have him.

Tolan cried out.

Someone laughed. The sound came faintly, a taunt, and he cried out again, anger flowing through him, filling him.

They were not going to have him like this.

And yet, how was he going to do anything to stop them?

Exploding outward, Tolan sent his shaping away from him with as much force as possible, trying only to shove the attackers away.

For a moment, he thought he might have succeeded.

Then shaping began to assault him.

It came with an onslaught of energy, first the wind battering him, the sense of water swirling around him, the Shapers Path trembling under earth, and fire with a rising heat. There was only so much of this that Tolan would be able to withstand. As he tried, he cried out again. His voice was muted in the night, hollow and empty, and it was as if his attacker knew he was unable to do anything.

And he *was* unable to do anything.

Through it all, shapings slammed into him.

As they did, something else came with them.

There was another shaping, but what was it? Where was it from?

The shaping was familiar. It was like the kind of shaping he used, the same way he pulled upon energy when he was shaping, focusing on the elementals.

He was not alone.

The disciples of the Draasin Lord were there.

His father.

Tolan had to hold out, but could he?

He squeezed the ring, focusing on spirit, using the only element he could shape through a bondar. It flowed outward, a powerful shaping that surrounded him, and thankfully, it held.

Tolan pushed away.

Then his shaping began to fail.

In that moment, another shaping exploded. Then another. Then another. And another. Each of them was incredibly powerful.

Tolan could barely look, afraid to turn his attention to whatever might be coming, knowing if he did look, it would mean that he was captured.

"Open your eyes, Tolan," a soft and gentle voice said.

Tolan blinked. "I don't want to."

"It's okay."

When he opened his eyes, he discovered he was face to face with his father.

"Are you ready to come with us now?"

Tolan glanced over at the Academy. After everything, considering what he had done, the ways that he had served the Academy, protecting it when others would have done it harm, was he ready to leave it?

He hated that leaving seemed to be his fate. He hated the fact that it seemed as if he had little choice in the matter. And he hated the fact that Ferrah wouldn't know where he was going.

Leaving didn't mean he couldn't return, did it?

It might. He had to admit the possibility was there that

it might. And if he couldn't return, the last time that he had seen Ferrah might have been in the hallway outside of the library. The last words that he had told her had been a lie—that he was going to return.

Tolan swallowed. "What choice do I have?"

15

A SENSE OF SHAPING CHASED HIM AS THEY STREAKED AWAY from Amitan. The darkness engulfed him, and there was a part of Tolan that still clung to the sense of the elements all around him. It wasn't the sense of the elementals, and it wasn't the sense of the element bonds, but it was the true sense of the elements. He'd never experienced anything quite so pure before. And in this case, he wanted to know it again.

There came the ongoing buildup of energy. Inquisitors were shaping, out in the darkness. He'd not been able to withstand their attack, and Tolan didn't think he'd be able to do so if it was only up to him. Now the Grand Master and Grand Inquisitor had called back the Inquisitors, searching for unity, Tolan had to better understand what was taking place.

That was his mission.

As much as anything, he understood the Grand

Master wanted more from him. He might not have said it, and he might not have been able to say it, but Tolan knew the man. Well, at least as much as anyone could know the Grand Master. He wanted Tolan to uncover the key to what the disciples were planning. While he wasn't sure if he'd be able to do that, he thought he could uncover the key to what the Inquisitors were planning.

And the more he thought about it, the more certain he was that they were planning something.

They streaked along the Shapers Path, moving quickly, shaped by wind and earth with a hint of fire mixed in, all the elements converging in a way that Tolan could feel flowing through him. He was fully aware of that power, and because he was, he let it wash over him.

No one spoke. What was there for anyone to even say?

They were running.

Tolan was running.

As they neared the path that would guide them toward Ephra, once again his father veered north.

This time, it would lead him away from the main part of Terndahl, toward an emptiness, and back toward where they'd been attacked before.

In the distance, something tugged at Tolan, a strange sensation, and something that left him troubled.

He couldn't determine what it was, though he could feel it.

"You need to hurry," his father said.

"I'm sorry," Tolan responded. He had been quiet up until that point, and he didn't realize that he was slowing while running, but now he did, he looked around. "Do you feel it?"

"What you're feeling is the edge of the waste," his father said.

"I don't remember it like this before," Tolan said.

He tried to ignore that sense, but as they traveled, he couldn't help but feel as if something different was taking place. The more he focused on that strangeness, the more certain Tolan was that it was real.

All he knew was that it was off. He was different than when he'd been here before. And, the more he thought about it, the more it reminded him of the strange sensation he'd noticed when he'd been near the Inquisitor they'd encountered.

"Tolan," his father urged.

Tolan took a deep breath, letting it out in a heavy sigh. There was no point in arguing with his father about this. He had to keep up with them. In order to do what the Grand Master needed, to go where he was needed, to find out what he was asked to uncover, Tolan was going to have to accompany them. And to be successful, that meant he was going to need to open himself to a willingness to travel with the disciples of the Draasin Lord.

Unlike the last time, Tolan wasn't sure he had the option to go back. The last time, he'd believed he could go and find the Grand Master, that he could share with him what had happened, and he had believed that in doing so, he would be able to get help. This time, the Grand Master was responsible for what was taking place. This time, the Grand Master had made his allegiances known.

Which meant Tolan couldn't go back.

This was his only option.

He let go of the emotions he was feeling. He let go of the helplessness. He let go of the strangeness, trying to ignore it, knowing there was not much more he could do.

When they reached the end of the Shapers Path, his father carried him on a powerful shaping of wind and fire, traveling to the north. As Tolan thought he would drop them to the ground, they continued to soar onward, more and more power guiding them. It seemed as if his father wasn't taking any chances this time. The sense of energy used was greater than what Tolan remembered from before. Bondars had to be involved.

And then they started to descend.

It happened gradually, and in the darkness, it was difficult for Tolan to make out anything that would help them understand where they were. They were north, though he had no idea how far to the north they'd traveled.

The only thing in the far north was the Maileen mountain range. His parents had brought him there when he was younger, testing him to see if there would be any way for him to reach earth or wind or even water. Tolan had failed, and now he was coming with his father, he couldn't help but wonder if they had done that as part of their testing to see if he belonged with the Draasin Lord.

When they reached the ground, a hint of color was starting to cross the sky as daylight started to surge. Wind whistled around him. The distant mountain peak rose high overhead, marking the northern edge of Terndahl. They had headed this way, veering away from the waste and from where Tolan had expected his father to have led him. This wasn't the domain of the Draasin Lord, at least as far as he'd have known.

He was underdressed for the weather, and without any connection to fire, he would have been cold, bitterly so. Thankfully, with his connection to fire, he didn't suffer quite as much as he would have otherwise. He shaped fire constantly, holding onto that connection, and his time with the furios and learning to hold onto fire shaping had made him skilled.

"There's a reason the Academy never found us," his father said.

"Beyond the mountain?"

"Something like that," his father said.

"I thought you went beyond the waste."

"As you've already seen, there's nothing beyond the waste."

Tolan wasn't sure that was quite right. When he'd been to the waste before, there'd been a sense of something, though he didn't quite know what it was. There was a part of him that wondered if it was an elemental, some marker of power, but if that was what it was, how could it be out in the vast expanse of the waste where there was no elemental power?

From here, they walked, and as they went, he continued to wish for different clothing, a cloak or boots or something other than the thin wool of the Academy uniform.

"You haven't asked about your mother."

The three disciples were in front of them, and Tolan

glanced toward them for a moment before turning his attention to his father. "Should I have asked about her? If she worried about me, she wouldn't have left me."

"We were needed."

"So you said."

"You don't understand the role we played."

"You make bondars," he said to his father.

"Where did you hear that?"

"I didn't hear it anywhere. I found evidence for it and have memories of it."

"You shouldn't have any memories of it."

"Because you stole them from me?" There was more bitterness in his voice than he had intended, and yet, he couldn't help the fact that he felt as if he'd had memories stolen from him, memories he should have known, things he should have been able to experience. Had they stripped away the memories that would have revealed who they were and left only those making it seem as if they had a happy life?

"We shielded you from memories that would have been harmful."

"Like the ones of you making the bondars."

"If the Academy learned the technique has not been lost..."

"How do you know how to do it?"

"Because it's been handed down through the generations."

"What generations?"

"Ours." His father fixed him with an unreadable expression.

"So, I will be able to make bondars?"

"If you choose to do so. The technique isn't so difficult, but it's learning the intricacies of it. It takes someone with specific abilities to do that."

"They can make copies of bondars at the Academy."

"They can, but that's all they are. Copies. They aren't nearly as potent as those made with a specific purpose. And the bondars the Academy possesses are only those that have a specific type of power. They lose something because of that."

"And what sort of bondars do you make?"

"All kinds," his father said.

Tolan thought about the memory he had, the vague recollection of watching his father as he worked, creating the bondar. It was tied to runes and shaping, but also tied to elementals, he was certain of that. There had been nothing else within that memory that would share with him what his father had done or how he could replicate it, yet he couldn't deny his interest in attempting to create a bondar. If he could do so, if he could use power like that, it would be valuable. Not just to him when he couldn't shape quite as strongly as he wanted, but to those with him. Not all shapers could reach each of the element bonds equally.

Then there was the potential to be able to create bondars with specific purposes. That had a different kind of value. He could imagine ways of twisting the elementals, and using various runes, together to grant even more power.

Tolan looked up the slope of the mountain that they were climbing. As he did, he shivered.

"There is a delicacy to creating them. I always enjoyed that. Even when we lived in Ephra, I found much satisfaction in creating bondars."

"Why were you in Ephra if you were serving the Draasin Lord?"

"Ephra was the easiest location to reach. Trade moved through, which meant it would be less suspicious when people came to me for the bondars I made."

"You always served the Draasin Lord?"

"Tolan—"

"Just answer."

"I've always served. As has your mother."

"Because of the bondars?"

"Because of many reasons," his father said. "The bondars are but one."

"What other reason did you have?"

Before he had a chance to answer, the disciples glanced back at him. One of the men, a tall, dark-haired man with dark skin, said, "We will send word that you're coming."

His father nodded. "Thank you for the escort."

"Nothing was lost, so…"

With that, they turned and hurried forward, moving on a shaping.

"What was that about?" Tolan asked.

"There was some question about whether or not we should go for you."

"Why?"

"Some viewed it as risky, but the Draasin Lord thought we needed to reclaim you."

"Why would he have cared?"

"Because he knew we wanted to reclaim you," his father said. He turned to Tolan. "I know you don't necessarily believe me, but everything we've done has been out of love."

"Including abandoning me."

"You weren't abandoned. You were of the age to take on an apprenticeship and Daniels was there, perfectly capable of offering the apprenticeship. You were supposed to stay in Ephra, and from there, when the time was right, we would have come for you."

They had a plan? Tolan wasn't sure why that surprised him. "Master Daniels attacked me."

"He wouldn't have attacked you."

"Maybe you didn't know him quite as well as you thought."

"We've lost communication with him, but he has served well over the years. It was why we thought it was safe to leave you with him."

"Then you made a mistake. He tried to kill me. He almost got away with it, but I managed to…"

He wasn't about to tell his father what he had managed to do. Not at this point. Not until he better understood more about his father and what he might do.

Instead, he looked around. They continued to follow a wide path around the base of the mountain, twisting as they made their way steadily upward. Not much farther from here, snow began to fall. Tolan would be uncomfortable, regardless of his ability to shape. Shaping could only keep him so warm.

"What happened with him?"

"The Academy has taken care of it," Tolan said.

"Perhaps that's for the best," his father said.

"Perhaps?"

"If he really did attack you, then perhaps it's for the best."

"It is *for* the best," Tolan said.

"Did he work with you?" his father asked.

"What?"

"Did he work with you? When you were with him, did he treat you well?"

Tolan shrugged. "I suppose he did."

"And then when you went to the Academy, he didn't."

"I don't think he knew I went to the Academy." As far as Master Daniels had known, Tolan had been in Ephra. He'd been sent off to Amitan for some sort of additional training. It had to have surprised him to realize Tolan was no longer in Ephra and that he had gone to Amitan as well.

"Perhaps he isn't lost," his father said.

In the distance, there was a strange break in the road. Boulders loomed in front of them, massive and abrupt. It was almost as if they had been…

Shaped.

There was no question in Tolan's mind that these had been shaped. The only question was why.

As they approached, his father stood before them. "On

the other side of the stones, you will find questions. You'll also find answers."

"This is a doorway?"

"Oh, yes. On the other side of it, you will hopefully gain understanding."

"Hopefully?"

"You have questions, and I have not been as forthright with you as you deserve. There are answers you need. They are answers you deserve. And perhaps I am not the one to provide them to you."

"Who, then? The Draasin Lord?"

His father tipped his head, though Tolan didn't know if it was a nod of agreement or something else.

Power built from him, that of a shaping, and the stones began to shift, rumbling softly as they pulled off to either side. The path opened wide enough for the two of them to walk through, though in single file rather than side by side. His father glanced over at him. "Unfortunately, it takes considerable strength to open the gateway. Even in this, I am limited."

He started through, and Tolan followed cautiously. The walls pressed against him, and he was acutely aware of how much power it would have to take to move this amount of stone. It was more than just a shaping.

Could he do it? Earth shaping was something he had some control over, but would it be enough to move these massive boulders out of the way? Perhaps with a bondar, he'd be able to do so. He wondered if perhaps that was why his father created the bondars the way he did.

There was another way Tolan might be able to do it,

but he wasn't sure his connection to the elementals was enough that they would grant him that level of control. And it *was* control. To be able to use the elementals in order to open up a doorway like this, he would have to have some level of control.

As he went through the doorway, the stone pressing on either side of them, Tolan resisted the urge to look back when he felt a rumbling behind him. There was a distinct sensation of the stone moving. As it did, he fought off the desire to push outward and shape. If he were to try to do so, he would probably end up overexerting himself.

The doorway stretched an impossibly long distance. Tolan found himself going on and on. He kept waiting for there to be an ending, but there was none. It was like walking through a tunnel. In that way, it reminded him of searching for the Convergence, though in this case, he didn't have the sense of power he had otherwise.

His father kept walking steadily. The farther they went, the narrower the walkway became. That wasn't just Tolan's imagination. He could feel the stone pressing against him the more he went, and he worried what would happen if it were to squeeze him. There was enough pressure here that it would overwhelm his ability to hold it off.

"How much farther do we have to go?"

"Not much," his father said.

Tolan found that difficult to believe. It seemed as if the tunnel stretched out in front of them, never ending.

Strangely, it ended.

Tolan blinked. Bright sky greeted him. Clouds hovered

in the air. There was warmth, none of the cold he'd been experiencing in the mountains, and lush meadow stretched in front of him.

Tolan glanced back. The rock behind them closed.

They were on the far side of the mountain.

How was that even possible?

"You *shaped* our way through the mountain?"

"If only I could take credit for it," his father said, smiling. "Others performed the shaping first and made it easier for the rest of us to do it. We merely borrow from that shaping, and we create a way through. A pathway, if you will."

"That's how they have never found you?"

"As far as Terndahl and the Academy is concerned, there is nothing but mountains upon mountains stretching in the north."

"But…"

"Come with me, Tolan," his father said.

He guided him forward, and Tolan stared around him. There was no sign of the disciples who had left, which meant that they had shaped themselves off to wherever they were going to go. Then again, they would've had to open the doorway themselves in order to reach this place. As he looked back, he wondered if he would be able to shape open the doorway if he wanted to return or whether he was at the mercy of his father being willing to open it once again.

Turning his attention back to the meadow, something strange occurred to him.

Not only was there grass and flowers and the normal

life that he would expect within the meadow, but there was movement down there.

Elemental movement.

He noted ara as it brushed against his skin, a fluttering sensation in the wind elemental. There was the soft pressure from an earth elemental, and he struggled to think through the list of elementals that Master Minden had shared with him, trying to come up with a name for what he detected, but for the first time, he failed. The air was warm, and he recognized the sharl elemental, that for heat and humidity. Distantly, he noted a sense of water. There had to be elementals in there, too.

And despite the fact he detected those elementals, there were others. Countless others. He could feel them pushing against his awareness, pushing against his connection to the element bonds, and all he had to do was reach out for them and he thought he might be able to grasp that power.

Tolan resisted the urge. Doing so would be dangerous, and he didn't want to risk the elementals for the sake of grasping for more power.

"You detect them, don't you?" his father asked.

"How can I not?"

"Many who come here cannot. It takes time to recognize the elementals who are free."

Free—and not wild. Not dangerous. And not coerced to follow.

Perhaps his father had been telling him the truth about the Draasin Lord.

If that were the truth, then what other truths could he learn?

What more could he uncover studying here, where a connection to the elementals existed? Looking around, Tolan knew this was exactly what he had wanted. He had wanted to better understand the elementals and had wanted to know whether there was something more to them than what he had already discovered. There had to be something more than what the Academy believed about them. Everything he had seen told him there was.

And this was the temptation he feared.

Regardless of what the Grand Master said, he didn't know if he'd be able to spy as they wanted. Not if the elementals were freed in this way.

"How is this possible?"

"The more you're here, the more you will understand."

"What should I recognize?"

"You should begin to recognize the elementals are not controlled the way you have been taught to fear."

The made their way through the meadow. As they went, Tolan couldn't help but detect the sense of ara flowing around him, swirling as if in order to draw his attention. It seemed almost like the elemental was playing with him. He focused on it, recognizing that sense, and reached outward, attempting to connect to it.

There was a brief stirring, little more than that, and then it faded. Whatever had been there was gone. Tolan didn't think that he'd imagined it, though. The sense of the elemental had been real.

He wanted nothing more than to stand in place, to use

his connection to the elementals to see what he could understand, and perhaps recognize whether there was anything that he could do to help them.

In this place, it didn't seem as if help was even needed. The elementals were free in a way that they weren't in Terndahl.

"You should keep coming," his father said.

"I'm sorry. It's just that—"

"I understand."

Tolan stopped. "That's just it. You don't understand. You left me behind for you to have this experience, but you kept it from me."

Now he was here, Tolan began to wonder if perhaps this was a mistake. He had questioned it before, but seeing this place, seeing the elementals as they were, he couldn't help but wonder if there was something more that he didn't fully understand. Why would his parents keep something like this from him? Why would they hide the potential of a place like this?

"It was kept from you for a reason."

"You keep saying that, but I still haven't seen a good one."

"Perhaps you haven't," his father said.

Tolan thought he might explain more, and yet he did not. He meandered through the meadow, reaching a hard-packed path. Tolan didn't see anything in the distance that would suggest a place where they would find the Draasin Lord—or his mother.

"There aren't many Shapers Paths here?"

"The Shapers Paths come with a cost," his father said.

"What cost is that?"

"It comes with the cost of putting power out in the open. We don't have so much we can risk."

His father continued onward, saying nothing. Tolan followed, glancing around as he went, looking for any sign of other shapers. He didn't detect anything. There might be others out here, but if there were, there was no sense of them pushing upon him. Any sense that he had came from the elementals.

There was an odd thing to be aware of.

"Where are all the shapers?" Tolan asked.

"You will have your answers soon," his father said.

"Where are all the others?"

His father glanced over. "Like I said, you will have your answers soon."

Maybe there was something he was missing. He had believed he was being brought someplace where he would learn about the Draasin Lord.

The path led up a gentle slope, and in the distance, Tolan began to catch sight of buildings. They were nothing like those found in Amitan. Many of the buildings in Amitan had been shaped into existence, the spires and structures all created with power. These had a similar sense to them, but they were smaller, closer to the ground, and there was no sense from them that power had been wasted.

Tolan stopped, staring. Some of them were of a pale white stone that seemed to gleam in the sunlight. Others were of a grayish, almost black stone, and those drew his eye almost as much. In the distance, near the city, he could feel the sense of shaping, the first time he had detected anything like that since emerging on this side of the mountain.

"What is this place?" Tolan asked.

"This is where you wanted to see."

"This is the rebellion?"

His father smiled slightly. "It's not quite a rebellion. It's more a collective of like-minded people."

"Like-minded people who seek to overthrow the rule within Amitan."

"A rule that is damaging."

Tolan wondered if that was true or not. It was hard to know whether that was the case. In Amitan, the Academy had existed for a thousand or more years, long enough that the shapers had helped establish peace and prosperity. Shaping had made all of Terndahl powerful. Through shaping, they had maintained peace, other than with the Draasin Lord. That peace extended between Terndahl and neighboring nations, allowing the nascent empire to continue to spread. There were other parts of the world, but the empire hadn't spread their influence to them quite yet. Tolan never really understood why.

"It still sounds like a rebellion to me," he said.

"I suppose it would."

As they approached the city—and it was a city, far too large to be merely a village—he began to slow. "Will I meet the Draasin Lord?"

"Only if you want to."

Tolan frowned. "Why wouldn't I want to?"

"There is a price to knowing the Draasin Lord, Tolan."

"What price is that?"

"A commitment to serve."

Tolan started to smile when he realized his father wasn't joking with him.

"You will notice that everyone here has agreed to their service. Everyone follows the Draasin Lord. In doing so, we serve a higher purpose. You might not believe it—not yet—but the rest of us do."

"That's why you didn't bring me here?"

"We didn't bring you because it was dangerous to do so. With the way the Academy and Terndahl treat us, there is danger to anyone who follows the Draasin Lord. It was better for you to believe we were abducted."

"I don't think it was better for me."

"And yet, because you remained, you were able to learn from the Academy. You were able to continue to train, to gain an understanding of your abilities."

Tolan studied his father, and he thought he understood. He hadn't been left behind because they didn't want him. "You wanted me to be trained by the Academy."

His father held his gaze, not blinking but not looking away.

"Why?"

"Because there are things we have been unable to learn. Things that one like you would be able to learn."

"One like me?"

"A shaper of power, Tolan."

"But I wasn't a shaper of power."

"You weren't, but you were always destined to be."

16

The building at the center of the city had a gently domed roof. It was different than many of the others, made of the gleaming pale stone with a roof of darker stone, almost as if they had been joined together. It was the only one within the city that looked as if it had been built here rather than shaped. There was something about that which made it even more out of place, and left Tolan recognizing its significance.

"When we go inside, you will have an opportunity to decide."

"Decide whether I want to be a part of all of this?"

His father studied him for a moment before nodding. "As I said, none of this will be forced upon you."

"What is inside?"

"Perhaps answers, or nothing."

"This seems something like a Selection," Tolan said.

"In some ways, I think that analogy is accurate. What was your Selection like?"

"Surprising."

"Because you didn't expect to be Selected?"

"Because I'd never thought I should be Selected. I went out of support for a friend, and for no other reason than that."

"What we have come to understand about the Selection is that it is not always tied to one's ability. There is something to it that is tied more to—"

"Who they are," Tolan said. He nodded. "When I was Selected, I spent quite a bit of time trying to understand why."

"I suppose you did."

His father led him inside the door. Light glowed all around, flames that seemed to dance in place, and Tolan couldn't tell if they were shaped or whether they were elementals. Either way, the nature of the power here was considerable.

It was a wide room, with a ceiling stretching high overhead, curving into the darkness. Tolan searched for signs of anyone else who might be here, but right now, it seemed only to be him and his father.

"Why here?" Tolan asked.

"For someone who has come to this part of the world, this place represents an important first step," his father said.

"Why?"

"To understand yourself and why you have come."

They headed to the center of the room. From here, the

flame surrounded him, almost in a ring. Tolan couldn't take his eyes off it, and he wondered if there was something more to it than simply illumination. There was a way to find out, and he could do so by focusing on power around him, on the elementals, and on whether or not he could detect any shaping. While approaching the city, he had been more and more aware of the sense of shaping, but he hadn't seen anyone shaping as they had reached the city. It was almost as if his father had tried to protect him from it, to shield him from a shaping, preventing him from knowing whether there were others here.

Reaching for the power of the elementals, Tolan detected it in the flames. It wasn't a fire elemental, but there was part of that within the flame, enough that he didn't know whether the elemental was confined here, trapped so they could provide power to this shaping, or whether it lent itself to this place.

Earth was here, though that was less surprising. When he had approached, seeing the gleaming stone mixed with the dark roof, he had known that there would be an element of earth mixed within it, though it was here quite powerfully, perhaps as powerfully as the fire, though in a different form.

What about wind? There was no breeze, but there were other forms of wind—and wind elementals—than simply a breeze gusting around. He could feel the presence of wind, though he wasn't sure what elemental was represented.

Water was there, mingling with the others, and with

the presence of all four of the elementals, he couldn't help but think that the power present here had purpose.

Was there any sense of spirit?

Reaching for spirit came to him in a different way than reaching for the other elements. While he often did so by straining to grasp at the other elements, now he used an understanding of the elementals.

"You will wait here."

"What's going to happen?"

His father studied him. "Something very much like your Selection, I presume. I will be back," his father said, leaving him.

Tolan stood in place, looking around. He was missing something, though he didn't know what it was. As much as he wanted to trust his father— and regardless of the way his parents had abandoned him, he *did* want to trust him—there was a nagging part deep within him that left Tolan wondering if he truly *could* trust the man.

It was strange to focus on elementals in a land where reaching for them didn't feel forbidden. There was no shame in his ability to reach out to them, to try and speak to them, to call to them.

Not command them.

If he discovered that was what his parents were intending, regardless of what they might say, what would he do? He was determined that he wouldn't abuse the elementals the way that he had heard the Draasin Lord intended, but at the same time, he didn't want to force them into the bonds, either.

Standing here, the power of the elementals swirled around him.

If only the elementals were able to share with him more of what they needed. The only time that he'd really had a sense of the elementals, feeling as if he had some semblance of understanding what they might want, was when he had released them in the Keystone and they had followed him. When they had done so, there had been a sense of understanding from them, a connection to emotions. That hadn't been faked. There was no way that it could have been. What he had detected had been real, but it didn't make much sense.

The one elemental he was least aware of here—wind—began to stir, swirling around him. Tolan smiled, tipping his head to the way that the wind began to pick up, increasing in its intensity. "You've been hiding from me," he said.

The wind spun again, twisting around him, and Tolan smiled to himself. It seemed almost as if that was the way the wind would answer him, and in doing so, he couldn't help but feel as if there was something more he should know, but didn't.

"What is this place? They tell me they don't control the elementals here, but I don't know if I can trust that."

The wind twisted, spinning. It brushed up against Tolan gently, twirling his hair slightly.

"Is that your way of telling me I should have some faith?"

Tolan looked around. The flames continued to dance, though did they do so with more intensity?

"Are they hurting the elementals here?"

There came a faint sighing of the wind. As it departed, Tolan could practically hear a word whispered within it, though he knew that was his imagination. It had to be.

"*No...*"

If that was real, how would the wind communicate with him?

Then again, how would he have an awareness of the emotions of the elementals? There had been little doubt that was what he had experienced.

Breathing out a sigh, he finally began to relax. If the elementals weren't harmed, perhaps he didn't need to be worried about them in quite the same way. "Why did they have me here?"

He waited, hoping the wind would whisper to him again and that he could get a better understanding as to what his father had intended by bringing him here, but the wind said nothing.

What of flames? Fire was difficult, if only because it burned and destroyed, but he had a sense he could reach it, perhaps communicate with it. If he did, what more could he learn?

Tolan looked at the fire, studying the way it twisted and burned. It was saa, an elemental of some power, but it wasn't *just* saa. There was a shaping mixed in with it, and that shaping allowed the elemental to remain, almost as if it was here for a purpose, as if serving in some way. If only there was some way for him to reach the elemental and communicate, but in all the time that he had been summoning the elementals, he had never figured out any way of sustaining that conversation.

If he were to try earth or water, he suspected he would come up with the same thing. There would be no way to reach those elementals, no way to be able to communicate with them.

"You seem to have some familiarity with them," a voice out of the darkness.

Tolan couldn't even tell if it was a male or female voice, only that it came from somewhere nearby. Turning around, he looked to see if he could make out where it came from, but there was nothing.

"I don't know what you're talking about," he said.

Laughter echoed off the walls, a muted sound that drifted to him. Mixed with the laughter was a sense of shaping, though he didn't understand why anyone would mix shaping into a laugh.

"I think you do, though you hide it well."

Wind continued to swirl around him, and he could practically make out the translucent shape of the elemental in front of him. There was something to the elemental, and as he focused on it, as he stared, he thought he could make out the details, though perhaps that was little more than his imagination.

He turned away from the elemental, searching for the person who was here with him. He didn't like the idea that someone was hiding from him, certainly not in this place. Considering how little he knew about what was taking place here, he didn't want to have somebody sneak up on him.

"Can you speak to all of them, or is it only wind?"

"All of them," Tolan answered.

"Interesting. There aren't all that many who possess the ability to speak to the elementals."

"I think anyone can speak to the elementals. The real challenge is having them talk back to you."

There came the sound of laughter once again, echoing gently off the walls and then the ceiling before rolling back toward him. As before, he had the distinct sense that the laughter was shaped.

He wondered why it would be shaped, and thought it strange, but perhaps it wasn't so much for him as it was for the elementals.

He focused on them, detecting the sense of the elementals, and as he did, he felt something within that laughter that came across as soothing.

That had been the purpose behind it.

Whatever else, they were trying to soothe the elementals, and he couldn't help but wonder why. Were the elementals so dangerous that they would need soothing with a shaping like that?

With a start, he realized it wasn't just any shaping. It had been a shaping of spirit.

Tolan searched around the room, looking to see if he could detect anything that would help him understand the source of the laughter and whoever was shaping.

Could it be the Draasin Lord?

Who else but the Draasin Lord would want to soothe the elementals? Everything he'd heard suggested that he wanted to use the elementals.

From what his father had said, the moment he gained an awareness of the identity of the Draasin Lord, he was committing himself to serving. Seeing as how he wasn't sure he wanted to serve, he wasn't sure committing himself was the right strategy. Until he knew better, it would be safest to avoid seeing the identity of the Draasin Lord.

That might be why they were remaining in the shadows.

But his father had also said this was something like the Selection. Perhaps it was a test. Could they be trying to determine whether he *could* reach the elementals before revealing the identity of the Draasin Lord?

"Who are you?" Tolan asked.

"Who are you?" the voice said.

"I'm Tolan Ethar."

"I'm familiar with your name, but that wasn't the question."

"That's who I am."

"Names are but a part of who we are. Have you found yourself, Tolan Ethar?"

"I didn't realize I was lost."

"And yet you come from Terndahl, where all are lost."

Tolan realized he was turning in place, trying to keep pace with the voice, trying to figure out where it was coming from.

Where was his father?

Had he left him here intentionally, knowing he would face this shaper?

It was more reason not to trust his father, though he had plenty of reasons already.

"Not all are lost in Terndahl."

"Perhaps that's true. You have come to us from Terndahl. I don't know you well, Tolan Ethar, but you don't strike me as lost so much as someone who has yet to be found."

"That doesn't make any sense."

Another peal of laughter echoed, and once again there was shaping within it.

It was what he had been waiting for. This time, he focused on the source of the shaping, searching for it, thinking if he could uncover where it was coming from, he might be able to track down the person.

He turned toward where he detected the shaping. "You can come out of the shadows."

"Can I?" The voice came from behind him and Tolan spun, feeling as if he was chasing nothing more than shadows. "Are you ready for me to come out of the shadows?"

"Are you the Draasin Lord?"

"If I were, would you want me to come out?"

"I don't know," Tolan said.

There came another peal of laughter, and again Tolan turned toward it, searching for the source by tracking the shaping, but as before, he failed. There was the sense of shaping, but the moment he turned toward it, that sense faded, almost as if he was following something—or someone—else.

"Wisdom. It is wise to know there is danger in the unknown."

"Are you threatening me?"

"I suppose my concealment could be perceived as threatening, and yet, have you been in any danger in your time in these lands?"

Tolan shook his head, but he didn't know if this person could even see the movement. "No."

"And you should not have. There is no danger to you, not unless you mean danger to us."

"Are the elementals really free here?"

"No freer than you or I are free."

"Does that mean that you are intending to hold me here?"

"It means that the elementals—much like you—can only go as far as is safe."

"Where isn't it safe for me to go?"

"I thought Terndahl was no longer safe for you."

He tensed. Would they know what the Grand Master had asked of him? If they did, then he'd have to learn how. "Why?"

"From what I understand, there are those who fear what you've managed to do. They believe you follow the Draasin Lord."

"They know I don't serve the Draasin Lord." At least, those who mattered knew he didn't.

Tolan cut himself off, realizing how foolish it was to be arguing with some person hiding in the shadows who may or may not be the Draasin Lord, about his arguing with the Inquisitors about him knowing the Draasin Lord.

"The Inquisitors can be most disturbing. You did well holding out as long as you did."

"How do you know how long I held out?"

"Do you think we have no presence in Terndahl?"

"How? The Academy is—"

"Not nearly as secure as most would like to believe. You have questions, Tolan Ethar. I would like to see you have answers."

"Who are you?"

"Back to that question again?"

"Why won't you reveal yourself?"

"The same reason you haven't revealed yourself."

"How have I not revealed myself? You have always known me."

Tolan waited, half expecting the person would show up. If they did, what would the Draasin Lord look like? He imagined an enormous and incredibly powerful shaper. He had envisioned this person growing up afraid of the Draasin Lord, and now he had the opportunity to see him, what would it be like?

He should be afraid… but strangely was not.

No one showed up. There was nothing, no sign of the shaper, nothing other than the voice that spoke to him in the darkness. Tolan continued to turn in place, looking for signs of the shaper, and yet he found none.

"Are you going to remain hidden?" he called out.

At this point, he no longer expected the person to show up, doubting they would say anything further. What purpose would there be to come out of hiding when they could continue to torment him from the darkness and shadows?

The sense of the elementals continued to push on him.

It was vague, steady, and yet, there was more power trapped within the elementals than he had ever detected before. Perhaps there was something about this place, the freedom they offered the elementals, that was different than other places.

"I thought you didn't want to see the Draasin Lord."

"You haven't told me if you are the Draasin Lord or not."

"Perhaps I haven't. What would you do if I were the Draasin Lord?"

"I don't know."

The voice echoed again, and once again, there was a sense it was close. Near enough that he felt as if he should be right there, and yet he still couldn't detect where that voice came from.

"It would be nice if you would help me uncover this person," Tolan whispered to the elementals. He doubted any of them would respond to him, but if they did, perhaps he wouldn't have to do the work in disrupting whatever shaping was taking place here.

A surge of elemental energy came, filling him. It drifted up from all the elementals, not just from the window nearest to him. As it did, he detected the emptiness where there should be something else.

That was where the shaper was.

The elementals had answered him.

That shouldn't surprise him. Still, it did.

Tolan turned in that direction, moving slowly. By the time he'd turned all the way around, he looked straight toward where that void was. The chances were good he'd looked at that void several other times and hadn't known the shaper was there.

"Show yourself," he said.

"Are you sure you want me to?" The voice came from behind him, but Tolan didn't turn. Despite the fact he heard it behind him, he suspected the person was in front of him. The void told him that. The *elementals* told him that.

"Show yourself," he said again. "The elementals have already shown me where you are."

"Traitors," the voice whispered.

With that, the figure stepped forward, though it seemed on a shaping of power he couldn't fully decipher. There was complexity to it that he couldn't identify, something surprising to him with as easily as he had begun to detect shaped power.

As the figure approached, it seemed as if a veil parted, revealing them. The Draasin Lord was not looming and imposing, as he had expected. They were of average height, a slender build—feminine. Dark hair hung down their back.

The person who approached, smiling at him, was not who Tolan had expected.

"Mother?"

His mother smiled at him, and the warmth he remembered, the affection he had always seen while growing up, shone in her eyes as she looked at him. "There you are, Tolan."

"You're the Draasin Lord?"

17

His mother made a steady circuit of the inside of the space. As she did, Tolan was aware of the shaping she used. It was a steady and powerful sort of shaping, one that built, searching out from her before sweeping back toward the center of the room. He could feel its effect as she used her connection, letting it linger with the elementals before moving on once again. There was something strange about the shaping, something quite powerful, and yet simple as well.

"You can't imagine how long we wanted you to return."

Much as he had with his father, Tolan wasn't entirely sure how to react. His mother might say they had wanted him to return to them, but they had done nothing to bring him back. "You knew where I was."

"We knew you were safe."

"Safe."

"We were needed here, Tolan."

"Are you the Draasin Lord?"

He studied her. With her wearing a grey robe, a silver band around her neck, and her dark hair hanging straight down her back, she seemed almost like royalty. It wouldn't be a big stretch to believe she was the Draasin Lord, and yet, that wasn't the woman he had known. Why would he ever have believed he was the son of the Draasin Lord?

Years of taunting came back to him. It was far too easy to think of people like Velthan and the way he had tormented him, coaxing others to do the same, all of them accusing him of siding with the Draasin Lord, accusing his parents of the very thing Tolan had attempted to defend them from, yet now he found not only were they true, but his mother was the Draasin Lord.

"What do you think the Draasin Lord is?"

Tolan shook his head. There was a building sense of the element energy around him mixed with that of the elementals. Looking around, he didn't see anything that suggested the elementals were there, not as he had when he'd first come.

This was similar to the Selection. That was what his father had said.

Why would his mother be a part of it, then?

She watched him, seemingly waiting for his answer.

"The Draasin Lord is a person of power who wants to free the elementals from the bond so he—or she—can use that power in a way that destroys others."

"My greatest regret in leaving you there is that you are filled with their ideologies."

"That's your greatest regret?"

"Perhaps not my greatest regret, but unfortunately, you view the world the way they view the world. You view it in terms of element bonds and the elementals needing to serve those bonds."

"How should they be viewed?"

She turned back to him. A wide smile spread on her face, stretching to her eyes. "There are many ways to view the elementals, and yet I could see it from you the moment that you first came here, the way you observed them, that you recognize the elementals are here."

"I don't know how I couldn't recognize they are here."

"You'd be surprised at how few people are capable of detecting the elementals. It's not a failing on their part. It's just a matter that the elementals make themselves known to those who understand them. But it's more than that with you, isn't it, Tolan?" She took a step toward him and stopped in front of him, smiling. "With you, there is something more than just an understanding of the elementals. You can speak to them. That is truly a rare gift."

"As I was telling Father, I don't think it's nearly as rare as you would like to believe."

She shook her head. "Perhaps not the speaking. Any fool can utter words, and the elementals certainly get to decide how much they will pay attention to what they say, and yet you don't just speak to them. You listen."

Tolan focused on the elementals around him. "What choice do I have but to listen?"

"There's always choice, Tolan, and when it comes to the elementals, so many over the years have thought the obvious answer to the question you asked was that they should force the elementals into the bond in order to serve them."

"The elementals don't care for the bond," he said.

"They don't, and I'm curious how you know."

"I could feel it."

"Feel it?"

This was his mother. It was one thing talking to his father, holding back when he was dealing with him, but quite another to refuse to share with his mother.

Still… there was something about this that didn't feel quite right. He wasn't able to quite place why that should be, only that he could feel it.

"I have felt the elementals when they were forced into the bonds before."

"What does it feel like?"

"Pain. Fear. They don't care for it."

His mother looked around the room, her gaze pausing on the locations of saa spinning gently within the room, drifting to the translucent shape of the wind elemental, and onto the dome overhead. "The elementals don't care for the bonds. They question when they will be allowed to emerge once again."

"I don't get it," Tolan said. "From what I've read, the elementals used to be separate from the bonds."

"They were, and the world was cleaner then."

"Cleaner?"

"Perhaps it would be better to say it was easier. Few people understood the nature of shaping at that time. Since the elementals were forced into the bonds, more people have been able to reach the power of the element bonds, and yet, all that does is allow more people to subjugate the elementals. Those rumors of the Draasin Lord you have known are more about control. I would suggest the people you learn from are the real Draasin Lord."

"The Draasin Lord wants to control the elementals for power."

"What do you experience when you see the elementals?"

Tolan turned his attention to the fire elemental nearby. It was mixed with a shaping, so it wasn't even a completely pure experience, yet even in its current form, Tolan could feel it. There was a playfulness about it, and it seemed almost amused with him, amused with the fact he was having this conversation with his mother, but at the same time, he could tell there was something else deep within the elemental.

As he focused on the elemental, he couldn't figure out what other emotion was there.

"You stare at it as if you will uncover some secret."

Tolan tried to understand the elemental, but there was no answer within it. Tearing his gaze away, he turned back to his mother. "Won't I?"

"Possibly, but the elemental isn't going to share with you any hidden secret about the element bonds. Pushing the elementals into the bond has changed them, has allowed others to reach the bonds who wouldn't otherwise, but it has weakened the world."

His father had said the same thing at the edge of the waste. Tolan didn't know if that was true or not.

"From what I understand, there was a time when shaping was different."

His mother smiled. "There was a time. The Academy was still new. The very first Grand Master understood it."

"Did you study there?" He hadn't thought so, but then again, there was so much he hadn't thought about his parents that he no longer knew.

"I spent some time at the Academy, but never studied there."

"Why not?"

"Because my ability to shape was different."

"You seem capable of shaping now."

"I think I've always had the ability to shape, it's just that what I was able to do with it was different. In my case, I recognized there were voices that seemed to call to me, power whispering in my ear from within each of the bonds. When I pulled upon that power, unusual things took place."

Tolan understood what that was like. It was the same thing for him when it came down to shaping. "You were talking to the elementals."

"I was, though I didn't know it at the time."

"And Father? Does he talk to elementals?"

"Not quite so strongly as I—or you, so it would seem."

"But he makes the bondars."

"Yes. He told me you uncovered memories of that. I'm surprised you were able to do so."

He studied her, thinking back to the visions he'd had when over the years. Within those visions, he thought he would have answers.

The visions.

That was the key to the Selection.

There were visions.

"You tried to shield them from me."

"I tried to shield the creation of the bondars from anyone who shouldn't access it," she said.

"How could you be the Draasin Lord?"

"Back to that, again?" Her voice seemed different, a little bit softer. More ethereal.

"It's sort of important."

"Perhaps, though I would argue it's not nearly as important as you would make it out to be."

"Why? The Draasin Lord has been leading attacks on Terndahl for years."

"Do you believe that?"

Tolan frowned. "I saw one of the attacks. I was there in Amitan when the disciples decided to attack."

"That is unfortunate. I don't think you were ever intended to have witnessed our actions."

"Now you're not denying it?"

"It's complicated."

Tolan grunted, looking away from his mother. All of this felt strange, but there was one thing that wasn't complicated, and that was the fact he thought he understood what he was able to do but didn't understand why his mother would downplay that.

With all of this, learning how to find the disciples of the Draasin Lord, he'd already accomplished what the Grand Master had asked of him.

Could he find more?

The question he should be asking was whether he even wanted to find more. Or whether it would even matter. As he focused on what he detected, he could help but feel as if something were off about all of this.

He kept coming back to his father telling him this would be like the Selection.

He didn't know.

"If it's so complicated, why don't you simplify it for me?"

"It all comes down to what you view as the Draasin Lord."

"I think we've established that."

"We've established what you believe the Draasin Lord to be. The Draasin Lord has been meant to be a representative for those who understand the elementals. For those who have that connection to the elementals, who, like yourself, have felt the question within them about the nature of power, they are guided toward the Draasin Lord, given an opportunity to find others like them."

Understanding came to him and he looked around, feeling the nature of the elementals. They were there, powerful and filling the room with their energy. "You use the Draasin Lord as a calling."

She nodded.

"What about this place?"

"It's a place of power. The elementals come together here, joining us, and occasionally, they grant us their strength. They do so willingly, unlike the elementals forced to serve in Terndahl."

Something about the way she said it struck a note with

Tolan. It reminded him of something he'd seen in Amitan. Could it be the same?

There was the power he detected here, and there was no question within him that the power here happened to be significant. With such significant power, there would almost have to be something more about this place than what it seemed.

"A Convergence," he whispered.

Could that be the key?

His mother frowned at him. "How is it you know that term?"

"There's one in Amitan."

"You shouldn't know that."

"I stopped one of the master shapers from attempting to use it to free elementals."

She cocked her head to the side, frowning deeply. "We haven't had anyone operating in Amitan."

"I had the sense he was doing it mostly to try to summon power. I think he wanted to rival the Draasin Lord's power."

"It would take someone considerably gifted with a connection to the elementals in order to do so."

"Why?"

"As I've told you, the people who come here, the people drawn here, find their way to us because of their connection to the elementals and because they recognize the elementals are suffering as they are forced into the bonds. There aren't nearly as many as we would like, but we suspected those who come here have the ability to speak to the elementals, if only a little."

"Do the elementals speak back to them?"

"Not in so many ways. According to what we've seen, there used to be people who had the ability to talk to the elementals and to have them talk back, but such connections have been rare recently."

"Connections?"

"There were connections between the shaper and the elemental. Some were incredibly powerful."

"Such as the draasin."

"That's one."

"And you as the Draasin Lord?"

"It amuses me you keep referring to me as the Draasin Lord."

"Aren't you?"

"No more than you are the Draasin Lord."

He tensed. "I'm not the Draasin Lord."

"With your connection to the elementals, you might as well be as much of the Draasin Lord as I. All that title is meant to reflect is a connection, a sense of power, and not much more. In that regard, you truly are as much the Draasin Lord as I am."

"That means Terndahl would come after me."

"If they know how you access your power, there would be nothing else they could do."

His experience with the Grand Master suggested otherwise. "But I can shape."

"Your shaping comes from the elementals. That is what makes your power unique."

Tolan didn't think that was it. When he had been through the Inquisition, he had learned to reach the elementals in a different way, but he also had learned to reach his power in a different way. It had come to him, filling him, and now he no longer struggled to reach for that power, to know how to shape. He might not be able to perform everything the master shapers could do, but in time—and had he stayed at the Academy long enough—he might have been able to discover he could.

"My power came from the elementals, but it no longer does."

"You say that as if there is a danger in it. Shapers connected to the elementals have quite a bit of strength. It's one that only can serve at the leisure of the elementals."

"What about those like me?"

"I'm afraid your experience is misguided. You still draw upon the elementals."

Tolan shook his head. He knew the source of his power. That was one thing he had grown increasingly confident about. He had seen the way he reached his shaping power and knew it was more than just the elementals. It had not always been that way, but now…

It was what Master Minden had wanted him to recognize. The more he'd been working with his shaping ability, the more he had begun to truly understand what he could do and how that ability was different.

"You're saying everyone who comes here has power from the elementals."

"Everyone draws their power from the elementals. It allows them strength."

"What about those who reach power through the element bonds?"

"Most are able to do that as well, but typically what we've found is that people who are connected to the elementals, and who draw power from them, aren't quite as connected to the element bonds. They can do so when using various artifacts—"

"Like the bondars. That's why you make them."

"That's right. The bondars are used for those who can't reach for shaping on their own."

He debated how much to argue with his mother about the nature of his shaping. He didn't know if it even mattered. "I can shape without bondars."

"Because you use the elementals."

"I did at first, but I don't any longer."

She frowned at him. "You can shape?"

Tolan nodded. "I can shape."

"How is it you have this ability?"

The question seemed to have layers to it. He struggled to identify what else there might be within those layers.

"I discovered it within myself."

"How?"

"I had no choice." When he had been in the Inquisition, he'd believed the change in his shaping ability had come from something his parents had placed around his mind, some way they had shielded him, preventing him from reaching shaping, but perhaps that wasn't the case at all. Could he have found it on his own?

"What did you do to me when I was young?"

"We did nothing."

"You shaped me somehow. You wanted to hide from me the fact you were shapers. And the fact you had access to the elementals."

"We didn't try to hide anything from you, Tolan. We were trying to help keep you safe."

"Which you did by spirit shaping me."

"Are you sure?"

That had to be what had happened to him. It was the only thing that made the most sense about what he'd needed to do in order to break free, to free his mind from whatever had been happening. He had thought it was his parents, but what if there was another reason for it?

"Why tell me all this now?"

"Am I telling you or did you already know?"

Tolan hesitated.

She smiled. "I'm telling you because you're ready."

"I'm no more ready now than I was before."

"Perhaps not, but the answer might be that we are ready."

"Ready for what?"

"There's a reason we've gathered in places like this. We have wanted to help free the elementals, let them loose from the elemental bonds, and yet, more needs to be done. If we don't do anything more, places like the waste will die."

"It seems like the waste has already died."

"The waste is diminished, but it's not dead. It can be reborn, much like other places can be reborn."

"Other places?"

"Do you think Terndahl is the only place where the elementals were forced into the bonds?"

"I don't understand."

"There are other parts of the world, Tolan, and other places where the elementals have suffered because of fear. Our intention is to free the elementals, to release them from captivity. In order to do so, we must understand how they are trapped. And your father tells me you have some experience with that."

"I do," he said slowly.

"We aren't going to force you to do anything you aren't comfortable with."

"Good, because it was starting to seem like you intended to use me to attack in Terndahl."

"What sort of attack would you expect?"

"I don't know. That's why I question your motives."

She smiled at him. "As you should. As you always should."

"Even though you're my mother?"

There was a pause.

In that moment, Tolan had a glimmer of strangeness, one that suggested something else took place beyond what he knew.

The Selection.

That was what his father had said.

If that were the case, then he had a vision in the Selection.

There *was* a Convergence here. Or was there?

Was his mother even here?

Tolan shook that thought away. She was in front of him. She was real.

"Mothers can make mistakes. I think we did when we left you behind. I suspect you could have learned far more had you stayed with us."

"Had I stayed with you, I doubt I would have discovered my connection to shaping."

"You would have learned about the elementals sooner."

He stared at her, not sure having this discussion was how he wanted to spend his time here. A part of him wanted nothing more than to return to the Academy, but he didn't know if he'd be able to cross back through the mountain.

"What is it you want from me?" That was the reason they had brought him here. She might speak as if there was some altruistic purpose and might try to make it seem as if she intended to help only the elementals, but Tolan couldn't help but think there was some other purpose she wasn't sharing.

"You mentioned to your father that you know of the Keystones."

"I've encountered one."

"They are places of great power."

"So I understand," he said.

"And these Keystones trapped the elementals. If we could release them, we would have—"

"Angry and rogue elementals wandering throughout Terndahl."

She frowned at him. "I don't think you understand."

"No. I do understand. If we release the elementals

from these Keystones, then there is a real danger to others. I've seen it." And as hard as it was for him to admit, rogue elementals could be dangerous. They could be violent. He'd seen the way the elementals would fight for freedom, and though he didn't blame them for that, it would be incredibly difficult to restrain the elementals if it came down to it. People would get hurt. Possibly people he cared about would get hurt. "I support helping the elementals. I support freeing them. Doing it has to be done in the right way. If we free the elementals, we have to make sure they won't harm anyone else."

"I'm afraid that isn't going to be easy," she said.

"Then we shouldn't do it."

"You would leave the elementals trapped?"

"I would leave them where they couldn't harm others until we knew for sure whether they could be released safely."

"And I would free them, unmindful of the dangers it posed, recognizing they have suffered long enough."

Of all the things Tolan had been through, and all the experiences he'd had, he would never have expected he would be debating with his mother the benefit of freeing the elementals.

And it wasn't that he disagreed. He felt the elementals should be freed, and the more he saw them, the more he had the opportunity to recognize them in a setting like this, the more obvious it was to him they shouldn't be trapped.

Still, if he allowed the elementals to be freed the way his mother and father wanted them to be, he imagined another situation much like what he had experienced in the Academy, with elementals violently breaking free of the bonds and those without any shaping ability coming into danger of harm.

There had to be some way of freeing the elementals where others wouldn't have to suffer.

"What do you propose?"

"I don't propose anything. I'm just telling you what I'm willing to do."

"I thought you had an affinity for the elementals."

Tolan turned his attention to the flame. He focused on the wind, and then earth, and then water. As he did, he couldn't deny he had a connection—an affinity, as his mother said.

"I do have an affinity for them," he said. "If your intention was for me to be used to release the elementals so they could destroy Terndahl, then I won't do it."

He turned back to her. There was a flicker. A movement. Nothing more than that.

Within that flicker, he realized what he detected.

Spirit.

Someone—or something—used spirit on him.

This *was* a vision.

"You're not even here, are you?"

She watched him, a sad smile on her face.

And then she disappeared.

18

Tolan strode through the meadow. The flowers were beautiful, and they gave off a hint of fragrance, a perfumed aroma reminding him of Ferrah, making him miss her far more than he had realized he did. Even Jonas. It had only been a few days since he had left, but he couldn't shake the questions he had. What was happening at the Academy now the Inquisitors had been called back?

Even though he was outside and standing under an open sky, the sun shining down and a gentle breeze brushing against his cheeks, the distant sense of water nearby, he still felt as if he was a prisoner.

It was a strange sensation, and he was surprised he would feel that way, but he couldn't shake it. His vision of his mother had told him he had to stay, but then, his father had warned him of that, hadn't he? He had told him that the moment he learned the identity of the Draasin Lord, he would be forced to serve.

Tolan didn't know why he'd seen his mother, or why it had been a vision like that. His father hadn't given him any answers, and had seemed surprised that his vision would manifest as his mother.

The elementals didn't hold him, though he didn't expect the elementals to do so. He could feel earth beneath his feet, and with every step, there came a rumbling, almost a sort of welcoming, as if the elementals were pleased by his presence. Wind whistled around his cheeks, caressing him gently, and he felt that as a welcoming touch as well.

The sun shining overhead gave a sense of warmth, and even in that was the sense of the fire elemental. The burbling stream carried with it a different elemental. And those were just the ones he could easily reach. There were other elementals here, and though he didn't attempt to grasp them, he knew they were here. The more he focused on them, the clearer it became that they were comfortable. They were free.

What his father—and his vision of his mother—wanted from him was to allow other elementals to have that same experience. Could that be wrong?

Tolan worked through what he knew about the elementals and the element bonds. Strangely, it felt as if he was in the wrong place to get the answers he needed.

Which meant he would have to leave.

Having not known what happened to his parents for so long during his life, he wasn't sure he even wanted to leave.

Yet, they had left him before.

In a twisted sort of way, Tolan thought he understood, though that didn't change the fact their departure from Ephra had left him in danger. They might've thought he was safe with Master Daniels, but they hadn't bothered to come check, and they hadn't known he was Selected.

When had they discovered it?

Maybe that was something he should've figured out before now. When they had realized he'd been Selected probably was about the same time they had come looking for him.

And here, after all these years, he had happy memories of his parents. Perhaps those were as artificial as a shaped memory, nothing that could be considered real.

"I need to go," he said, talking to all the elementals and none. More likely than not, none of the elementals would respond to him. It was likely they were all bound to his parents and the others on this side of the mountain.

Even if he wanted to go, how could he? He'd seen how difficult it was to get into this place. Reaching here would require a shaping of the kind Tolan didn't know if he was even capable of doing. Did he have enough power to do something like that?

He had a hard time thinking he did. While he had shaping ability, he didn't have strength, not like what would be needed in order to get out of here. And it wasn't just shaping ability, either. Even if he were able to use the elementals, he wasn't sure they would be of much use to him when it came to accessing the kind of power necessary to get through the mountain.

The other alternative would be to shape his way free,

to travel the way the shapers of old once did, but in that case, Tolan didn't have the necessary strength.

A flicker of red, a flash of fire, caught his attention.

He looked in that direction, frowning to himself. Could that have been hyza? He hadn't seen that elemental in quite some time, not since he had freed it from the elemental bond, and it was one he was surprised he hadn't seen before now.

Tolan started toward it, trailing after the fire elemental, noticing the trail that the fire elemental seemed to make. He kept pace with it, not wanting to get too far behind, and as he went, he was careful not to track too closely, giving the elemental some space.

It led him beyond the meadow, and surprisingly, he found he was drawn back toward the mountain where he had been let into this place.

A sense of shaping caught his attention, and he turned.

Several shapers made their way toward him and Tolan hurried toward the rocks, masking himself within them. He whispered to earth, drawing upon an earth shaping, hoping the earth elementals would be willing to help conceal him. He didn't want his parents to know he was here, contemplating escape. There would be time enough for that later, and he would rather have them not know he was planning anything just yet. Not that he had any way of figuring out how he could escape. Getting out of here would involve far more than what he thought he could do.

The voices drifted, muted by his shaping. He hurriedly turned the shaping inward, using the technique learned when he was in his Inquisition. It masked the shaping, hiding it. They passed by without noticing him.

When they were gone, a powerful shaping built, splitting the stone, and they headed into it. Tolan was tempted to chase after them.

If he would have, he would have to keep near enough that he didn't end up risking getting crushed by the stone as it collapsed behind them, which was reason enough to not try. He didn't know if he could be quick enough, and if it came down to it, he certainly didn't know if he was powerful enough to withstand the stone as it collapsed around him.

Tolan released his shaping, turning to study the wall. Maybe there was something there he could uncover that would help him determine the way to get into it. If it was all about shaping, using the power of the elementals, that was something he thought he could do.

According to the vision he'd had of his mother, the shapers here didn't have the same strength with the element bonds as those in the Academy or in Terndahl, which meant this was the kind of thing he should be able to do. He didn't need considerable shaping strength in order to get through the stone. The one thing he did have was a connection to the elementals, and the necessary strength in that.

Only, as he focused on the stone, thinking of the earth elemental that would be necessary for him to be able to cross over, he wasn't sure he even knew where to start. Which elemental would give him the necessary strength to cross?

Another flicker of red caught his attention and Tolan spun, looking to see if the fire elemental was really there or not.

He didn't think it was his imagination.

Standing on the pathway, leading up to the mountain, was hyza.

The elemental was larger than when he had seen it last, though it could have been another elemental. There were plenty within each type of elemental, but he had a sense this was the same one that had escaped the bond, the same whose escape he had somehow facilitated when dealing with Aela.

"Why did you bring me here?" he asked.

Tolan didn't expect there to be an answer and, indeed, didn't get one. The elemental instead turned and loped off, heading up the side of the mountain.

Tolan frowned but decided to follow the elemental. It was mostly curiosity, but it was possible the elemental would have something he could learn from it.

He had grown to trust elementals when they guided him like this.

Scrambling up the side of the rock, he wished for a bit more strength, but it didn't seem as if hyza was trying to move farther away from him. It was almost as if the elemental waited for him, taking its time, giving Tolan a chance to keep up.

As he scrambled along the rock, he kept looking up, searching for why the elemental would guide him. There had to be some reason for it, something he thought Tolan could find, but there was only more rock.

"I don't think I can climb over the mountain," he said, hollering up at the elemental. He didn't know if hyza would even know what he was saying. And if the elemental did, he didn't know whether there would be any recognition of it.

He continued after the elemental, climbing step after step as he made his way along the rock face. Every so often, a cluster of flowers or a small scrub of plants grew, but surprisingly, Tolan recognized their presence even before he saw them. It was almost as if he could feel them, their pressure pushing against his awareness, a combination of his sensing ability mixed with perhaps his elemental connection.

Tolan lost track of time and how long he was climbing. His arms began to grow tired, burning with the effort. He found himself taking breaks, and still he decided to continue. Getting down from here would be far easier than the climb. He thought he could shape himself down, using a combination of wind and perhaps fire, but he wanted to know why hyza had brought him here.

He had a sense hyza was waiting nearby, not trying to run beyond the pace Tolan could keep. Whatever the elemental intended for him was ahead.

Was it nothing more than a way to get through the mountains without trying to open the doorway?

If that were the case, that would be valuable enough. If he could find an alternative route, he wouldn't need to be dependent upon earth shaping and someone willing to open the doorway for him.

That didn't seem quite right, though. Why would hyza

guide him this way? If it was a doorway, hyza would have other ways to travel.

There had to be something else.

Higher and higher they went. Heat was building, though it might only have been the heat from the climb. Sweat streamed down Tolan's back and his hands were beginning to throb from gripping the stone. It was nearly a vertical climb, and though there were good handholds, it made for slow moving. It amazed him that hyza was able to climb so quickly, almost as if this was nothing. To an elemental, it was possible this *was* nothing.

Was it his imagination, or did the sun seem to be burning more brightly?

Tolan took a break. He looked up, his breaths heaving, and searched for hyza, seeing where the elemental had gone. He found it crouched on a small cropping of stone.

The elemental watched him, its glowing bright red eyes attempting to meet his.

"What is it you want me to see?"

A hint of a voice whispered through the back of his mind. "*Patience.*"

Had he imagined that or had the elemental spoken to him?

Tolan cocked his head to the side, studying the hyza elemental. It had to be his imagination, didn't it? There was no way the elemental had spoken in his mind.

"Patience?" Tolan leaned back, looking to the ground below.

He been climbing long enough and far enough that it was quite a way down. He couldn't see anyone moving, and at this point, suspected his parents had begun to look for him. Would they have some way of tracking him, using their connection to spirit—or possibly even a bondar? He suspected there would be some way for them to find him. After all, they'd found him at the Academy. But if they had wanted to find him, they should have done so before now.

"I don't have much patience. I'm away from the Academy. Away from my friends. Essentially a traitor to one side now." Tolan met the elemental's eyes, and though it felt strange to talk to the elemental, at the same time, he couldn't shake the idea hyza was listening. If only hyza could answer him, then maybe this wouldn't be so strange or useless. "And now I'm here. I've become the traitor I claimed I wasn't." Tolan breathed out heavily, shaking his head. "And maybe that's not even the case. I want to ensure the elementals are safe, it's just... It's just I don't know what the right way to do it is. I don't want people to get hurt because we are freeing the elementals from the bond, but at the same time, I don't want the elementals to remain trapped within the bond." He looked up, shaking his head and laughing to himself. "I doubt you understand any of this. Lead on, hyza. I will follow."

"*Patience*," a voice whispered deep within his mind again.

This time, Tolan was certain he hadn't imagined it, but why would he need to have patience?

More than that, he had heard the elemental.

There was no doubt it was the same word, and that it had been repeated.

The only thing he could think of was that hyza wanted him to hear and wanted him to understand, but what else could he learn from the elemental?

Hyza started back up the rock, and with renewed determination, Tolan hurried after, scrambling to keep up. He moved with renewed energy and found he was shaping, drawing upon earth to make him stronger, wind to make himself lighter, water to restore the pain in his fingers. Was he supposed to be doing that as he went? He wasn't even aware of the fact he was shaping; it seemed to flow out from him almost instinctively, yet it felt right.

Every so often, hyza would wait for him, looking down as if to watch, and Tolan nodded, trying to signal to the elemental he was still there and keeping pace, but he didn't know if he would be able to keep at it for much longer. Even drawing upon the elements, his strength was beginning to wane.

It was probably a good thing he hadn't tried to follow the shapers into the doorway. If he would have, and the door would've shut, he'd have ended up crushed. There was no question he would've been squeezed by the stone, slammed into nothingness.

He realized hyza was missing.

He didn't see where it had gone.

Tolan crawled forward, summoning a reserve of strength, borrowing from earth in order to do so. His hands throbbed; whatever shaping he'd used to restore himself had made them better, healing them with water so he didn't have to suffer quite as much as he had before.

The rock ended.

Tolan pulled himself up and lay there, looking up at the sky, staring at the sun. It shone down on him, a perfect circle. No clouds were in the sky; nothing marred the crystal blue beauty. In some ways, it reminded him of when he had gone with Master Marcella to the ocean and she had tried to coax him into learning to shape water by forcing him into it.

It was the kind of sky begging to be seen. It was almost as if he could walk across it, though in this case, maybe it was more likely he could swim across it. If there was a Shapers Path, then he could easily imagine traversing it and feeling a part of something greater.

Then again, lying as he did on the ground, his back pressed into the stone, the wind whispering around his face, the heat overhead, and a distant sense of water burbling from a stream as it ran down the mountainside, he saw a very different sort of power. It was the power of the elements and the elementals. They came together here, a place of power.

A place of Convergence.

That was why his parents were here. They used this place of Convergence, drawing upon it in order to have even more power, but what else did they use it for? Certainly nothing that helped others. Supposedly, they were after the elementals, seeking to free them, and yet, Tolan couldn't help but think any help they had given the elementals had been not nearly as honest as he thought they needed.

A sense of movement caught his attention and Tolan rolled.

Hyza perched across from him. The elemental was only a few paces away, looking much more like a fox than it had before. It had an enormous head, pointed ears, and elongated muzzle. Despite all of that, it was the eyes that always seemed to draw his attention. It was the eyes that glowed with power and strength and a sense of purpose. It was an emotion he wasn't sure he shared.

"Is this all about freeing the elementals from the bond?"

The elemental stared at him. As his eyes seemed to burn into Tolan's, he couldn't help but feel as if the elemental was trying to communicate with him, to send word of something, but what? Tolan didn't know if he was bright enough to detect it.

"Are you going to tell me I need to do everything I can to free the elementals from the bond, too? I've done what I can. I just don't know there's much more that can be done without harming others."

"*Patience*," a voice whispered once again, this time not quite so deeply in the back of his mind.

"Patience with what? With working to free you from the bond or with all of this?"

Hyza didn't answer.

Tolan laughed to himself.

This was foolish. He was probably imagining the word he heard whispered in the back of his mind. It might be only what he thought he wanted to hear rather than what he heard. There was no way the elementals were truly speaking to him, was there?

After a few moments of lying there, not moving,

collecting himself and trying to regain his strength, he crawled to his knees.

He stood looking over the ledge, down at the land his parents had claimed, lands they used as their base of operations, claiming the power of the Draasin Lord. And maybe they weren't the Draasin Lord. Or maybe they all were the Draasin Lord, much like his vision of his mother claimed. Either way, all of this felt wrong.

Worse, the Grand Master wanted him to share more about the Draasin Lord, but Tolan didn't think he could. Even if he disagreed with what his father asked of him, he didn't disagree with their desire to free the elementals from the element bonds.

He turned back to hyza, but the elemental was gone.

Tolan was too tired to keep chasing it. He focused on fire, wondering if the elemental had disappeared altogether. Maybe this was nothing more than a game of chase, and he'd been caught up by the idea the elemental could talk to him, but in reality, there might be nothing here to understand.

As he sensed for the elemental, he could detect it nearby, not nearly as far as he thought it would've gone.

Tolan started after him. The rock sloped up a little bit more, not as much as it had before. It no longer required him to scramble vertically up the side of the mountain. He took a few deep breaths, steadying himself to be ready for whatever might come, seeing if the elemental was trying to show him something, but he needn't have bothered. There was nothing he could detect. The only thing he was aware of was that hyza was in front of him.

Not just in front of him, but nearby.

Tolan took another step, following the path that wound between two rocky prominences. As he went, earth pressed upon him, wind gusted, and he hesitated.

There was a sense of significant power.

Where was hyza leading him?

He needed to approach more slowly. If there was something dangerous here, he needed to be prepared for it, needed to make sure he didn't get caught up in whatever it was the elemental was doing. Until he had some way of effectively communicating with the elemental, it probably wasn't safe to just blindly follow like this.

Another few steps. He pushed through the stone, scraping by on either side. The wind pushed against him, but Tolan managed to withstand it. Once he was through, he paused.

There was an enormous sense of heat nearby.

Where was it coming from?

He couldn't tell, though he could sense it.

"Hyza?" He whispered the elemental's name, wishing he would've stayed closer to it. At this point, he no longer knew what he might encounter. He had thought it was going to be nothing more than hyza, but what if something else was here?

Heat was the most prominent feature.

Not just heat, but wind. A hot wind. It swirled around him, threatening to lift him up. Tolan realized they were in some sort of valley within the mountain, with nothing but rock all around. Water trickled down the side of the mountain, from streams all around them. The wind that swirled created a vortex of sorts, starting from some unseen height and spiraling downward.

The only thing he didn't really understand was the sense of heat.

Then a voice whispered in the back of his mind. "*Patience.*"

Tolan started forward. If he was to have patience, then hyza was still here, and if hyza was here, then whatever the fire elemental wanted to show him was here.

Could it be this sense of power? Was that why hyza had come?

Tolan paused.

Shadows began to move and he darted back, pressing his body against the stone, staring at the center of the clearing. An enormous shape unfurled, drawing itself out.

As it did, Tolan's heart stopped, skipping a beat.

The shock at seeing what lay in front of him was almost more than he could bear.

A draasin, and an enormous one at that.

Why had hyza brought him here?

"Because I am the Draasin Lord."

19

THE VOICE THE DRAASIN SPOKE WITH WAS NOTHING LIKE any voice Tolan had ever heard before. It filled him, and it seemed to come from everywhere all at once. It was almost as if it bounced off the rocks, bouncing off the water trickling down the face of the rock, echoed through the air, and carried through the heat radiating off the massive draasin. All of it seemed to carry the sound of the draasin's voice.

And all of it seemed to come from deep within him.

Tolan didn't know what to do. He could barely move. The creature was impossibly large, a scale he'd never even considered. When he had been near the Keystone, attempting to draw out a draasin, there had never been anything like this. That draasin had been flame and fire, heat, but a smaller creature. Still large, but nothing like what he saw unfurling itself now. It had enormous leathery wings practically glowing with the heat. Sharp spikes protruded all along its neck and the back of its head. Deep golden eyes glowed, seeing everything with a bright-eyed intensity. Sharp talons at the end of four legs tapped at the ground, creating a rhythm Tolan hadn't noticed before now. Now he was aware of it, it was the only thing he could feel. It seemed to fill him, as if it were all he should feel.

"How is it I can hear you?"

"Because I choose it," the draasin said.

Not just draasin. Draasin Lord. That was what the creature had said.

Could this truly be the Draasin Lord?

There were rumors the Draasin Lord had trained at the Academy, but those rumors would only work if it were a human. There was no way an elemental had been at the Academy, but then, if anything were to be a Draasin Lord, it would be this creature.

"Have I offended you?" Tolan asked, looking for hyza. He had been brought here for a purpose, and the challenge now was in discovering what that purpose was. If he could uncover why hyza had decided he needed to come here, then perhaps he could understand things better.

"You have not offended me. You have been brought to me for service."

It couldn't be a coincidence the draasin would use the same term his father had used.

"Do you know my parents?"

"Should I?"

"I don't know. They claimed they were acting in service of the Draasin Lord."

"Perhaps they were. I grow weary of trying to keep track of your kind."

"My kind?"

"Shapers. Humans. Those who play at understanding power but do not."

"I don't think they tried to play at power."

"Perhaps not, but they play at having power they do not. There are many who have attempted to play at power they should not have."

"They tell me they are trying to free the elementals from the bond."

"As they should."

Tolan struggled to believe what he was looking at. Part of it was his difficulty in believing the draasin was here in front of him. The other part came from the fact it seemed as if the elemental had guided him here.

There had to be some reason hyza had brought him here.

The challenge would be in discovering what that reason was. Whatever reason the elemental had brought him here had to do with him, and with some connection he had to the elementals.

"What do you need from me?" Tolan asked.

"What makes you think we need anything from you?"

"You brought me here. You wouldn't do that unless you needed something."

The draasin made its way toward Tolan, and as it did, the enormous creature radiated heat off its body, more than Tolan could withstand. It was powerful and gave off more significant heat than nearly any of the other elementals were able to create. He'd been around many of the other fire elementals, and none of them radiated heat quite the same way as the draasin did.

"You can't enjoy the gift you were given?"

"There's another reason. More than just a gift." He was certain of that, though not why. "What reason would you have for bringing me here?"

It was more than just trying to discover the reason for bringing him here. Hyza had brought him here for a purpose. It wasn't about just being here; hyza had brought him away from the other place.

"You haven't revealed yourself to them," Tolan said.

The draasin paused for a moment. As he did, there was another surge of heat and a strange fluttering of a connection deep within Tolan's mind. He was aware of the elemental in a way he was not with any of the others. Whatever the draasin was doing was allowing him a greater understanding of him than even hyza had.

Images flashed in Tolan's mind. Dozens of them. Hundreds. Within those images, he recognized elementals. There were elementals for all different elements, not just fire. They flashed in his mind, one after another, an unending onslaught of them. In every image he had, in every vision the draasin gave him, the elementals were free. They were not a part of the elemental bond. Other images flashed through his mind, and Tolan thought he caught sight of people, but that seemed surprising.

"I don't understand," he said.

"Wait," the draasin told him.

More images continued to appear, flowing through his

mind, one after another. Within those images, it seemed as if the draasin wanted to show him something else. He didn't notice elementals quite as often. In one, he caught sight of a draasin, though it was smaller than this one. Two people—a man or woman—were on either side of the draasin, and in a fleeting moment of the vision, Tolan could feel what they were doing.

A shaping.

The vision disappeared, but not before the sense of what he had experienced washed over him. They had forced the elemental into the bond. They had forced the *draasin* into the bond. In that moment, Tolan had known just how brutally they had done it. It had been a painful thing for the elementals, particularly for the draasin.

Other elementals came, and in one, he saw hyza forced into the bond, and in another, he saw earth elementals, names he once had known. So many came through his mind, and so many disappeared, forced down, changing the bond, making it stronger, but at the same time, changing other things.

In that regard, it was like what his father had suggested. The elementals forced into the bond had changed the elementals.

The visions didn't end. More came to him, one after another, and he had to brace himself as they did. It was almost as if he had to see all the elementals forced into the bond, as if he had to experience it for himself. There was no reason to have to do that. He could feel the pain. He didn't need to see another… Then another…

"Enough!"

The visions faded and Tolan took a step back, breathing out. "What was your point in showing me that?"

The draasin huffed at him for a moment before opening his wings. "For you to know what I have experienced."

"You experienced all of that?"

The draasin pulsed outward with heat. "I did."

Tolan thought about his experience with the visions, thinking about what he had seen within them. If the draasin had felt everything that had happened to each of the elementals, it meant he had been there.

"Why didn't you do anything?"

The draasin let out a streamer of flame. "When it began, it was out of a desire to understand. The shapers thought they were adding to the bond and helping the elementals return to them. At that time, the bonds and the elementals were felt to be connected in a way we needed to restore."

"They aren't connected?"

"Not that way."

"What changed?"

"Shapers who were doing so began to recognize how the element bonds changed for them. At some point, he decided all the elementals needed to be placed within the bond. They claimed it was for our safety and theirs, and there were enough elementals who went willingly. Not all did."

Tolan couldn't believe what the draasin was telling him. "The elementals knew what they were getting into?"

"They did not. Not exactly. If they had known, they

wouldn't have gone quite so willingly. How could they have known they would be trapped within the bond and not allowed free?"

Something about what the draasin was telling him struck a chord for Tolan. "You knew them." He looked up at the draasin. "The shapers who did this. You knew them."

"I knew them well. They were our friends."

"Why would they do this?"

"Fear. Power. A misunderstanding."

The draasin turned away from Tolan, and he sensed the massive creature's emotions for a moment. There was sadness and fear mingling within it. "They tried to come for you."

The draasin turned in his direction, one massive eye glowing. "They tried."

"How did you avoid it?"

"Not all shapers attempted to force us into the bond. Some fought. Many died."

Tolan shivered. What was the point of sharing this with him? Were they trying to get him to know just what the draasin had gone through? It was terrible, but at the same time, it had happened so long ago, there was nothing he could do.

"Nothing?" The draasin started toward him, lowering his head so he could look into Tolan's eyes. "You are the first in years who has attempted to reach the elementals. You shape outside of the bond."

"I what?"

"You shape differently. It's why I called you here. It is

why I showed you what you needed to see."

Tolan hesitated. "You brought me here." It was more than that. "You showed me the vision."

"I can show you more, if you would like."

"More visions?" Tolan shook his head. He didn't want any more visions similar to what the Draasin Lord had shown him—or of his mother. He would see her, but seeing her in that way left him feeling as if he'd been used. That and the other set had been enough, and he didn't know he could tolerate another onslaught of those images rolling through him, forcing him to see the way not only the draasin had been treated, but the other elementals as well. "I think you made your point well enough."

"If I made my point, you would be willing to assist."

"You don't understand what you're asking."

"I have lived for thousands of years."

"Fine. Maybe you do know what you're asking, but I don't know what I can do. They wanted me to go and release the Keystones. Doing so might release the elementals, but it also is dangerous to the people around. If I do that, the people around the Keystones will be injured. They will view the elementals as dangerous and violent, the way they currently do."

"They're not dangerous and not violent."

"None of them?"

The draasin didn't answer.

"I didn't think so. Even with humans, there are some who are helpful and some who are not. Some dangerous and some not. I imagine it's the same with the elementals."

"Staying within the bond for as long as they have has

changed them. Those of us who can have done what we can to stabilize them, but there are limits to how much we can do from outside the bond."

"What would you have me do, then?"

"Find a way."

"Find a way. Just like that. I don't think you fully understand what you're asking."

"Perhaps not, and yet, I can tell you don't know what you are ignoring."

Visions flashed into his mind again. This time slower. There were free elementals pushed into the bonds. Elementals that had remained hidden were forced away, dragged into it.

"How?"

Rather than answering, the draasin sent him even more visions. As they came to him, Tolan tried to keep them straight, to understand what he was seeing, but he could not.

And then came a dark-cloaked figure.

"The Inquisitors?" he whispered.

More visions appeared. Power surging. Elementals forced away. Tormented. Through the visions, Tolan could feel the torment, as if the draasin wanted him to know.

Tolan looked up at the draasin. He didn't have any choice. Though his father had wanted him to see the free elementals, to understand the Draasin Lord, *this* was why he had needed to come.

Had Master Minden known?

Another image flashed, and this time it reminded him of something. A Keystone.

Were the Inquisitors placing more Keystones?

That didn't make any sense, but it was tied to what the draasin showed him.

"How can I help?" he asked.

An image flashed into his mind. Within it, he had a sense of power. It was a sense of the various elementals, and they were drawn to it.

Tolan knew exactly what it was, though not why the draasin would show it to him.

"The place of Convergence?"

"We call it something else, but yes."

"I don't understand."

"You ask how you could free the elementals without them harming others."

Tolan nodded.

"This is the key. It's a place where even the elementals understand. Released from the bond, the elementals will seek familiar things. This place would be familiar to them."

If the elementals would be drawn to the place of Convergence, perhaps he could help them. He'd seen how they used the Convergence here, though he didn't really understand it. They drew the elementals to it, giving them freedom.

"If that's the key, then why not use the one here?"

The draasin snorted, steam bursting from his nostrils. "What must happen is not in this land. It would not serve the necessary purpose. This one."

Another image. It was the Convergence within Amitan.

If he went there, it would mean he would have to get into the library, and he would have to somehow find his way down to the Convergence, and from there…

It would be difficult. It meant returning to the Academy with the Inquisitors having returned. But he could ask Master Minden for help.

"That's what you wanted, isn't it?"

"You must do this."

"Because of my ties to the Academy?"

"Because of your ties to the elementals."

The draasin stared at him for a long moment, and Tolan felt a mixture of emotions from the creature. The draasin looked nothing like he had expected. He was so incredibly large, and so incredibly powerful, he had to wonder how anyone had ever forced the draasin into the element bonds. With power like the draasin were able to summon, wouldn't they have been able to fight?

"We fought," the draasin said.

"I'm sorry."

"You don't need to be sorry. You need to understand that though we fought, there was only so much we could do. Fighting pitted us against people we cared about."

Tolan had a sense he was telling him that because whatever else would happen, fighting might mean Tolan was pitted against people he cared about.

"How am I even supposed to get there?" Tolan glanced down at the rock, thinking about the mountain. "I don't know the trick to shaping my way through."

If he tried to go, he'd have to answer questions from his parents, and he would have to explain why he suddenly wanted to leave. He didn't have those answers yet. He had what the draasin had shown him, but nothing more than that. And what he had seen didn't necessarily mean he would be able to do anything to even help.

The Inquisitors might be involved, and there might be Keystones, but how would he find them?

The Convergence. It was all tied together. Reach the Convergence, understand what the Inquisitors were doing, and find a way to help the elementals.

In doing so, he would be working against them. Despite how they might serve the Academy, that was reason enough to do this. Even without that, he had to do this. If elementals suffered, he would help. How could he do anything else?

"There is no trick."

"You'll teach me how to cross?"

"No. I will bring you."

With that, the Draasin Lord lowered his head. There was a sense from deep within Tolan, from the connection he now had with the draasin. He needed to climb onto the creature. He looked at the draasin, unable to believe he wanted him to do this. A part of him—a very large part—wanted nothing more than to do it. If he could travel with the draasin…

Was that what he wanted—or was it what the Draasin Lord wanted of him? He'd been shown visions by the draasin, given images that he thought he needed to have, something similar to the Selection... and now he didn't know if he could help.

This was for the elementals.

How could he *not* help?

Tolan climbed onto the draasin's back. "Others will see you."

"I've lived for a thousand years. None see me unless I allow it."

With that, they took to the air.

20

Landing on the other side of the mountain happened quickly. Tolan found himself gripping the draasin's spikes, trying to avoid falling, though he had done so the entire time they'd been flying. Everything about the journey had been unsettling. The trip had been fast; they'd streaked across the sky, the wind whistling past him so fast he could barely see. His eyes watered and the heat rising off the draasin seemed to increase the farther they went.

There hadn't been an opportunity to understand how the draasin intended to conceal himself. Power bloomed from the draasin, enough that Tolan was convinced there was something to it that made it so he wouldn't be able to see the creature, and yet, the draasin moved so quickly, he wasn't able fully figure it out.

When they landed, he sat on the draasin's back for a moment, remaining there as he looked around the landscape. There was something here he was supposed to see, though what was it?

"Where did you bring me?"

"To someplace familiar," the draasin rumbled.

They were in a forest. Trees towered overhead, and somehow the draasin had managed to land in the middle of them, somehow navigating between them so they came down in a clearing.

Tolan climbed off the draasin's back, and in doing so, he felt a connection to the earth that hadn't been there before. It rumbled through him, filling him with another sense of awareness.

An earth elemental.

Surprisingly—or perhaps, not surprisingly—he recognized immediately where they were.

Outside of Ephra.

"You brought me back to my home."

"If I go any farther, it risks exposing my presence, but this is where you are needed."

"Why am I needed here?"

The same images he'd had before flashed again into his mind. With each one, he could feel the elementals disappearing, though how would there have been so many free elementals to begin with? On this side of the mountain, there was no sense of free elementals as there was in the land his parents occupied.

But then, there wouldn't be. They couldn't be free—not really. The Trackers would chase, as would the Inquisitors. The elementals would be trapped and forced into the bond. Perhaps all those times they had experienced rogue elementals had been something else. Not rogue at all, but free.

"Serve the Draasin Lord," the draasin said, his voice rumbling.

"And by that, you mean the elementals." The draasin locked eyes with him and Tolan knew he would do what was asked. How could he do anything else? "What about you?"

"I will return and wait for you to succeed."

"Back to the mountains?"

"Back to where I was."

"You weren't in the mountains?"

"I came to you out of need."

"You don't stay near the others."

"The others call themselves the Draasin Lord, along with the followers of the Draasin Lord. There is no reason for me to be there."

"Other than they seek the same things."

"They do, but they do it through a different means."

"You don't support them?"

"They are supported, but don't need my support."

"Who supports them?"

"The others."

Once again, images flashed through Tolan's mind, one after another, and with them came images of the elementals. They were who the draasin referred to. They served his parents and the followers of the Draasin Lord.

"You don't mind that they refer to themselves as the Draasin Lord?"

"Why would I mind?"

"Because they're stealing your title."

"I'd rather have them draw the attention than me."

Tolan found himself smiling. "You're using them."

"I'm not using them. I'm allowing them to do what they're already doing."

Tolan chuckled. "You're using them. That's okay. I won't tell them."

The draasin stared at him for a moment before flapping his massive wings and taking to the air. With that, he disappeared. There was a moment of disappointment for Tolan, but it passed. He shouldn't be disappointed he didn't have more time with the draasin. He'd already been granted far more than almost anyone ever was. And he knew what he needed to do, if not how he needed to do it. Find the Keystones. In order to do that, he needed to reach the place of Convergence.

Tolan looked around, debating what the right strategy would be. From here, he could travel close to Ephra, and if he could skirt around the city, he could avoid notice, and then he could reach the Shapers Path.

Instead of going anywhere, he decided to focus on the sense of the elementals here. This was a place where they'd either escaped before or had always been free. Having been on the other side of the mountain, and the lands controlled by the Draasin Lord, he thought he could use what he had learned in order to see if he could free elementals.

What would happen if he released the elementals here? They were near enough the border of Terndahl that it was possible nothing would happen. Perhaps the elementals would drift out over the waste. If they did, then they might be safer. What he wanted was to see if there were free elementals. To find that, he would have to search for them. It was far easier to do it in the park near the Keystone, but then, he had used the bondars.

Focusing on earth and fire, he thought of hyza. At first there was nothing, but a sense of earth drew him. He continued his focus and felt an echo of power. Pushing more into his shaping, he held onto that sense of earth, letting more and more awareness flood outward.

Earth began to emerge. Tolan watched. There was a violence to it as it rumbled, dragging itself clear of the ground.

Oshal.

It had been here. He had done nothing to free it.

The elemental surged, tossing Tolan off his feet. He went rolling, trying to scramble back, but the elemental lunged toward him, using some strange combination of whatever power it possessed. In doing so, it sent him staggering off his feet again.

"I'm here to help you," Tolan said.

The elemental shifted its focus to him. As it did, the earth tossed him.

He held his hands out, trying to soothe the elemental, but it didn't respond. It was almost as if it was ignoring him. Given what had happened to the elementals, the way they were forced into the bonds, he thought that might be the case.

Could he try something different?

What had he detected with his vision of his mother?

She had been using a shaping that had soothed the elementals. If he could somehow soothe him, he might be able to coax oshal into calming.

It had been spirit, but spirit was one element Tolan didn't know how to shape nearly as well as the others.

He had to try. Focusing on shaping, trying to stay away from oshal as it rumbled, tossing the earth, he strained to reach the connection to spirit. It was a different sense for him than others. With the other elements, reaching his shaping was a matter of embracing the connection within it, but with spirit, it was almost like submitting. He didn't have any other way to describe it than that. He remembered how it had felt when he was in the middle of his vision, during his Inquisition. Could he reach for it?

Tolan attempted to submit.

The ground rumbled around him and the power of whatever the elemental used threatened to overwhelm him. He staggered back, trying to stay clear of it. In order to focus on what he needed to do, and on submitting to spirit, he needed a moment to clear his mind. Running from the power of the earth shaping made it difficult to do that.

There had to be some way to hold onto his connection to shaping in order to get ahead of the elemental.

When the sense of the elemental rumbling toward him changed again, Tolan darted off to the side. He gave himself a moment, staring at the elemental. Oshal was little more than a stack of rocks, and when he had experienced it before, he hadn't noticed it was as quick as it was

—or as powerful. Then again, maybe it was only powerful in this location.

Somehow, he needed to find a way to soothe the elemental.

He focused on the memories of the images that he had from when he had relaxed and allowed himself to reach for spirit. It was there, somehow, and all he had to do was reach for it.

It came to him slowly.

Tolan pushed out with spirit. He focused on his intent for the shaping. As he did, it struck the elemental.

Soothing.

That was all he wanted. He wanted to calm the elemental, to send a wave of relaxation through it, and then he could figure out if there was another way to work with it.

Rather than soothing the elemental, it seemed almost as if he'd aggravated it.

That hadn't been the intention. Perhaps he didn't have nearly as much control over shaping spirit as he had thought. What had happened during the vision of his mother when she was shaping spirit? Tolan had been aware of it and had felt the nature of the elemental and how they'd responded to it. He needed to do something similar.

Pulling on that power again, he summoned it from deep within him. It came slowly, and once again, he sent it pushing outward, reaching the earth elemental. As he did, it paused.

That was more than what had happened before.

He needed to use that.

This time, when he sent his connection to spirit, he twisted it, focusing it toward the elemental and trying to add his intention behind it. He needed oshal to know he wanted to help it rather than harm it. He wasn't trying to force it back into the bond.

That was why the elemental was fighting. It was afraid Tolan would try to force it back into the bond.

"I want to let you stay free," he said, hoping he could shape spirit into the words. If he could do that, then perhaps the elemental would understand him. Without being able to do that, it was possible the elemental wouldn't have any idea what he meant or intended. "The draasin wants me to help you."

This time, he sent an image through the shaping, trying to do the same thing the draasin had done for him, giving him an understanding of what he was doing. That sense came slowly, and as it did, he pushed a little bit more. Tolan put more of an image into the shaping, sending through his request to the elemental.

"Please. Relax or others will discover you."

That, as much as anything, was his fear. If shapers from Ephra discovered he was here and that there was a free elemental, there was a real danger they might come and try to suppress the elemental and push it back into the bond.

The elemental began to ease. Pushing out another shaping, the elemental began to slow. The violence began to abate. No longer did it try to toss Tolan off his feet.

He watched, waiting to see if the elemental would do

something else, but nothing more came. Approaching slowly, he made his way toward the elemental, holding his hand up. Shaping flowed from him and he held his breath, fearful he was making a mistake. If the elemental decided to harm him this close, there would be nothing Tolan could do to prevent it.

"I don't intend to push you into the bond," he said again. "Let me help you."

It was easier to put the spirit shaping into the words the more he tried. The elemental responded, almost as if he understood him better when Tolan used spirit mixed with his shaping.

And here he had thought it was a simple thing to speak to the elementals. It wasn't simple at all. Not all would understand. It required more than he had been doing before.

"You don't have to go into the bond." He was nearly up to the earth elemental. Power radiated from it, and this close, Tolan could feel the earth rumbling beneath his feet. It was deep and powerful and tinged with a hint of anger.

He sent a soothing shaping through the elemental again but had no idea if it would even be effective. This close, the elemental seemed more receptive to him. Pushing out another shaping, he let it flow into the elemental, and once again, there came the sense of relaxation, as if the elemental was finally beginning to ease.

"How are you free? How have none ever encountered you?" That was the part of the elemental he had to understand. "Why not travel where it would be safer?"

There came another rumbling and increased agitation,

and Tolan realize he'd asked the question while shaping. It meant the earth elemental understood him.

There had to be some way to understand it. He had been aware of elemental emotions before, and he had spoken to the draasin—though the draasin seemed to be something different than most elementals. Older. More powerful. Possibly more intelligent. Could he somehow have used spirit in order to allow a communication from the elemental?

Rather than pushing a specific message, Tolan shaped spirit. He didn't force it on the elemental. He held it there, layering it around oshal, trying to use it so he could feel the emotions from the elemental and so oshal would know his.

Despite the earth elemental's power and size—it towered above him, a finger of rock that seemed impossibly high—the primary emotion he suddenly felt was fear. It was terrified to be forced into the bond.

How could those ancient shapers have thought it was a good idea to force the elementals into the bond? If they were as scared as this, they would have had to have been aware of it, and yet they had done it. The draasin's visions had shown him the people of that time had been connected to the elementals in a way that should have allowed them to know forcing them would cause pain.

What had the draasin said?

They had been friends.

How could they have done this to their friends?

"I won't harm you," he said.

Earth rumbled, a steady sort of sound, and Tolan

breathed out, letting out a spirit shaping once again. As it left him, heading into oshal, he pushed out his desires. Not to trap the elemental. Not to harm it or force it into the bond, but to leave it free. To help the elemental.

Was this what the draasin had wanted? It seemed almost as if it had wanted him to be aware of the elementals in a different way.

It was more than the Keystone. It was more than a place of Convergence.

Somehow, he had to get back into the Academy. He needed Master Minden.

"Stay safe. I will do what I can to protect you and the others." As he said it, he knew it was true. He would help the elementals.

The earth rumbled, power rolling through him, and it turned.

As it did, Tolan thought he heard a faint word whispered at the back of his mind, a rumbling sound deep and grating, like stone shifting. *"Thanks."*

It might be nothing more than his imagination, but he smiled, nonetheless.

The elemental left, making its way from Ephra, away from shapers who might find it and attempt to harm it. Tolan hoped freedom would last.

He had spent enough time with oshal. It was time to return. He didn't think he had enough strength to search for additional elementals, but that wasn't the point. He had to find what the Inquisitors had done—and find a way to stop them.

As he made his way through the forest, meandering

between trees, Tolan came to the place where he had first seen hyza. The ground was no longer blackened and charred as it had been, but the trees that had been here were gone. Their burned husks remained, little more than that, and a wide swathe of forest had been cleared. He made his way through it, casting a glance to the city in the distance, and veered around it. There was a brief temptation to head back into Ephra, to make his way to what had been his home, but he ignored it.

Instead, he headed toward the Shapers Path. He headed toward Amitan.

Reach the Convergence. Then he could find what the Inquisitors had done. And then he would free the elementals.

21

HEADING BACK THE CITY WAS AN ACT OF DIFFICULTY. TOLAN was careful not to travel too quickly, not wanting to draw the wrong kind of attention. He still didn't know if his parents and the other disciples might come after him. How long would it be before his father realized he'd decided to leave?

Tolan thought he had a bit of a break before his father realized he'd escaped, and even then, it might take them a while to decide whether to return. Was Tolan reason enough for them to come after him?

He moved carefully, and yet, even as he went, the sense of the elementals was there, all around him. Perhaps that was the message he was supposed to take, that there were so *many* elementals around. The draasin certainly seemed interested in showing him that, but when he reached the Academy, what was he going to find?

Now he was heading back, he had to focus on what was there.

The Inquisitors. That's what was there.

Returning to the Academy meant encountering the Inquisitors. It meant trying to prepare for whatever the Grand Master had asked of them by returning. And it might mean trying to find a way to free the elementals without the Inquisitors knowing what he was doing.

He knew he needed to do what he could to help the elementals, but to do that meant he would have to face the Inquisitors and pit himself against the Academy.

Was this what the Grand Master had wanted? Was this what Master Minden had wanted?

He didn't know.

When he reached the outskirts of Ephra, he paused. From here, his old home was near enough that he could practically feel it calling him back, and yet, Tolan had no interest in returning. Ephra had not been his home in quite some time. Even when he'd gone back with the Selection, he hadn't felt like he belonged. It was almost as if he was out of place.

How much of that was because of his parents? He'd never blamed them for it before, but learning they were somehow tied to the Draasin Lord, he did blame them now. It was their fault he'd been taunted by those who'd once been his friends, but it was about more than that. They had blocked off his understanding of shaping, preventing him from knowing what he could and should be. Had he not gone to the Selection, he never would have uncovered his potential.

That as much as anything angered him.

From here, he could reach the Shapers Path near Ephra. That was what he planned on. But when he looked over at Ephra, he realized something was not quite right.

There was a strange sense within the city.

Why should that be?

It took him a moment, but he felt something akin to the sense he'd when near the waste.

He hadn't been here in a while, not since the Selection, and even when he'd been traveling with the disciples, he'd been moving quickly enough that he'd not spent any time considering his former home. Now he was here and looking upon the city, he could feel for himself that something was not quite right.

Despite himself, Tolan felt a draw into the city. As he wandered between some of the outer buildings, little more than farmhouses, he paused, looking around. He would be a little bit out of place. He was wearing his cloak from the Academy, and it called attention to him, but that could not be helped.

He had no goal in mind. He just wandered. His path took him along familiar streets, and at one point, he found one of the nearby streets that would have brought him back toward his childhood home, but Tolan ignored it, turning away. The memories he had were not what he had thought. They might've been happy memories—at least at the time—but they were missing something. The truth.

As he meandered, there came another sense, and this one was from where he would have found Master Daniels' workshop. He chose not to go in that direction, either. As much as his parents, Master Daniels had deceived him as well.

A part of him was tempted to go toward Tanner, to find his old friend to check on him, but he decided against it. If he did, it would only draw attention to the fact he had come to the city. If anyone came looking for him, they would know he had been here, and he did not want anyone he cared about to be harmed. He wasn't sure about how Tanner viewed him any longer, but he preferred to keep with his view of the friendship, the memory of the person he'd been.

If he were to turn down another street, he could reach the Ephra Academy of Shaping, a place in which he had never been allowed to learn, and for so long, he had thought it was a deficiency within himself. Maybe it still was. He hadn't reached his shaping until he had gone to the Academy, freeing his mind, using the bondars to better understand how to access the elements, but perhaps it was all because of his parents.

Tolan turned away.

He wasn't here to reminisce and think about the perceived slights he might have experienced over the years. He needed to move past that. He was a shaper now, and there was little doubt in his mind he would be able to become a master shaper, graduate from the Academy, and then… Tolan didn't know what he wanted.

Perhaps that was part of the reason for this journey, part of the reason Master Minden had sent him, encouraging him to go. Maybe she wanted him to know what he was supposed to be so he could eventually find himself.

Was it to be a master librarian like her? According to the Grand Master, he had the potential, and because he had some ability to see the portraits, it had opened him in a way to that power, though Tolan wasn't sure if that was even what he wanted.

If it was, what then?

Would he spend his days in the library, finding a research topic the same way the master librarians did, copiously taking notes, never changing anything, only researching and observing?

That was not what he wanted.

Despite the fact it was a place of—and he would have a position of—respect, Tolan wanted more for himself.

How could he not after everything he'd experienced?

More than that, he wasn't sure if he could be content at the Academy in such a fashion any longer. After having seen the elementals free—truly free—he didn't know if he could be in a place where they were not.

There was a strange presence here. It had more to do with the elementals than he had realized. There was an emptiness. When he had lived here after all those years, there had never been this sense of emptiness, though perhaps he had not been attuned to it at the time.

Even now, he wasn't sure if it was the fact he was attuned to it or whether it was something else, and that something had changed. Perhaps that was all it was and if so, he thought he needed to understand it. If it was nothing more than the way the city had always felt, then he needed to get an understanding as to why. If there was another reason, if it was about something that *had* changed, Tolan thought he needed to understand that, as well.

He continued to wander the streets and opened himself up to spirit.

Of all the elements, spirit seemed the one that would offer him the most understanding. As he focused on it, he could feel the way it flowed around him. He could detect the connections between the elements, but strangely, it was different than what they had been before.

That couldn't be a coincidence. Then again, if it wasn't, then why was it happening now? What was he detecting?

Perhaps it was merely the fact he'd been spending time on the other side of the mountain, in a place where the disciples of the Draasin Lord existed, where a proximity to the elementals gave him a greater understanding of their presence—or absence.

Then again, perhaps it was something more.

What if something *had* changed?

Tolan wandered slowly, carefully, and continued to press outward, using his connection to spirit in order to do so. It was there, the faint sense of spirit existing all around, and he thought he could use that to help him reach an understanding of what was taking place, but it failed.

Perhaps he needed a different approach. If it wasn't only spirit, could he add aspects of other elements to it?

He had never really tried combining spirit with the other elements, not the way he'd tried mixing shapings of earth and wind and water and fire. How would spirit mingle with them?

Without having any formal spirit training, it was possible he wouldn't really know, and equally possible that trying this on his own was dangerous.

He needed to get an understanding of what was taking place because the longer he was here, the more certain he was that something had changed within the city.

What if it had to do with the elementals?

Why would the elementals have anything to do with what he detected?

Standing in a small square—Araln Square, he realized as he looked around, wondering at the name for the first time and curious as to whether it was at all tied to the wind elemental—he focused on wind and spirit. He bound them together, tying them as much as he could, though was careful not to bind them too tightly. He wasn't sure whether mingling them in such a way made a difference or not. Perhaps there was nothing to it, but perhaps it didn't matter, and perhaps he could use it.

Hadn't he connected to the elementals using spirit?

Tolan had to think he could do something similar now.

In this case, he wasn't trying to connect to the elemental. It was connecting to the element.

That was different than the element bonds. Different than the elemental.

As he focused, he thought about what he'd experienced outside of Amitan the night he'd left the city, traveling with the disciples of the Draasin Lord. That night, he had felt a closeness to the elements, one that was different than the element bond, different than even the elementals, and together, it had given him a knowledge and understanding of things he didn't have otherwise. It was the first time he'd ever really felt that same proximity to the elements, a sense there was power within them by themselves, different than the element bond, and different than the elementals.

He needed that connection now.

Tolan focused on the way the soft breeze caressed his cheeks. There were people all around him and they left him alone, but he heard their voices. As he focused, he could almost feel them breathing. All of that went into the sense of wind in this place. Tolan continued to focus on it, reaching for that awareness, and as he did, he let that sense fill him.

It was there, a calling.

Tolan drew upon it, welcoming it.

As he did, he added a hint of spirit. Little more than that, just enough that he could push that sense into it.

Everything changed.

Not only did he have a sense of the wind, but he felt it connect. Not just his breath to the gentle breeze that blew through the clearing, but the breaths of all people around him. They were all connected. Wind was interconnected. He was interconnected to them, and they were interconnected to something even greater.

The recognition of it was amazing. Awareness filled him, power and warmth. He no longer felt quite as isolated. With the wind and how they were interconnected, he recognized the elementals would be as interconnected as he was to everyone else.

And that was what was missing.

Why should it suddenly be missing? The elementals had been forced into the bonds in Ephra and throughout Terndahl for many years. Nothing had changed.

Tolan continued to walk, and he found himself guided, caressed forward. With his hold on wind and spirit, he felt as if they both wanted to push him forward, urging him toward something.

He should have tried something like this with oshal, but he'd been so surprised by his success in freeing the elemental that he hadn't.

Tolan followed the urging of the wind, choosing to listen rather than object in any way. Not that there would be any way to object. It wasn't that he wanted to refuse the request of the wind. As he held onto this sense, this awareness, he felt even more certain he wanted to know what message the wind had for him.

He followed, making his way outside the city once again. He paused, looking back, curious if it was a mistake or not, but it didn't seem to be. The wind wanted him to go in this direction. Whatever was here was where the wind wanted to take him.

Tolan went where he was guided. And as he did, he hurried forward, obeying an increasing intensity in the way the wind pushed him, almost as if he needed to reach the outskirts of the city as quickly as possible. Away from Amitan.

It was the opposite direction from where he'd been heading, but connected as he was, feeling the sense of wind and everything around him, Tolan couldn't help but feel as if this was exactly where he needed to go.

It might not be back to Amitan, but perhaps it was something more.

In the distance, a haze grew. Tolan stared, frowning as he did. He didn't remember that outside of Ephra—at least not quite so close. It reminded him of the waste. The waste should be another day's walk from here, far enough away that he wouldn't be able to reach it easily without shaping. As far as he could tell, he wasn't shaping at all.

Tolan wasn't entirely certain if he was or was not. Perhaps he *was* shaping. Maybe there was no other way to detect the wind in this manner but by shaping, though the longer he listened and focused on the wind and the way it guided him, the more he felt he was not.

As the distant haze came closer, Tolan recognized it. It *was* the waste.

The waste shouldn't be here. It was far enough from the city that people could leave Ephra and not ever deal with the terror of it.

As Tolan approached, he saw that the line of demarcation with the waste had changed, shifting, and there were the dried husks of trees that appeared strangely fresh.

Standing there, the wind caressing him, he noticed something else.

The wind seemed to stop at the border between here and the waste.

Tolan lingered at the edge, letting himself feel the power as it flowed outward. He had rarely spent much time this close to the waste. Now he was here, he couldn't help but feel as if it was more dangerous than it ever had been. Perhaps that was nothing more than his imagination, but Tolan didn't think it was.

He cocked his head, listening to the wind. Perhaps there would be a message within it that he could hear, but as he focused, he was aware of nothing.

"What do you want me to learn? That it's moved closer?"

The wind continued to caress him, though it no longer pushed him forward the way it had. It was almost as if even the wind hesitated to send him any closer to the waste.

All of that had to be his imagination. And yet, Tolan couldn't help but think it was not.

He looked at the ground, and the abrupt change between the border of Terndahl and that of the emptiness—the bleakness—of the waste was striking and stark.

More than that, it seemed to be moving.

That had to be his imagination, didn't it?

But the border of the waste *had* moved once before. He'd been there when it had started, the way the border had suddenly changed, requiring the master shapers to hold it. The border had gone from straight to irregular.

There was an emptiness here. Having been connected to the elementals as he was, he recognized the reason for such emptiness.

The elementals.

For the waste to be retreating like this, it meant the elementals had been removed.

Keystones.

This was what the Inquisitors had been doing. They

had wanted the power of the elementals, power that wouldn't be found any other way. Trapping the elementals had moved the waste. And the draasin had known.

That was what he'd felt when he'd encountered the Inquisitors while leaving Amitan with the disciples.

If removing the free elementals had done this, what would it mean for Terndahl?

What would happen to all of Terndahl?

The idea terrified him.

22

After searching along the edge of the waste for a Keystone and failing, Tolan hurried back toward Ephra. More was taking place than even the Grand Master would have known. He had wanted the Inquisitors back, but in doing so, had given them even more access to the elementals of Terndahl—and to finding a way to trap them.

He *had* to reach the Convergence to stop this.

Moving beyond the far side of the city, Tolan sensed for the Shapers Path, finding it where he expected. With a burst of wind and fire, he landed upon it. His mind raced with what he'd seen and how he would frame it for those in the Academy.

It was possible the Grand Master wouldn't believe him. Master Minden would. If necessary, he'd go to her, see what it might take to convince her, and then…

Free the elementals.

He raced along the Shapers Path. Under the bright sun,

there was a hint of warmth, and Tolan used fire and wind to speed along the Path, giving himself an added boost of speed. He had followed this Path several times now, enough that he had at least a sense of where he was going, though there were branchings leading off it, heading to other places throughout Terndahl. Tolan ignored each branch point, following the road where he needed to go, and by the end of the day, he was already nearing the city. As Amitan loomed into view, Tolan barely slowed. There was no point in doing so. He needed to reach the Academy.

Just at the edge of the city, a strange sense emerged.

Power bloomed, shaping power, and Tolan recognized it.

It was the shaping power he'd detected the night he'd left. It was more than just a shaping, more than just a calling of spirit. This was something else. Could it be how they formed the Keystones?

There was shaping within the Academy, though it was muted compared to what he normally expected to see. Throughout the city, he detected an occasional flicker, a sense of the shapers living there. Their shaping wasn't that powerful—certainly not enough to account for what he detected.

Heading in during the remaining daytime risked exposing him, so Tolan dropped down from the Shapers Path, wandering through the city. He didn't want to come in too abruptly.

The city was like Ephra. Buildings surrounding him,

many of them with a sense of shaping coming from them, and others carrying with them the sense of having been shaped. Quite a few of these buildings had required the assistance of the Academy in order to have been built, and that power flowed through them, an incredible sense that filled Tolan. He couldn't help but marvel at the control those shapers would have needed to have in order to build some of these homes. He had never really noticed that before, but as he wandered, not holding onto a shaping, merely allowing his awareness of the elements to fill him, it was quite clear.

Perhaps it was nothing more than the fact he'd never allowed himself to have such awareness.

Tolan took a deep breath, letting a shaping flow out from him. It was spirit, and he unleashed it without fully meaning to. Using spirit, he was better able to determine whether there was anything here he needed to be concerned about. He added a hint of earth to it, his experience staying tied to wind giving him the idea. The two elements mingled, giving him a greater understanding of everything around him.

Earth alone could be powerful, a and as Tolan's first skill had been earth sensing, he was familiar with the ways in which it could be used. Adding spirit to it changed not only his connection and what he could do, but also the sorts of things he was able to detect.

As he went, his combined spirit and earth shaping swept away from him. It touched upon the various people he passed. Many of them gave off no sense of anything other than their connection to the world, but others had something more. It took Tolan a moment to realize they were the ones who could shape.

With that realization, he stopped.

He could use this combined shaping to detect other shapers?

Could that be what the Selection was all about?

It seemed far too simple, and yet, the Selection *did* involve the Inquisitors, and because of that, there was an element of spirit within it. He'd believed the need for the Inquisitors came from the fact they were able to erase the memories of those who failed, but perhaps that was not it at all.

Tolan continued along the street, using this new shaping as he pushed it outward. If only he could figure out some way of uncovering those who might pose a threat to him. If he could find other spirit shapers, then he would know who the Inquisitors were and who he needed to avoid.

As far as he could tell, the shaping did not allow that degree of understanding.

There were far more with shaping ability within the city than he had realized. Much of it touched his combined shaping softly, barely more than a tap, as if their connection to the element bonds was faint, whereas others were stronger, the detection more of a pulse, a burst of power flowing from them.

Those were the ones who had real power, and the ones he thought he should steer clear of. It was possible they were still with the Academy. He wanted to avoid members of the Academy until it was time to make his way back into the building. For now, he wasn't sure it was safe.

Tolan wandered along the outskirts, heading toward one of the nicer buildings, and looked up when he reached it, unsurprised it was shaped into existence much like so many of the other buildings here, but also that there were several shapers of reasonable skill within it.

Tolan continued onward.

Strangely, as he went, there seemed to be a demarcation between those who could shape and those who could not. Beyond a certain point within the city, there were no shapers. He would've expected it would come on the outskirts of the city, but the sense of shaping was absent more toward the center of the city, closer to the Academy.

Were those who had shaping ability so fearful of getting close to the Academy that they stayed away?

It didn't strike him as anything he'd have expected from those he'd encountered. It suggested another reason.

Near the Academy, on the other side of that demarcation, came a different sense. It wasn't an emptiness. As he focused, he could detect shaping, but there was something else within it.

Tolan made his way slowly and focused on what he might detect on the other side. In a way, it reminded him somewhat of what he had detected near the waste. It was a barrier.

Perhaps he imagined it. The Academy was on the other side of that line.

Then again, he didn't know. Tolan continued to

wander along it, finding it encircled the Academy grounds.

It stretched beyond. There was a place of Convergence, a place of real power here, yet as he wandered here, he couldn't find any sense of the Convergence, and he couldn't detect anything suggesting real power.

Maybe he was missing something.

Tolan wandered as the day turned into night. It shifted over slowly, at first, the sun setting in the distance, streaks of color turning the sky orange and red, giving him a sense of fire fading in the sky. As the sun went down, there came a shifting, darkness rising, and with it, a strange sense of elementals with it.

Tolan suspected that was little more than his imagination.

He waited another few moments, letting the sun completely fall and darkness begin to linger, and looked around for movement in the city. At first, it came slowly, and then increased, giving Tolan reason to head toward the Academy. It was time to make his next step.

As he approached, his heart racing, he focused on shaping.

Heading toward the Academy at this time of night reminded him all too much of what it had been like when he'd been here the last time. There had been a secretiveness, a silence, and though he didn't fear the Academy itself, it was what was inside that worried him.

Continuing on his way, he paused at the edge of the line of buildings leading up to the Academy proper. From here, he could make out the towers rising in the distance.

On the ground, he couldn't see the runes on the towers quite as well as from the air, and even at night, wasn't sure if he would be able to see them clearly. It was better he didn't even try.

Tolan instead wondered if he could use those runes.

He hadn't given it much thought before, but there had to be something about them he could borrow from. In order to do so, it would require him to draw upon power he wasn't sure he was capable of mastering. It was the kind of power the Grand Master had warned him he might not be able to access.

He focused on fire. Fire was easy, and came to him quickly. He wrapped himself in it, holding onto a sense of the shaping. This close to the Academy, he was hopeful he could hide himself if others within the Academy might be aware of his shaping. As he did, he focused on the sense of the fire tower, the rune marked on the outside. He strained, pushing outward with a shaping to reach that rune, wanting to pour power into it.

Tolan was concerned he might push too much into it. If he did, he risked harming himself.

There came a steady buildup, more than he could shape on his own, and far more than he could use even with the furios.

Tolan began to ease off his connection to those runes, not wanting to hold onto too much power. It was tempting, but at the same time, that temptation meant he was bound to do something foolish. He didn't want to unleash fire in a way that would be damaging not only to him but to the fire bond.

How about earth? As he shaped it, he focused on the earth tower and the rune there. As with fire, it reverberated, slowly building, a rumbling starting deep within him. Tolan released it, fearful he might explode power outward.

He looked around the Academy. Something within him trembled. There was power he was able to access, and not at all what he had expected. There was no way he should have been able to reach for power that easily, and yet, by focusing on the runes on the towers, he could.

Hurrying across the courtyard, Tolan reached the main entrance. Inside, he paused, looking around. It was mostly empty, a few older students making their way through the halls, and they didn't pay him any mind. He hadn't been gone all that long, certainly not long enough to draw too much attention, and not at all as long as he had been when subjected to the Inquisition. This was practically easy.

Tolan debated where he would go.

He wanted to do this as quickly as possible. The library.

There was a risk of one of the master librarians being upset with his presence, but he needed to find Master Minden.

Once inside the library, he hesitated. There were more people here than he'd expected. He glanced up at the dais, noting the master librarians. They were not Master Minden. And they weren't Master Jensen. Master Stole and Master Havern were there, both with books spread in front of them, as the master librarians often did while working. He waited, looking around and debating how much he would push into the library, when he saw Wallace.

The other man remained leaning over his book, studying by himself, as he often did. While debating what to do, Tolan made a circuit of the library. As he went, he searched for signs of Master Minden. Even if he didn't reach the Convergence, he could tell her why he was here. He believed she would be willing to help.

He lingered along the outer wall, and as he went, he considered waiting for Master Minden, but didn't think he had the necessary time.

Master Stole made her way down the dais and Tolan ducked behind it, wanting to, if nothing else, hide from her. It was better than to have questions asked of him.

He lingered for a moment. As he did, he searched for the door leading down to the Convergence. It was masked, but as he found the runes marking it, he pressed his hand up against them, pushing power through them, and hesitated.

The moment he opened this door, the moment he pushed power through it, someone would be aware. It would be Master Minden, most likely, and he knew she could be upset with him for this, but he needed to do it.

Tolan completed the shaping.

The door popped open.

Hesitating for only a moment, he stepped inside, closing the door behind him. As he did, darkness swallowed him.

Then a surge of shaping washed over him.

23

Tolan hesitated. The shaping that struck him was surprisingly a mixture of elements. Through it, he felt spirit placed among it, twisting and spinning, the combined effort of the other elements working with it.

Tolan had used a shaping like this before, and recognized it. A shaping like this was meant to allow the shaper access to powerful elements, and allow them to know the way they worked together.

He waited, letting the shaping slide over him, but shifted the nature of his own protection in a way allowing him to defend himself. In doing so, he kept the strange shaping from striking him. He had to turn each of the elements at the same time, using them so they resonated at the same frequencies as the shaping approaching him, but he managed to match it, finding a way to use it so he wasn't going to be discovered.

This was the kind of shaping Master Sartan had

warned of, but he wasn't turning it on himself. He was inverting it, twisting it, but the shaping itself didn't work over him.

That power persisted, and he held onto it.

He was sure he was meant to know about it. He continued down the stairs, determined to avoid the nature of the shaping, thinking he had to have some way of figuring out who was forming it. If he could, he could figure out where it was coming from.

Lanterns along the walls glowed softly, seeming to pulse in time with his presence, and as he descended, they glowed a little more brightly with each step. That was unlikely to be only his imagination. The more he worked, the more certain he was he detected another shaping layered beneath the first. He was sure he hadn't imagined it. The longer he focused, the more certain he was that it was there.

Hurrying down the stairs, he reached the first landing, and from here, it wouldn't take long to reach the Convergence.

More light glowed softly here.

Tolan looked around, thinking he was bound to come across someone else shaping, but there was no one. The sense of power continued to build, though, and he might not know where it came from, but it was down here.

Tolan approached carefully. He wrapped one hand around the ring dangling from the necklace, thankful he hadn't given it back to his father when he'd seen him. He'd used it to hold onto his connection to spirit, knowing there had to be something within that shaping to help him.

There had to be something here. Had the shaper somehow hidden themselves? The sense of shaping was present here, pushing against him, creating a warning, almost as if designed to hold him back.

As he focused on the shaping, he began to recognize more within it. It was more than just a shaping designed as a barrier; it was a warning of sorts, a way of refusing a shaper's presence, a way of keeping them from reaching this place.

And the power within it was subtle. Without having been here before, Tolan wasn't sure he would have known to come, and might have been influenced by it.

Then again, it seemed almost as if not designed to hold him out.

He needed to figure out who was holding this shaping.

He continued through the open chamber. In the distance, the doorway blocking access to the Convergence loomed in front of him. Dozens of runes marked the surface.

This was a place of considerable power. As he stood there, holding onto his own shaping, keeping it wrapped around him so he didn't get caught up in the power, he gently pushed back against those shapings.

When he did, it reacted.

It was a strange sensation, almost as if the shaping was alive. It came at him, attacking the way he shaped, reacting violently, thrashing against his shaping. Tolan quickly retreated, removing the effect of his shaping, but it might already have been too late. As he shaped, as he pulled on that power, he continued to feel the effect of the strange shaping. It pressed in on him, attempting to cut him off from the shaping bonds.

Tolan stopped fighting. He let it cut him off from the shaping bonds. There was nothing he needed from them. He could shape without the element bonds and reach his shaping without them.

He held onto the barrier around him, using his connection to the elements in order to do so, and stopped fighting against the shaping.

The violence of the shaping retreated.

Tolan focused instead on the runes. There had to be power within them, and he needed to use them to open the Convergence.

Standing in front of the door, focusing on the power there, he debated whether this was what he really wanted to do. If he opened the Convergence, he would release the power within. They could use that to trap even more of the elementals and would destroy all Terndahl, even if they didn't mean to do it.

As he focused on it, he decided to shape the runes.

Power flowed out of him, hitting the nearest of the runes, and he continued to push shaping after shaping into it, using each of the elements. When he'd been here the first time, he couldn't have imagined doing this by himself. It had required all his friends in order to shape through it, and now he was doing it on his own.

And as he did, he realized it wasn't a particularly difficult shaping—only that it took power. It simply took access to each of the elements, and in that sense, it took considerable power with each of the elements, but it wasn't something Tolan struggled with.

He continued to shape, sending it into the runes.

He didn't have enough strength to open it on his own. Even with a shaping like this, as he pushed upon the runes, he still didn't have enough energy. He tried, but the shaping wasn't strong enough. Tolan released his connection, leaning back and looking around. Maybe that was for the best.

As he looked around, he felt the effect of a shaping once again. This time, there was something in it he hadn't recognized before. The shaping had spirit.

Tolan focused, searching himself. That spirit shaping had been used on him.

It was subtle, but strong enough that it overwhelmed his ability to ignore it. The touch was soft, gentle in a way he wasn't sure he would be able to recreate, and more than that, it pushed against the sense of the Convergence.

It was almost as if someone used it to hide the Convergence.

The longer he was here, the more he felt a desire to leave. Had he not recognized the sense of spirit, he might actually *have* left.

His breath caught.

The shaping was powerful, and more than he remembered when he'd been here before. Could the Inquisitors have learned how to find the Convergence?

Stopping them meant he had to find their Keystones—

and it meant reaching the Convergence. If only the draasin had taught him how to do that.

He focused on shaping. Opening it would require a difficult shaping, perhaps more than he could handle.

He began to understand the purpose behind the powerful shaping he detected. He had thought it was strictly a barrier. While it had that purpose, there was more to it. It wasn't just a barrier, and wasn't just a way to prevent others from finding the Convergence. It was designed to be a defense against anyone who might find it and to prevent them from opening this door. He had felt it the moment he'd begun to attempt to shape, the way the power pushed outward from it, washing over him, and in doing so, it came as a promise of violence.

And yet, Tolan needed to reach it. He had to stop the creep of the waste. He had to stop the Inquisitors.

He started to draw upon each of the elements. He focused that power, letting it flow from him quietly and faintly at first, and then with more intensity. He didn't focus on the door—not at first. Instead, Tolan kept his attention on the towers above and the runes within them. That was what he needed to reach.

Could he use that power from here? He didn't know if the protections would prevent him from doing it or not. It was entirely possible the barriers he suspected the Grand Master had placed would be enough to keep him from doing it.

Surprisingly, power flowed through the shaping, emanating away. As it did, he pushed it toward each of the runes. That power sliced through the shaping, as if intended for that purpose.

Tolan continued to push, letting the shaping flow from him, and when it struck the runes, power surged within him.

He didn't know how much time he had and didn't want to wait. He worried that doing so would somehow diminish him.

Focusing on the door, he exploded power into it.

It began to shimmer. Colors began to swirl, filling the shape of the patterns marked upon the door. As it did, he realized there was something missing.

He hadn't been shaping spirit.

He feared drawing upon the spirit rune, not wanting to gain the attention of the Grand Master before his actions here were complete. He didn't doubt the Grand Master would be paying attention to what he was doing, and had little doubt the Grand Master would recognize a shaping, so he needed to be careful.

But he had a bondar.

Once again, he wrapped his hand around the ring, pulling power through it. He wasn't sure if that was what his parents had intended for him to do, but it was effective.

The door swung open.

Tolan hurried inside, closing it behind him, and pushed his sense of elemental energy back through it. If nothing else, he wanted to seal it so no one else could reach him and use the Convergence against him.

He paused, looking around. The pool of the Convergence spread in front of him. Last time he had been here, Tolan had been so focused on survival, he hadn't had the opportunity to fully appreciate the pool itself. Within it was a silvery liquid. Even as he looked at it from here, there was something thick about it, something unusual. It wasn't plain water, not like he would have expected from other pools. This was something else. There was power here. He'd felt it even then, and his connection to his ability to shape had increased in the last few months, so he was far more aware of that power now.

It was almost as if he could use it, draw shaping from it, the same way he could draw shaping from a bondar. It was strange to think of it like that, but it struck him as if it were some extra-powered bondar.

That was what he needed from it. He needed the power of the Convergence, and he needed the connection to that power in order to be able to reach the Keystones.

Tolan didn't know how much time he had before someone realized he was here. The moment they did, he would either have to depart or he would have to hide. Considering he wasn't sure he would even know how to hide, that might not be much of an option.

He needed to know where the Keystones were. That was the first step.

What would that involve?

Focusing on spirit. Could it be anything else?

He had learned that spirit allowed all elements to connect, and that through spirit, there was an interconnectedness.

What was the key to shaping spirit here? When he'd

been here before, there had been something of a summons, an effort by Jory to pull power from the Convergence. That wasn't what he wanted to do here. It wasn't about pulling power out. It was about pushing power in, using that to help him connect and get a better understanding of the nature of the power available within the Convergence, the connectedness the Convergence could help him find, and the Keystones the Inquisitors had placed.

He pushed on his shaping, sending it into the Convergence. As he did, he sent a request. The shaping poured into the Convergence. It was almost as if it absorbed it, accepting it, drawing it deeper and deeper.

A singular focus remained in his mind—find the Keystones and the trapped power of the elementals. When he could do that, he would be able to stop the Inquisitors.

There was no real response.

He needed a greater draw to trigger something within the Convergence.

Using the bondar, he pulled upon power, sending that out and away from him. There came a sense of energy, a flowing sort of power drifting out from the bondar, into him, and then into the Convergence. Tolan poured more and more power into it but could tell he didn't have enough. He needed a connection to something greater.

How was he going to reach that power?

There was another option.

If he used that option, he would most definitely draw the attention of someone else, either the Grand Master or the Grand Inquisitor, or perhaps even the Inquisitors.

Tolan reached for the spirit rune.

It was somewhere above him.

He was aware of it, could feel it, and as he held onto the bondar, sending power out from it and toward the distant sense of the rune, he knew he would be triggering more than the rune. He would be triggering the protections the Grand Master had placed.

There was no choice otherwise.

Tolan forced a shaping into the rune.

When he had tried before, he hadn't enough power to use it. Perhaps it was more that he didn't have enough control over shaping in order to use it. Either way, he recognized he was unable to use the power stored within the rune.

And he still might not be able to.

This time, though, he used a bondar, attempting to trigger the power within the rune with it.

Energy flowed.

It filled him, the power of the elements, mixing with the element bonds, mixing with him, and giving him a sense of something more. It was a hint, little more than that, and as it came to him, he felt as if there was something more to it.

Tolan focused on the Convergence, shifting the shaping he was using. He sent it down into the Convergence. Power poured out from him, hitting the Convergence. He shifted the way he shaped and began to use the connection to the rune along with the power of the Convergence. Together, it gave him a greater sense of power and connectedness.

Tolan felt overwhelmed, but refused to move. This was what he needed to be doing.

A sense of something more—something greater—came to him, buried within the Convergence, as if he had always been meant to find it. Understanding and knowledge and connectedness came to him. In that moment, a flash of recognition surged through him.

As it did, he saw the element bonds. He saw the people accessing them. He even saw the elementals.

They were lost, trapped, and afraid.

And he saw *where* they were trapped.

Tolan held onto that knowledge, trying to hold it.

Strangely, darkness swept toward them.

Tolan focused on where the clusters of the elementals could be found. They were all along the edge of the waste. Could he use the Convergence to learn how to remove the Keystones?

Another surge of knowledge struck him.

Now he had to hope that knowledge stayed with him. At least he knew where he needed to go first.

Before he could do anything else, a shaping exploded behind him.

24

RELEASING HIS CONNECTION TO SPIRIT, TOLAN INSTEAD focused on the doorway. He wanted to prevent anyone entering, regardless of who it might be. It didn't matter who was coming. All that mattered was he needed an opportunity to hold them back.

He used his shaping, forcing it against the door, sealing it, but there wasn't enough power available.

Was there another way to attempt this? He focused on the runes overhead and quickly connected to them. Having done so now more than once, he was able to connect to a greater magic. He pulled on it and pushed that energy against the door, attempting to seal it.

There might be something more he could do.

Focusing on the Convergence, he drew that out as well, adding to it.

Tolan stood, holding onto that power. How long would he be able to maintain his connection like this? He didn't know if he would be able to withstand an attack long enough to be of much use. There had to be some way of separating himself from the shaping, to hold it in place, but it wasn't a technique he knew.

"You've returned."

Tolan jumped, spinning, and realized Master Minden stood on the other side of the Convergence.

"Master Minden?" Could she be the one responsible for the shaping? She had considerable talent, though he had never seen her use it to the full extent of her ability. He wouldn't be surprised if she could somehow use shaping in such a way that allowed her to create a defense against people like him. "How long have you been here?"

He hadn't noticed anyone here when he'd first come, but there was only the one way in.

"I'm surprised you returned as quickly as you did."

"You didn't want me to."

"It's not a matter of want. It's a matter of needing to find your purpose, Shaper Ethar."

Tolan shook his head. "I was worried I'd betray the Academy by going with my father, and worried I would betray my parents by staying at the Academy."

He continued to hold onto power, pressing it against the door. Even as he did, he could feel his strength beginning to wane. This was an incredibly powerful shaping, and he didn't have enough experience with similar shapings. Had he spent more time at the Academy, it was possible he would be better equipped to handle a shaping like this, but he hadn't been able to properly study.

"Most people don't have such concerns. And yet, you aren't most people, Shaper Ethar."

"Why are you here?"

"I suspect I'm here for the same reason as you."

"The elementals?"

"Is that why you've come?"

"I needed to. There's something happening…"

"There's always something happening," she said softly. Her gaze lowered to the pool of silvery liquid. "I have visited this place many times over the years. There's something peaceful about it, and when I'm here, I get the sense I can find myself."

"Why would you need to find yourself?"

"When you have served as long as I have, sometimes you begin to worry you will lose your way."

"And what way is that?"

Rather than answering, Master Minden began to make her way around the pool. When she neared him, she paused. "How long do you think you can maintain that shaping?"

"You can feel it?"

"You are using considerable power, Shaper Ethar, but you lack experience. Time will teach that, I suspect, though I begin to wonder if we have the necessary time."

"I was just trying to—"

"Find yourself?"

Tolan glanced at the door. "Something like that."

"And did you?"

He shrugged. "I… I don't really know."

"That's good. It would be unfortunate if you claimed you knew yourself before you were ready."

"I don't know what that means."

"That is also good."

"Are you going to force me to return?"

"It doesn't appear anyone forced you to return."

"I came for understanding."

"To the Convergence?" Master Minden asked, once again lowering her gaze to the silvery pool. As she did, Tolan noted a shaping slipping away from her. There was power in that shaping, and as it drifted from her, she continued to hold onto it, letting it slip deeper and deeper into the Convergence. She didn't appear to do anything drawing upon that energy, and instead, just poured it out.

"It was where I thought I might gain the understanding I needed."

"Then why are you holding onto the shaping?" She spoke softly, but there was power in her words. She knew exactly what he was doing, and if it were anyone else, he might have been more concerned, but something about Master Minden had always been friendly.

"I don't know who's coming."

"I suspect if you were to use the power you're holding, you'd be able to identify them. I could tell you it is the Grand Master and the Grand Inquisitor, along with several of the master shapers."

Tolan's heart sank. It would be difficult to explain to the Grand Master why he had come to the Convergence again.

"I was under the impression you and the Grand Master were on good terms."

"I think we are."

"You think? You aren't certain?"

"Well, after having left, I worry I won't have done what he wanted me to do."

"And he wanted you to infiltrate the disciples of the Draasin Lord."

"That is what he wanted."

"You returned, which tells me you decided otherwise."

Tolan said nothing, continuing to hold onto a shaping.

"Or perhaps you made another choice."

"I…"

She smiled at him. "Twist your shaping as you would invert it when you protected yourself from the spirit shaping. Once you twist it, you can find that you will knot it, and when you do, you can separate the shaping."

"What?"

"I didn't think I would need to repeat myself with you, Shaper Ethar."

Tolan focused on what she had said. He twisted the shaping and then inverted it, much the same way he did when protecting his mind. This time, rather than focusing on himself, he focused upon the door. He forced it into a knot, and then withdrew.

The shaping held.

Tolan took a step back, releasing the power he held.

"Why did you help me?"

"Not all of us view the world the way the Academy views it."

"But you're a part of the Academy."

"As are you, Shaper Ethar."

"I don't understand what you're getting at."

"What has your experience been with the elementals?"

"They aren't what others believe."

"And how is that?"

"They're not dangerous."

"Oh, they are dangerous, but they're dangerous because of what shapers have done to them."

"They're afraid of the bond," Tolan whispered.

"They are."

"You know?"

Master Minden turned to the Convergence. Her shaping poured out from her, heading into the silvery pool. "When you come here and have an opportunity to draw on power, you begin to recognize there is more to the bonds than most would believe. I have visited this place many times throughout my life. Each time, I'm painfully aware of the way the elementals suffer within the bond." She squeezed her eyes shut. "Their being forced into the bond ages ago was felt to be for their benefit, a way to protect them, and yet, it was a mistake."

"Why can't others see that?"

"Others *have* seen it over the years, and those who do will begin to understand there might be another way, but still others fear losing the strength the element bonds provide. With the elementals within the element bonds, power has grown beyond what it once had been. Most fear to lose that power."

"We're losing something else. The Inquisitors are using that power again."

"And how is that, Shaper Ethar?"

"Ephra is going to fall to the waste."

"Do you think it's only Ephra?"

Tolan glanced down at the Convergence. He had a memory of what he'd seen, the places where that power had been, and yet he didn't know any other places where it needed to be released. "It's not?"

"Unfortunately, it is more than just about Ephra." She glanced toward the door. "Most view the disciples of the Draasin Lord as violent and seeking to free the elementals to rule them."

"I don't know if that's what they want, but they aren't afraid to use the elementals to attack."

"Their release must be done carefully."

"They'll still be used."

"Do you think the elementals can be ruled by someone?"

"I don't know."

"Unfortunately, it *is* possible. And yet, the ones who have used the elementals in such a way are not the disciples of the Draasin Lord."

"Who is it?"

"The Academy."

"Are you saying—"

"I'm saying that while many others view the Academy as protecting us from the disciples of the Draasin Lord, unfortunately, we must protect ourselves from the Academy. We must protect the Academy from doing what it has done all these years."

"That's why you're here?"

"Change must happen from within. There is much good within Terndahl."

"I…" Tolan wasn't sure what to make of what she was telling him. And yet, it fit with the same things he had been thinking about. Somehow, he had to find a way to be both the student at the Academy and the son his parents had raised. As difficult as that might be, he couldn't help but think he could find a way to do both—and not betray both.

If he did, he would be deceiving the Academy, but also ran the risk of deceiving the disciples of the Draasin Lord, and the fact he had returned to the Academy might be perceived as him having done so.

Was that the fate he wanted for himself?

"Will you tell the Grand Master why I did this?"

"Do you want me to?"

He could talk to the Grand Master himself, but worried if he took the time, he would lose the knowledge he'd gained coming here. He would lose the chance to undo what the Inquisitors had done. And he would fail the draasin.

"What has he told you?" Master Minden asked, as if knowing his thoughts.

"He?"

"The draasin."

Tolan stared at her. "How do you know?"

"You have his touch upon you. It's subtle, but most definitely there."

"He is… amazing."

"There are only a few alive who have been allowed to see him. You should consider yourself blessed for the fact he opened himself to you."

"I don't know why he would have."

Master Minden smiled at him. "No? I can see quite easily why he would have. You have proven yourself, Shaper Ethar. You have demonstrated you don't fear the elementals. You have demonstrated an open mind, and because of that, you have shown yourself to be something the draasin respects."

"I think I know how to help Terndahl," he said.

"Good."

"I can't do it from here."

"I suspect you cannot."

"If the master shapers catch me, they might prevent me from doing what I need to do." He hesitated. "You could help."

"I am but an old woman now. Perhaps in my younger days, when I was stronger, I might have posed more of a challenge, or perhaps were things different, I might…" She smiled. "It doesn't matter, not as it once did."

"How am I supposed to escape?"

"Spirit."

"I don't understand."

"Then let me help."

She turned once again to the Convergence, and as she

did, she focused a shaping upon it. It built steadily, a rising sort of power, and flowed into the Convergence. As it did, she pulled it out and held onto the power of the shaping. She waited, watching Tolan, and he had a sense she expected him to do something similar. Was he capable of doing it?

He focused on his shaping of spirit, squeezing the bondar, but she shook her head.

"You must do it. Only you."

Tolan released the bondar and used a sense of spirit. He pushed that into the Convergence and the energy reverberated, filling him. With it, he followed the direction of Master Minden's shaping and used that to help him. She nodded, and they turned to the door.

"Now, sweep it outward, and do so with force and intention."

"What sort of intention?"

"You are looking to dissuade them from following."

"I don't want to harm them."

"Did I say anything about harming them? Had he not called the Inquisitors back, this would be much easier, so I believe we can blame his pride for what is to come."

Tolan smiled to himself, though he wasn't sure how attacking the Grand Master would end for him. "Isn't there another way out of here? You weren't here when I came."

"You wouldn't be able to leave the way I arrived."

He frowned at her, thinking that a strange comment, but brushed it aside. He instead focused on the shaping, thinking of his intention, and decided his intention was to simply explode outward, to blast the people on the other side of the door, knock them out before they were aware it was him. With the power of the Convergence, Tolan had to believe he could do it.

He hesitated, then he pushed out a shaping.

There was a sense of resistance as he did, and when it struck the others on the opposite side of the door, Tolan continued to push. It continued to meet resistance, and he drew more and more from the Convergence. At first, he wasn't sure if he was going to be able to succeed, but the power overwhelmed the others on the far side of the door, and then he exploded through.

Nothing else moved.

Tolan swept out with his sensing, using earth and spirit, and was able to determine there was no movement on the far side of the door.

Master Minden pushed out her shaping, drawing spirit from the Convergence, and she pushed a little harder than Tolan had. As she did, it slammed into something on the far side of the door that he couldn't detect.

"I added a touch to ensure you have adequate time to get out of the city."

"Thank you."

"Do what needs to be done, Shaper Ethar. And then, when you are done, return to me."

"What if it's not safe?"

"I think you will find it is perfectly safe. There is much you still need to learn, and I think I must teach what I can."

Tolan nodded. She started back around the Convergence, leaving him, and he approached the door. He had knotted off the shaping, but as he approached, he could feel the shaping begin to separate for him, a little at first, then a little bit more. As it did, he pushed the door open, noting the fallen forms of a half dozen shapers, the Grand Master and Grand Inquisitor among them. None of the masters from each of the element towers were there, and though he recognized these others, he also found there were those he didn't recognize. There were no Inquisitors among them.

Tolan hurried back up the stairs, stepping through the door and closing it once again. He sealed it with a shaping, attempting to delay, just a little bit more, anyone who might follow him. When he was done, he made his way around the edge of the library. He looked around, curious if there were any students here, though unsurprised to find there were none. As he stepped out into the hallway, there was a temptation within him to go and find Ferrah, to tell her where he was going and what he needed to do, but that could come after.

For now, he needed to take the action that would give him the opportunity to return.

When he was done, then—and only then—could he come back.

Hurrying out of the Academy, he found himself once more under the darkened sky. And he knew where he needed to go.

Tolan shaped himself up to the Shapers Path, taking a deep breath, and then raced upon it, running through the darkness, making his way toward Ephra—and to danger.

25

The waste crept up on Tolan faster than he would've expected. He reached it by morning and was tired enough that he wanted to do nothing more than to have a moment of reprieve. If he could take time to rest and recuperate, he thought he might have the necessary strength to complete what he saw as his assignment.

Tolan didn't know if he dared take that time. Now he was here, he could see the waste had shifted, moving from where it had been even the day before. There was no way that was coincidental, and it meant whatever was taking place was accelerating.

Surprisingly, the Shapers Path took him very nearly to the edge of the waste. That had never been the case before. When he had come here before with the Academy, there had been a significant walk to reach the edge of the waste, but now it was practically up to the Path.

More than ever, Tolan felt certain he needed to do something.

A part of him thought this wasn't his responsibility and he could alert the Grand Master or others at the Academy, convince them this needed to be repaired, but he doubted they would understand what was needed for the repair. How could they believe the elementals needed to be freed in order to restore these lands?

Even if they believed, it was unlikely they would be willing to do anything.

Tolan approached slowly. He focused on what he could detect around him, but there wasn't much, certainly not as much as he needed, and yet, the time at the Convergence had told him this was where he needed to be. This was where elementals were trapped, and in other places like it.

He thought them Keystones, but there was nothing like what he had seen in the clearing outside of Amitan. If there was a Keystone, it was different.

The connection to the Convergence had helped him know where the Keystones were, but now he was here, finding them proved more difficult than he would have expected. How was he going to uncover those Keystones?

Tolan focused on the elements. If nothing else, his time connecting as often as he now had to the various elements had given him a greater understanding of the connectivity that existed. It was the only thing he had he thought he could use. He swept out away from him, using a sensing drawing upon power from earth. He felt nothing more than the emptiness of the waste.

That wasn't the key.

There had to be something else, but would any of the elements work for him like that?

As he continued to probe, he continued to run into the emptiness.

What if he attempted it with all elements?

Pushing outward, reaching with earth and wind and water and fire, he swept that sense away from him. As he did, he added a hint of spirit.

Spirit changed everything.

Power surged from him, stretching away, and Tolan focused on what he could find within it. It came to him slowly, but there was the sense of the land around him. There was a sense of wind whispering. The heat from the sun. The water within him and even within the air. All of it combined, and Tolan continued to push out, focusing on it. It was there, near him, and all he had to do was reach for it. He pushed outward, using his sensing ability, focusing on what he could pick up on. As it swept away, he detected the strange barrier appearing from the waste.

He could feel it creeping backward, the power around him. It was as if the waste itself was drawing forward, creeping ever more.

Tolan stretched outward, looking for where he could detect that sense, and yet, what he detected was emptiness.

He needed to find something more than that. He continued to send out his connection to each of the elements, wrapping spirit around him, and as he did, he probed, looking for the missing elementals. That was the key. Where would they be bound together, trapped within the bond? If he could find them, free them, then—and only then—could he halt the progression of the waste.

The knowledge was within him. He knew it was. He had detected it from within the Convergence. He had to access those memories and recall what the Convergence had shown him, and if he could do that, then he might be able to uncover the secrets.

More power pushed out from him.

He reached the end of his own strength. Without bondars, there would be nothing more he could do.

If only he had the power of the runes at the Academy to draw upon.

Could he recreate them?

Tolan made markings on the ground in front of him, dragging his foot through the earth. The shapes filled his mind, and as he had used that power before, he knew he could draw upon it again. They were there within him, familiar from the shapes of the runes within him, and he made them in the same pattern as they appeared on the Academy building. He even added spirit, though didn't know if that made any difference.

As he did, Tolan pushed power out, sending it into the runes. At first, he thought he might not have enough strength, but then his power surged, flowing through him.

With the augmented power of these runes, Tolan pressed outward, searching for the disruption he had detected while near the Convergence. It had to be there, didn't it?

He continued to pull on that power.

And then he felt it.

It was near, and he made his way along the ground, heading carefully, looking for anything similar to the Keystone. When he came across it, it wasn't anything like what he would've expected.

It was runes.

They were similar to what he'd made, and yet, these were a bit different, and the power they pulled was forced downward. Something about it felt off. It was wrong, though Tolan didn't quite know how else to describe it.

Focusing on that pattern, he sent his own shaping into it.

The shaping pushed against him, as if attempting to refuse him and his ability to disrupt it. There was considerable power behind it. As he continued to push, he felt the ongoing resistance.

Tolan pushed again and again.

He drew upon the runes he'd made. With them, he thought he had enough.

Power exploded from him. The runes snapped.

And he was thrown back.

It took a moment for his mind to clear and for him to realize what had happened. The sudden change had come from his freeing of the elementals. They were no longer bound as they had been, and he continued to pour power out, pushing it away, and in doing so, he could feel a strange sense of relief.

That couldn't be the elementals, could it?

And yet, as he detected it, he realized that was exactly what it was. They were relieved he'd released this hold.

Strangely, he realized he'd been wrong. This wasn't the

Keystone, at least not like what he had detected in Amitan. This was something else, but no less powerful. The Keystone had held onto the power and trapped the elementals within it. This did something similar, but not quite the same. It still pulled the free elementals away, stripping them from this land, but it did something more.

What was the purpose of it?

He should have taken more time to study the runes. If he had, he could have better understood their purpose. Now he'd disrupted them, there was nothing about them he could make out anymore. The runes were gone, and any opportunity he might have at understanding what had been taking place here was also gone.

Could he find another?

Tolan continued to focus on his runes, the power he'd placed. As he did, he pushed outward again. Now he knew what he was looking for, it was easier to find it again.

There was another, not too far from where he had been.

Tolan paused in front of it. This one had a strange shape, and it was nothing like the elements and the runes he'd placed. This was something else.

He stared at it, trying to focus on it, wanting to remember what it was he had detected. It would make it easier to find it again. After staring for a while, Tolan thought he knew how to copy these runes. There was danger in it, and he worried if he were to copy them, he would end up somehow drawing a strange power, but he wanted to be able to research them as well.

As before, Tolan pushed power out, sending that into

the runes. As he did, it took a little bit more strength to destroy them.

Depending on how many more there were, it might be almost more than he could manage. Tolan focused, drawing power through the runes he'd created, and searched for evidence of others. He suspected there were others, and as he focused, he found them... And felt a growing shaping.

Tolan released his connection and looked around.

Someone shaping nearby might be involved in creating these runes, but they could also have come for another reason. He continued to hold onto his connection to the marks he'd made on the ground and used that, along with a hint of spirit, to push out, thinking if nothing else, he might be able to discover what was out there.

Another surge of shaping came.

This time there was a distinct signature to it.

Inquisitors.

Tolan wasn't sure he would have enough strength or access to shaping to deal with the Inquisitors. This close to the edge of the waste, he feared what might happen.

He glanced up, looking at the Shapers Path, and decided to shape himself up to it. At least from there, he had the opportunity to escape if it came down to a need to run.

He used a mixture of wind and fire, as he often did, and streaked up toward the Shapers Path, landing on it. Looking down at the ground, it seemed as if the advancing border of the waste had changed, perhaps no longer moving quite as aggressively as it had before.

What if that was only his imagination?

He didn't think so. It didn't seem to him that it was anything but the waste no longer pushing as it had.

Another shaping exploded near him, and then another. Tolan shivered.

He couldn't stay here. He was exhausted from a lack of sleep and even more from all the shaping he had been doing.

He started to make his way along the Shapers Path when a barrier surrounded him, preventing him from going anywhere.

He hadn't even felt it. There was a surge of power, the kind of power he'd not expected. It trapped him, holding him in place.

Another shaping exploded near him, and then another. With each one, Tolan knew there would be no escaping.

Worse, he knew he had made a mistake. He should have told someone—anyone—where he was going and what he was going to do. Even if he had told Master Minden, that would be better than what was now happening. Now he was at the mercy of whoever caught him.

Another shaping, and a figure shimmered into existence near him.

Aela.

"I am surprised you continue to pose challenges," she said, smiling at him.

"What are you doing?"

"I am the Inquisitor while you are nothing but a student."

"You attacked me."

"Do you think that should concern me? As I said, you are nothing more than a student."

"You're responsible for these markings," he said. "You're responsible for destroying Terndahl."

"What markings?"

Another shaping struck, and as it did, Tolan could feel the power within it. How many more would he have to endure? He didn't know if he'd be able to withstand too many more shapings—or shapers.

Surprisingly, he could see none of them. That had to be related to what they were doing and the kind of shaping they were using, but whatever the shaping was, it was not something he recognized. Perhaps that didn't matter. All that mattered was they had the numbers.

"What are you going to do with me?" he asked.

"Seeing as how you have continued to press? I think it's time to remove you as a threat."

"I'm not any sort of threat."

"Ah, Shaper Ethar, you have proven you are more of a threat than you should be, especially as a student."

A shaping began to build from her, and he recognized the power within it.

Spirit.

Other shapings started, one after another, all of them surrounding him. Within each of them came the sense of spirit, and it continued to build.

Tolan focused his shaping, using each of the elements and turning it inward, trying to protect himself, but at this point, and against so many shapers, it might not even matter. The numbers were all that mattered, as was the fact he was exhausted, having used far more of his power than he ever had before, and now it put him into a situation where he was going to end up overwhelmed by their spirit shaping.

All he could do was attempt to hold on.

He had the bondar of spirit, and he tried to use that, wrapping it around him, but even with that, he wasn't sure he had enough strength to make a difference. Tolan continued to wrap himself with it, and when the first shaping struck, it was deflected. So were the next and the next. One after another they came, each of them hitting him, reaching him, and as they did, Tolan continued to struggle, knowing there might not be much he could do. He resisted as much as he could, holding back, fighting the attempt of the shaping to strike him.

Aela watched him, a hint of a smile on her face.

He reached for the power of the runes he'd made, but even those weren't going to be enough. Already Tolan could feel Aela's power was going to overwhelm him. There was too much, and he struggled against it, straining to refuse the shaping, but could he hold out?

He wasn't sure what choice he had. He would try. That was about all he could do—try.

Anything more would be chance.

Tolan felt the effects of the spirit shaping continuing to slip toward him. They were far more than he could withstand.

And then one started to reach him.

He didn't need to see Aela to know it was her shaping. He could feel it was her. She was slipping into his mind, trying to change him. As she did, he fought, but he failed.

"I wonder if you can't be useful."

"No!"

She merely smiled. "As I said, you will be useful."

As the shaping continued to press upon him, and as Tolan continued to fight, he feared losing himself. What would she make him do? He'd seen the way spirit shaping could work, having dealt with it firsthand against his friends, and he didn't like the idea it would be used against him in a similar way. He'd thought he was protected from spirit shaping, and thought he wouldn't be subjected to that power, and yet, here he was, forced down by it.

Would they make him harm people he cared about?

Would it even matter if they forced him to act against the elementals? He cared about his friends, but he also cared about the elementals, cared about what he detected from the bonds, and the way he felt the pain within the elementals. They suffered, and that was not something he could support.

Eventually, it would be something he cared nothing about.

By shaping his spirit, she would be taking it. She would be changing him. There would be nothing left of Tolan, merely a husk, everything he was changed, compromised, and he would be gone.

He thought of all the elementals he'd encountered ever since reaching the Academy. Even the elementals he'd encountered before coming to the Academy. While the draasin was impressive, it was hyza that had been there the most. The elemental of fire and earth had followed him, had been with him, and...

He still was.

Distantly, Tolan could feel the elemental. It was almost as if he were there with him, within his mind, trying to work with him, to give him additional strength.

Could Tolan borrow from it?

He had wanted the power of the element bonds, but he had also wanted the power of the bondars. Could he use hyza something like a bondar?

With the idea, power began to flow through him. It was the power of earth and fire, and Tolan solidified his connection. He formed a seal around his mind, forcing Aela out. As he did, her eyes widened.

He would fight, and do everything in his power to withstand her if he could. It might not matter, but he'd try.

He continued to force outward, using his connection to hyza.

Awareness of the elemental filled his mind. He could feel the elemental, and sense the willingness of the elemental to help him.

Tolan cried out, but this time, he felt as if there was a possibility of success.

Yet, regardless of how much power hyza might grant him, it still wouldn't be enough to overpower so many shapers. Tolan didn't even have an idea of how many were here.

"You have far more skill than I would've expected for a

student. Perhaps the rumors about you are true and you really do serve the Draasin Lord," Aela said.

"I serve the true Draasin Lord," Tolan cried out. This time, he did so with a desire to connect to hyza, to use the strange awareness the elemental granted. It was considerable power, and it connected him to the elemental, granting him an awareness of the way the elemental was thinking and feeling. There was fear within the elemental, but this time, the fear was for Tolan.

He drew upon the elemental's power. It solidified the barrier around his mind and he pushed outward, forcing the shapers back.

It still wasn't enough.

Then, he felt something else.

A shaping.

Something in the shaping resonated with him. It was familiar, and he realized it came from one of the disciples of the Draasin Lord.

Tolan felt another surge of emotion. This time, it was hope.

All he had to do was hold on, and then another shaping came. Then another.

As they did, the pressure upon him began to fade. One after another. It was as if the disciples had figured out a way of attacking those he couldn't even see.

Within a few moments, Aela seemed to realize what was taking place, and she turned her attention, but Tolan used that moment to attack, sending out a blast of fire, focusing on hyza. He drew that power outward and Aela fell from the Shapers Path.

Tolan didn't give her a chance to recover. He jumped, wrapping his arms around her as he fell. Wind whistled around him. When it did, he felt a cushioning, and he crashed to the ground far more slowly than he would've expected.

Aela got to her feet, shaking herself free, shaping building from her. Tolan tried to create a barrier, but it was all he could do to hold onto the barrier around his mind.

She stalked toward him.

"Do you think you will be able to stop this? Do you think I am acting alone?"

"You aren't going to succeed."

"You don't even know what we're trying to do."

There was movement behind her and the power of shaping, but Tolan couldn't take his eyes off her to focus on it.

"What are you trying to do?"

"There is power in the world greater even than that of the element bonds. Those of us who have discovered it will use it."

Tolan shivered at the way she said it. Having felt the effect of her spirit shaping, he had little question as to the way she would use any sort of power. It meant whoever she intended to use that power on would be subjugated the same way she'd just attempted to subjugate him.

And it meant the elementals would be forever trapped, held within the element bond, or perhaps worse, forced to serve.

"The others will stop you."

"Others? By that, you mean the disciples?" She smiled. "I admit I'm surprised you were able to withstand the Inquisition as long as you did, and yet now you reveal yourself."

"I didn't serve the disciples. I still don't."

"And yet you're hoping they will be the ones to stop me?"

"You're attacking Terndahl. Even if the disciples don't stop you, when the Grand Master learns—"

She lashed at him with a surge of power. He was thrown away from her and landed on his back. He looked up as she stormed toward him, power flowing from her, and Tolan tried to hold onto the barrier around his mind, but he was failing.

"The Grand Master has served his purpose. He will serve no more."

"He will stop you." Tolan scooted back, trying to get away from her, but there didn't seem to be any way to do so. He scrambled back, moving along the ground. As he did, the earth scraped across his back, painful and biting. "When he learns you attacked Terndahl, he will stop you. The Academy will stop you."

"The Academy will soon be under different authority."

She took another step toward him and Tolan squeezed his eyes shut, focusing on hyza. As he did, he sent a single request.

He didn't want the elemental harmed. Regardless of what happened, the elemental needed to get away. He didn't deserve to suffer simply because he had stayed, thinking to help him.

Run.

The thought surged toward the elemental, and Tolan prayed it was enough.

As Aela's shaping built, Tolan braced himself. He opened his eyes, looking up at her. He would force her to meet his eyes as she shaped him, forcing her to know what she did when she destroyed his mind.

She didn't seem to care. She sneered at him, power building, spirit flowing through her. One like her didn't deserve that kind of power. Spirit should be held by those who understood it.

Her shaping began to sweep toward him. It was all Tolan could do to hold her off.

And then his barrier began to collapse.

26

As Tolan felt his barrier collapse, he braced himself for the inevitable impact.

It never came.

Instead, a roar exploded, heat blasted around him, and a blur of flames slammed into Aela. She cried out, trying to redirect her shaping, but hyza overpowered her, ripping through her shaping—and her.

It was a brutal and bloody end, but it was an end.

Tolan got to his feet. He could barely stand, and hyza approached. After a moment, the elemental dropped to his haunches, looking up at him.

"Thank you."

The elemental turned his head, studying him, and seemed as if he was going to say something, but a shaping built near Tolan and he turned, half expecting to find something dangerous. Instead, it was a familiar shaping.

"Father," Tolan said with a nod.

His father looked around. "What happened?"

"I had help."

His father looked around, frowning. "What sort of help?"

Tolan shrugged. "The kind of help that mattered." He studied the fallen form of Aela. He had a hard time feeling any sympathy for her. Still, he didn't know he completely understood what she'd been doing. There was something she was after, and she had been working with someone else, though Tolan didn't know who that might've been.

"Are you ready to return with us?"

There was another sign of movement in the distance, followed by a shaping. This one came almost like a warning. The Grand Master.

Tolan turned his attention back to his father. "I can't."

"I told you what the price of your visiting our lands would be."

"I understand the price, but I can't. I won't betray you. But I need to return to the Academy."

"We can't take that chance, Tolan. Even for you."

Tolan took a deep breath. Would he have gotten this far, and have seen everything he had, only to have his father be the one who dragged him away?

"I can serve better here," he said.

"What do you mean?"

Tolan motioned to the edge of the waste. "They've been doing something. Some attack. Whatever it is caused the waste to move. I can help remove the runes, but I think I need to head back to the Academy to understand what else is taking place."

"They won't allow it."

"Who *they*?"

"The rest of the disciples."

"Did they think I'm going to betray the Draasin Lord? I've met him, and won't betray him."

His father stared at him for a moment. "What do you mean, you met him?"

"The Draasin Lord."

His father studied him. "You met what you were supposed to see in that place. It's a vision, nothing more than that."

"That's not what I mean. I met him."

"You met him?"

Tolan nodded. "I understand not many do."

"No," his father said with a whisper. "And none of us have."

"None?" He found it difficult to believe none of the disciples of the Draasin Lord would ever have met the Draasin Lord, but the way his father looked at him suggested that was the case.

"We've seen evidence of his passing, and we can communicate with some of the elementals who suggest he's out there, such as the elementals you met when you were with your time in our Selection. Other than that, we have not been able to find him."

Tolan smiled to himself. "I think he has to choose to reveal himself. He's the reason I'm back here. The Draasin Lord returned me to Terndahl."

His father's breath caught. "Not only did you see him, but you *rode* him?"

"How else would I have returned?"

"I didn't know. I thought perhaps you had more potency with shaping than we had realized. That or bondars. Though the Academy bondars are weaker, they still can have some potency."

Tolan smiled. He had seen that firsthand. "If only I did."

His father looked along the line of the waste. "If you show us these runes, then you can return."

Another burst of shaping came. Closer this time.

"Use this." He drew out the runes he'd used, shaped into them, and let power flow. "Is that enough?"

"It should be. You have gained more skill than we expected."

Tolan glanced behind his father. "I…" He shook his head. "What will you do?"

"Remove them. And then, perhaps we can understand what we can do to prevent others from forming." He took a deep breath. "We have been searching for the key to the waste for many years. Perhaps that can be your contribution."

"It's not just that there is an absence of the elementals?"

"It's more than just an absence of the elementals. There's something that has changed. We've tried to return elementals to the waste, but even when we do, they either can't or won't remain."

Tolan focused on what he could detect of the runes and guided his father to one of them. They crouched down next to it, and he studied it for a moment before getting to his feet.

"You did well, Tolan."

"You're not going to bring me back. I get to choose my fate."

"You're right. Much as I chose mine and your mother chose hers."

He still didn't know what had happened with his mother, only that his father hadn't talked much about her.

"Is that why you left me behind?"

His father smiled. "It's complicated, but we knew if we brought you to the other side, we would be committing you to a path. It's one you need to choose for yourself, not to have chosen for you." He reached out a hand as if to shake Tolan's, and rather than shaking it, Tolan pulled his father toward him in a hug.

"Be safe. Know we will keep an eye on you and know you are welcome to return when you have finished with whatever you need to do," his father said.

Tolan looked around the edge of the waste. There were several other disciples making their way along the border, but none focused on him. Instead, they were wandering along the edge, and his father went to talk to the nearest of them before making his way back toward Tolan.

When they were gone, Tolan remained where he was. It didn't take long for the Grand Master to appear. There were other shapers nearby, but they spread out, searching. Hopefully, they wouldn't find any of the disciples.

When the Grand Master saw Aela, he frowned. "I hoped things would turn out differently," he whispered.

When the Grand Master looked up at him, he frowned. "Was this their doing?"

He shook his head. "She attacked me."

"You would not have killed, Shaper Ethar."

Tolan wasn't so certain what he would do anymore. All he knew was that he had survived. "I didn't."

"That is all you will tell me?"

"The Inquisitors were placing something like Keystones to trap elementals and their power. I don't know what they intended to use it for, but I don't think Aela was acting alone."

The Grand Master eyed him for a long moment. A shaping swept away from him and toward Tolan. He wrapped himself in a shaping of each of the elements, protecting himself.

"She was not."

"You knew?"

"Why do you think we wanted her to return? There is more taking place than you know, Shaper Ethar. We lost the opportunity to discover that now."

Tolan looked down at Aela. The sense of the waste was shifting again, moving back to where it should be. "Maybe, but we prevented something too."

Not we, but he. Without him—and the draasin urging him—the elementals would have remained trapped.

"I can see why she chose you."

"Who?"

The Grand Master tipped his head to the side a moment before turning his attention back to Tolan.

"Master Minden. When you return, be sure to tell her I know she's using you."

"I can return?"

"Don't you want to?"

The sense of other shapings built all around him, though he had no idea where they came from. Were the master shapers attacking the disciples—or was it about the Inquisitors?

"Shaper Ethar?"

Tolan tore his attention away, meeting the Grand Master's eyes. "Very much."

"Good. Then I would suggest you go. And don't make the mistake of shaping me again."

Tolan sucked in a sharp breath. The Grand Master knew he had shaped him.

"I won't."

With that, he hurried away and took the opportunity to jump to the Shapers Path and started along it. It wasn't long before he reached Amitan. When he did, it was late in the day and he entered the main door, heading to the student quarters, and to Ferrah.

He found her in the library, as he suspected he would. She was bent over the table, looking at a book, and when he came in, she jumped to her feet.

Tolan hurried over to her, wrapping his arms around her and giving her a quick kiss. "I'm sorry I left when I did."

"You don't have to explain. When the Inquisitors returned, I understood." She looked around the library.

"The Grand Master came to me. He said you were going to take his assignment."

"I tried. I failed."

He would tell her more later. She deserved that from him. For now, that was all that mattered.

And when it came to the Grand Master, perhaps that was the only answer he needed, too. When the other man returned, Tolan didn't know how he would react. Now he knew the Grand Master was aware he'd shaped him, he feared… What, exactly? The Grand Master could have punished him outside the city. It was almost as if he didn't exactly mind that Tolan had done what he had.

Why was that?

Tolan scanned the inside of the library. It only been a day since he'd been here, and yet with the exhaustion, he felt as if it was much longer. Master Minden sat upon the dais, looking down at her books.

"I'll be right back," he started. "There's quite a bit more I want to tell you."

"You're not going to keep anything from me?"

"No."

Ferrah smiled, taking a seat and pulling her books back toward her. Tolan started toward the dais, and Master Minden climbed down, making her way to the row of shelves. He followed her, and when he joined her, she glanced over.

"Did you succeed?"

"I found what they were doing."

"They?"

"The Inquisitors. They used some strange runes on the border of the waste. They were changing it."

"Did you see these runes?"

Tolan nodded. "I saw them. I destroyed what I could and the disciples were going to take care of the rest. And I think I can repeat them."

"Great Mother," the master librarian said. "Could you have finally uncovered the key?"

"What key?"

"The key to everything."

"I don't understand?"

"Not yet, Shaper Ethar, but you will."

"How?" Tolan looked around the library before settling his gaze back on Master Minden. "The Grand Master followed us. He knows you were involved."

"Of course, he did. Which is why he told you to come to me. Now you and I must take on a different task."

"What task is that?"

"Discovering who the Inquisitors serve."

Grab book 5 of Elemental Academy: The Spirit Binds

The Inquisitors have been stopped, but the one who leads them remains at large.

Tolan discovers a dangerous plot against the Academy —and all of Terndahl—the Inquisitors have planned for far longer than any have suspected. The power involved is unlike anything ever encountered by those within the Academy. Tolan isn't sure he's capable of understanding what has happened, but with his connection to the elementals, he might be the only one able.

The key to what's happening is tied to something in Tolan's past. For him to stop the one who leads the Inquisitors, and to understand what they're after, requires him to know more about where he came from and why his parents left him in Ephra.

Stopping the Inquisitors is only the beginning, not only for to save Terndahl, but for Tolan to finally know himself.

ALSO BY D.K. HOLMBERG

Elemental Academy
The Fire Within
The Earth Awakens
The Water Ruptures
The Wind Rages
The Spirit Binds

The Cloud Warrior Saga
Chased by Fire
Bound by Fire
Changed by Fire
Fortress of Fire
Forged in Fire
Serpent of Fire
Servant of Fire
Born of Fire
Broken of Fire
Light of Fire
Cycle of Fire

The Endless War
Journey of Fire and Night

Darkness Rising
Endless Night
Summoner's Bond
Seal of Light

The Elder Stones Saga
The Darkest Revenge
Shadows Within the Flame
Remnants of the Lost
The Coming Chaos

The Shadow Accords
Shadow Blessed
Shadow Cursed
Shadow Born
Shadow Lost
Shadow Cross
Shadow Found

The Collector Chronicles
Shadow Hunted
Shadow Games
Shadow Trapped

The Dark Ability
The Dark Ability

The Heartstone Blade
The Tower of Venass
Blood of the Watcher
The Shadowsteel Forge
The Guild Secret
Rise of the Elder

The Sighted Assassin
The Binders Game
The Forgotten
Assassin's End

The Dragonwalker
Dragon Bones
Dragon Blessed
Dragon Rise
Dragon Bond
Dragon Storm
Dragon Rider
Dragon Sight

The Teralin Sword
Soldier Son
Soldier Sword
Soldier Sworn
Soldier Saved

Soldier Scarred

The Lost Prophecy

The Threat of Madness

The Warrior Mage

Tower of the Gods

Twist of the Fibers

The Lost City

The Last Conclave

The Gift of Madness

The Great Betrayal

The Book of Maladies

Wasting

Broken

Poisoned

Tormina

Comatose

Amnesia

Exsanguinated

Printed in Dunstable, United Kingdom

66352081R00221